# The Round Robin

*A Novel*

*Elizabeth Ruble*

ISBN 978-1-68517-067-7 (paperback)
ISBN 978-1-68517-493-4 (hardcover)
ISBN 978-1-68517-068-4 (digital)

Christian Faith Publishing
832 Park Avenue
Meadville, PA 16335
www.christianfaithpublishing.com

Printed in the United States of America

The following story is true. The names and places have been changed to protect people's identities.

# *Preface*

When WWII ended, and soldiers retuned home, family members were anxious to stay in touch with one another, so letter writing became the preferred way to correspond. My father, born in 1910, was the oldest of ten children, having four brothers and five sisters. My mother, born in 1913, was the second oldest of five children (three sisters and one brother). All survived the war except for Mom's brother who died in his teens before the war began.

The two families devised a plan of how to stay in touch with one another. In each family, a letter about current happenings would be written and sent to a specific sibling. That sibling would read the enclosed letter, write one about their family, and send both letters along to the next brother or sister. So, by the time the letter returned to the original address, there could be several letters in one envelope, especially Dad's, with news about the whole family.

Mom became the letter writer in our family. The letters became known as *The Round Robin,* and we usually received two envelopes every four to six weeks—one from Dad's family and one from Mom's family. In our home, we were excited to have it arrive, and in the evenings, Mom would read the letters from the different family members. We learned a lot about our extended family as *The Round Robin* traveled from Colorado to Wyoming, California, Oregon, Montana, and Indiana.

When my oldest daughter left home to attend the University of Colorado at Boulder, people would ask me, "What are you going to do without her?"

I told them, "I'm going to write her a letter!"

So began my personal handwritten letters, not only to her once a week, but also to my other two children when they left home to make their way in the world. My letters found their way from colleges and universities to different states to hospitals, to the battlefields of Iraq, to the continent of Australia.

For twenty-five years, I wrote those handwritten letters, and through them, I now write the story of my life—a life that has had a lot of diversity. I have lived in several different places, met different types of people, and had many different careers. Some of the diversity was of my own choosing; at other times, I was left feeling I had no choice. It's the story of my journey with my God.

# PART 1

## *Leaving*

I had been going to the mailbox every day for the last week, each time hoping it would be there. Everything I dreamed or hope to dream was depending on the application I had sent to a small college in Texas. Many of the seniors in my high school class had already received their acceptance notices and were making plans for the time they would be leaving to attend their first year of college in the fall. I wanted to be one of those seniors.

As I approached the mailbox, I prayed a small prayer to God that he would give me the desires of my heart. Opening the mailbox lid, I pulled out the random stack of mail, and there it was! A letter from Wayland Baptist College in Plainview, Texas. All my hopes and dreams lay within the answer inside that letter. For as excited as I was to open it and discover the outcome, I also knew I would be facing my father with his answer, and he had not approved of me applying or even thought of me moving away.

There were two things my father, Robert Wilson, wanted to give his children: a college education and for them to know the Lord Jesus Christ as their personal savior. Robert was the oldest of ten children. His father made him quit school in the third grade to work the family farm in Northern Montana in an area that was opened to homesteading. Over the years, he saw the value that an education offered, and he wanted it for his children, especially a college degree. However, he became very parochial with his views on life in raising children. I also came to value in my life my father's dreams, but I wanted to achieve them in a different way.

Church was the central part of my family's life. We attended services on Sundays (mornings and evening) and prayer meetings on Wednesday nights. We participated in all the different events in the life of the church. Growing up, it was just assumed my brothers and

I would attend the local college and work in the community. That was exactly what my brother, Logan, did. He has wisdom beyond his years and has been successful in his marriage and in his hometown community.

For myself, school was always hard for me. I did not really "fit in" with the local high school scene, and I wanted to go away to a private Christian school. I thought I would "fit in" a lot better, and there was so much about the world I wanted to discover. My father was totally against the idea, and for eighteen years of my life, I complied with all his wishes—until now.

What my father did not realize was I really did not want to go to the local community college in Gunnison, Colorado. I had set my heart on not going. It was a school where kids who loved to ski, hike, water-raft, and bike ride, and the town of Gunnison, situated in central Colorado, was a unique mountain town with an elevation of seventy-seven hundred where a college student could get a degree and enjoy their favorite sport at the same time.

My brothers and I never got involved in any of these outdoor sports because they were expensive, our family lived on a tight budget, and my father did not see the value in playing a sport. Our social activities revolved around the youth group at church and the school band. I had already spent four years at a high school where I never really "fit in," and I did not want my college years to be the same way.

I returned to the house and put the mail on the table, all except for the letter from Texas. I took it to my room, opened it, and read the words that I had been accepted for the 1966 fall term. I hugged the letter to my chest, thanked God for answering my prayers, and was so excited that a new life was ahead for me. Now it was time to tell my family. I returned to the kitchen and approached my mother.

"Mom, I'm so happy! I have wonderful news! The letter from Texas I have been waiting for arrived today. I have been accepted at Wayland for the fall term!"

"Gillian, I know this is wonderful news for you, and I'm happy that you were able to achieve one of your goals. You deserve some happiness in your life, and I know how disappointing some of your high school years have been. You also have supported and served this family in many ways, especially when I was ill and recovering from different hospitalizations. But to your father and I and this family, it is not good news. It hurts to know you would be leaving us."

"Mom, thousands of students leave home every year and go away to college. Yes, it is a sad time for families, but it is also a time to grow as a family. I love my family, and I know I will miss all of you. But I think going away to college is the experience I need to help me grow as an individual."

"Even when you know we won't be able to help you financially?"

"It is probably just that that will help me become less shy and more assertive."

"You would be going to a place we know very little about. It's only what we've heard from members of the youth group that have attended Wayland that we know anything about this college at all."

"Mom, it's those kids in the youth group that came back on their college breaks and shared with us high school kids what their college life is like that has me excited to want to go. I need your support! I need you to help me persuade Dad with my desire to go away to college."

"Even when you know the success to achieve academically and financially is all on you?"

"Mom, there is so much I want to experience about life and the world. I want to experience dorm life and try to become more involved with the different activities that a college life has to offer. Wayland has small class sizes, and they say the teachers offer a lot of assistance to help a student succeed. Dad's dream is for me to have a college education, and I want that too. But I want to achieve that goal at a small college with a culture I can thrive in, not hide. I've also understood Wayland offers student loans based on family finances that can be repaid upon graduation when a person is employed. I feel certain I would qualify for one of those loans. I plan on working at a job during the year and have been told I could apply for a job on campus since I will not have a car. Mom, will you please help me?"

"In many ways, I think it is time for us to grow as a family, and the college years is one way to do that. I believe it will be hard for your dad to accept the fact that not only are you leaving, but you could achieve a lot of what you want to experience right here at Western. There is the money issue also. But, since you have shared your dream and plans with me, I will do my best to help persuade your dad to let you go."

"Thanks, Mom! This is what I really want to do. Maybe this summer, you can help me sew some new outfits. I'd really like that."

"I'd like that too," my mother replied.

Mom and I began preparing supper, and we decided the best time to tell Dad would probably be after the family ate. When supper was over, I said a small prayer—"Jesus help me!"—and began to speak.

"Dad, I have something to tell you. Today, I received the letter from Wayland, and they have accepted me into the fall term."

He stood up and sternly said, "I told you I don't have any money to send you to Wayland and you're not going! You're going to Western! There is a good college right here in our hometown. You can stay home, find a job, and you can make it through with help from student loans!"

"Dad, I will not go to Western! I'll join the army before I do that!"

"No daughter of mine will be seen in the army!" He yelled, "I don't have any money to give you to send you down there!"

"Dad, I will work and apply for student loans, but Wayland is where I want to go. It is a small Christian school with the same values that our family believes in. It's a much better place for me 'down there' than 'right here' where I don't belong!"

During the summer months, as I worked at preparing to leave for Wayland, I shared more about myself and my dreams with my father. It took a while, but eventually, my dad saw how serious I was, and with tears in his eyes, he said I could go, but he could not give me any financial help.

I spent the summer working as a maid, cleaning cabins at a guest ranch a few miles from our home. I saved as much as possible while purchasing needed items recommended from the Wayland directory. Mom and I had a good time sewing new outfits along with a formal dress that was to be worn at the president's reception for incoming freshmen.

In August 1966, the family gathered at the bus station in Gunnison to say goodbye to me. After riding a bus overnight, I would begin my new life in Texas.

**2**

Wayland Baptist College is in Plainview, Texas, situated in the Panhandle about fifty miles north of Lubbock, Texas. The region has a semiarid climate with very flat land. During the years I attended Wayland, there were between 700–900 students enrolled. Today, it has reached university status and is now called Wayland University.

There is a story told of how Plainview got its name. A man asked a girl out on a date, and when he took her home, he wanted to kiss her goodnight. He couldn't find a secluded spot, so he kissed her in plain view. This geographical terrain was a huge change for a girl raised in the Rocky Mountains of Colorado most all her life.

I remember the first time I went to the cafeteria to eat, I was waiting in line and asked some of the students where they were from. One girl said, "Paris."

Another said, "Nazareth."

"Wow!" I replied. "I can't believe students would travel that far to come to Wayland!"

"Where are you from?" asked one of the girls.

"Colorado, and this is my first time in Texas."

Another girl explained that Paris and Nazareth were the names of towns in Texas. I had only been on campus a few hours and was already learning about the geography, towns, and cities in Texas.

I will always believe that the decision to go away to a Christian school was a good one. I enjoyed the small college-campus environment. The academic classes were small, and the professors were approachable and helpful to see that the students succeeded. I especially enjoyed dorm life. Living with a bunch of girls, sharing stories, watching television dramas, playing cards or board games on Friday nights with other girls who didn't have dates, and decorating the dorm for all the different holidays was a lot of fun.

I went to Texas with a deep faith, and Wayland helped me sustain it throughout my college years. There was chapel once a week, and all students were required to attend. During chapel time, the students were introduced to different preachers in the area. The senator and congressman from the state would speak along with writers, artists, and musicians. Almost everyone on campus attended church on Sunday mornings, a special Sunday dinner was served in the cafeteria at noon, and Sunday afternoons and evenings were free time.

I especially looked forward to Sunday evenings because the cafeteria was closed, and several of us girls would go out to a restaurant located in a mall near the school. My dad and mom could not help me financially with my education, but each week, I received a letter from home letting me know about the family, the different events in their lives, and within each letter was a five-dollar bill. With the five dollars, I was able to wash my clothes, and on Sunday nights, I could go out with the girls. So they ended up helping me after all in a big way.

In the late 1960s, Wayland built the new Harral Auditorium that would hold chapel each week along with academic and special music events throughout the year. To give the students on campus a special treat, the administration held a concert featuring Neil Diamond. I remember asking, "Who is Neil Diamond?"

No one seemed to know who he was, except that he was an up-and-coming musical artist.

Well, the students found him to be electrifying, singing his hit songs like "Sweet Caroline," "Cherry Cherry," and "Red Red Wine" along with all his other popular hit songs at that time in his career. There was a reception afterward where students could meet him, and that night, there were more demerits handed down because dancing was not allowed on campus. It was a great performance, and to this day, Neil Diamond remains one of my favorite musicians.

3

One of the newfound freedoms I began experiencing was making my own decisions. I didn't have to go and ask permission to go to the movies, go out with the girls, or what to do with my free time. This was a new experience in my life, and I remember the first time that freedom was put to a test.

It was my first Sunday on campus, church was over, the special noon meal had been served, and several of us were sitting around the dorm, deciding what to do with our afternoon. One of the girls suggested, "Let's all go to a movie!"

Another girl said, "Walt Disney has a new movie out titled *Swiss Family Robinson,* and I hear it's really good."

I replied, "You aren't all thinking of going to a movie on a Sunday, are you? That wouldn't be right since it is Sunday."

They all sat there and looked shocked by what I had said.

Someone else said, "Here in Texas, we think it is okay to go to a movie on a Sunday. You should come with us. It will be fun. I think you will enjoy the movie."

I really wasn't sure what to do. I had been raised all my life to believe that Sunday was the Lord's Day, and you didn't go to a movie on a Sunday. We certainly went on Saturdays, but not a Sunday. I had mixed feelings about going, but I finally agreed to go.

As I went into the theater, I was hoping God wouldn't strike me dead before I got back to the dorm. When I sat down in my seat and was waiting for the movie to begin, I started looking around to see who was there. I saw most of the people that were in church that day there and was really surprised when the pastor and his family walked in to watch the movie. I thought to myself, *Maybe this isn't wrong.* I really did enjoy the movie and was glad I went. I had survived my first big decision, and it felt good.

However, my choice in whom to date made life difficult on campus and with my parents. Ricardo was Spanish. I was white. We met while working in the college bookstore our sophomore year. We enjoyed talking and laughing about random things. It was just fun working together. I was excited the night he asked me to walk around the campus. When I got back from that walk, my dorm mom was waiting to talk to me.

"Gillian, I want to talk to you. Please come and sit with me."

I complied with her request but had the feeling I had done something wrong. Knowing that Ricardo and I had just walked and talked, I knew I hadn't done anything wrong.

"Gillian, it is not appropriate for you to be seen with Ricardo in a dating sort of way. You both come from two different backgrounds. This is an interracial situation, and I want you to seriously consider not having the relationship go any further. I'm sure your parents wouldn't approve of it either."

"All we did was walk and talk," I spoke. "We laughed like we do when we are working together in the bookstore. I just don't see anything wrong with what I did tonight."

"Regardless, it would be in your best interest not to accept any more invitations that would place you in that situation."

"I'll think about it," I told her and went upstairs. When I got upstairs, three or four of the girls were excited to find out the details of our walk around campus. Most of them said it would be okay if it was just a friendship and it didn't get serious.

I went to my room and was so confused. This was the first time a boy had asked me out to walk with him. It was my first official date. It was such a lovely evening with the fall temperatures arriving on the Panhandle of Texas. The air was cool, we were warm in our jackets with a full moon overhead, and we shared a little of where we came from and what our families were like. As he walked me back to my dorm, he made a comment about our walk.

"I had a nice time walking and talking with you," Ricardo said.

"So did I with you. It was a beautiful evening. Thanks for asking me out for a walk," I said.

"Maybe we can do it again sometime," he said.

"I'd like that," I replied as I slowly open the door to my dorm and went inside. Now, after feeling on cloud nine for just a few minutes, I was under pressure to make sure we just remained friends. That night is all I thought we would ever be.

Lying in bed that night, I remembered thinking, *It finally happened! It was so wonderful for a boy to think that I was special and worth his time in a special way.* I lay there, wondering about the word *interracial.* It had never been a part of my life. Growing up in all the trailer courts I had lived in, there were only white people, and I never had a Spanish or African American friend. In eighth grade, when we moved to Gunnison, there was a Spanish population, and many of them rode on the same school bus as we did. But I never had any association with them, and they mostly stayed to themselves. The Spanish people attended the Catholic church, and we attended one of the Protestant churches.

Ricardo was the first Spanish person to approach me, be friendly, and he enjoyed knowing me. As I went to sleep that night, I prayed to God for guidance with the decision ahead.

*****

The next day, when we met in the cafeteria, Ricardo brought his tray over and sat beside me. All the other students who were sitting at the table began to "ooh and aah" at us. Ricardo and I just laughed it off. But all week along, he sat beside me when we ate, and that weekend, he asked me to go to the movies, and I accepted.

I wrote my parents and asked them what they thought. My father was totally against it and would not allow it. My mother said to keep it as a friendship and nothing else. It was the Bible Belt in the 1960s, and we were not approved of as a couple. Ricardo was my first boyfriend, and people considered me worldly (imagine me a worldly person with only two dates!).

*****

In our junior year, the day before I was to head home for spring break, Ricardo walked me back to the dorm after the dinner hour was over and said he could not keep dating me anymore. He said it would be better for everyone if we broke up. I cried most of the way home on the bus, and several times, my parents heard me crying in my room. I did not want the relationship to be over. My dad came in, hugged me, and tried to console me.

"Gillian, it's the right thing to do. It is best for both of you, and I could never approve of you marrying him."

"Dad, I love him, and I know he loves me. It's other people who don't approve. What am I to do with the way I feel?"

"Gillian, you need to give yourself a chance to date other boys among your own race. You haven't even given that possibility a chance. And it would take away all the stigmatism that you are now facing by continuing to date Ricardo."

*****

For the whole week home on spring break, I was a mess, and now the time had come to head back to school and face everyone on campus without Ricardo. Getting closer and closer to Plainview, I decided I would try to be strong and give myself a chance with someone else if it would ever happen again.

To my surprise, when I got off the bus, Ricardo was waiting for me. He said he missed me a lot and he thought it over and didn't want us to break up. He loved me. I loved him. Somehow, we would find a way to make it work. All I knew is we cared for each other, and in the fall of 1969, our senior year, we were making plans for graduation and being teachers in Texas.

In 1969, the United States was still at war with Vietnam (1965–1975). It was also a very turbulent time of anti-war protests with many college-age students wanting nothing to do with the war effort. That fall, there was a high demand for military personnel, more than the regular military could provide, causing an acceleration of the draft.

On December 1, 1969, the Selective Service System conducted two lotteries to determine the order in which men born from 1944–1950 would be called to service in the Vietnam War. Ricardo received number ninety, considered a low number out of 366 drawn, and was told he was sure to be called in the fall. Our graduation plans changed, and we gave each other the freedom to date other people if the opportunity arose.

In August of 1970, I moved to San Antonio, Texas, where I received a teaching position at an elementary school. I purchased my first car, a two-door red-and-white Ford Fairlane that I thought was beautiful. I rented a two-bedroom townhouse apartment and advertised for a roommate. The ad was answered by another single young woman who was also a teacher.

As roommates, it was fun sharing our different teaching experiences, and on weekends, one could find us clubbing around San Antonio's night life or visiting her family in a nearby town. On Sundays, I found a church where I could worship and thanked God for the life he had given me. I was even thinking about working on my master's degree in education when the school year ended.

Ricardo graduated from boot camp in January 1971, and with all the places he could have been sent, he received orders to be stationed in San Antonio at Fort Sam Houston where he would receive schooling to be a dental assistant. We felt like it was fate for us to be together. We resumed our dating relationship and decided to marry the coming summer.

# PART 2

## *Alaska*

In June 1971, I resigned my teaching position and traveled back home to be married in the church I grew up in. My mother helped me with the wedding preparations; my best friend from college and my roommate in San Antonio were my bridesmaids. We planned a small wedding and invited church members. Ricardo, who was already stationed in Fairbanks, Alaska, flew back for the event while his mother and a few siblings drove up from Texas. My father walked me down the aisle but wasn't happy about the union. He was excited that we would be living in Alaska, a place he'd always dreamed he could see someday.

Our honeymoon was the trip back to Fairbanks. Driving my Ford Fairlane, we left Gunnison and traveled to Yellowstone National Park. Neither Ricardo nor I had ever visited the park, and we were hoping to see a gushing geyser, possibly its most famous one, Old Faithful. We found the park to be a beautiful wilderness area with surrounding mountains, geysers throughout along with lakes and rivers. Driving around Yellowstone, we passed by bison and deer but never saw a bear. We spent the night at a lodge in the park and, after breakfast the next morning, went and saw Old Faithful erupt before driving on to Seattle, Washington, where we decided to pass into Canada.

Crossing the border into British Columbia, we began diving through valleys with orchards and onto a small winding road which pasted several sawmills and log mining camps. It was amazing discovering how beautiful the province of British Columbia was with its high mountain ranges.

Driving into the beautiful port city of Prince Rupert, British Columbia, we were able to secure passage on a ferry boat headed for Haines, Alaska. Once on board the ferry boat, we traveled at night through the Inside Passage and stopped the next morning in Juneau, Alaska. Juneau is Alaska's capital and can only be reached by boat or seaplanes.

There wasn't time for sightseeing in Juneau, but we did enjoy discovering the beauty of the city with Mount Roberts in the background. Casting off from Juneau, we sailed another four hundred and seventy miles of the Inside Passage before we disembarked at Haines, Alaska, near Glacier Bay National Park.

On the road again, we still had to travel about five hundred miles of the Alcan Highway, which in 1971 was still a gravel road, and my Ford Fairlane was not the best vehicle for those driving conditions. We had one breakdown along the Alcan Highway, and we were very thankful it was in an area that had repair shops. I think business was good for them!

After traveling for a week, we arrived safely in Fairbanks, a former gold-rush town with a population of forty-five thousand. It was the largest city in the interior of Alaska, and it was home to the University of Alaska Fairbanks and the Fort Wainwright military base. This would be our new home for one year. I thanked God once again for giving me another part of my dream. I was on a great adventure, exploring the world with the man I loved.

Upon our arrival, I was excited to find out about our housing accommodations.

Ricardo said, "Gillian, we can stay at the on-base housing facility for a few days, but we will need to start looking for an off-base apartment since Wainwright doesn't have on-base housing for married men with my rank."

"Okay, we can start looking tomorrow. How much have you saved for the deposit and first month's rent?" I asked.

"I haven't saved anything. I even borrowed money to purchase our wedding rings. I've been too embarrassed to tell you," Ricardo replied.

"So you're telling me that I paid for the wedding and the trip to Alaska with what I could save on my teacher's salary, rent, car payment, and living expenses, and you living as a single guy on a base with most of your needs meet haven't saved anything at all?"

"I know it's a bad situation. I've never been a good manager of money. I just thought you would have the money to get us started," Ricardo said.

"Well, I still have money coming on my teaching contract, but I wouldn't be receiving that for at least six to eight weeks. You're going to have to come up with a plan on how we are supposed to live here. Ricardo, I can't believe you haven't thought about this or saved for it!"

"My friends that I borrowed money from for the rings can probably loan us enough to get started," Ricardo said.

"That's just great! I arrive and haven't even met or gotten acquainted with your friends, and now we must ask for a handout so we can begin living up here! Do you understand how embarrassing this is to me?"

"I understand you're disappointed, but that's the only way I know of right now on how to get us out of this predicament," Ricardo replied.

This was my first time to learn that Ricardo was not a good manager of money. So we borrowed money from his best friends, and I assured them I could repay them when I received the check. And I did.

I have the fondest memories of our life in "The Land of the Midnight Sun." We found off-base housing in an apartment complex which housed many other enlisted men and their wives. Before our marriage, my husband had established some good friendships with both single and married military personnel. Many times, you could find us hosting dinners and parties or invited to card games and barbecues. On Sundays, we attended the Protestant services at the non-denominational church on base. We had a close friendship with my husband's best friend, his wife, and their little girl. We enjoyed weekend outings, exploring the sights around Fairbanks, or just staying home and sharing meals and playing cards or board games.

During the summer months, many times, Ricardo would come home with a large salmon that one of the officers at the base dental clinic had caught on a weekend fishing trip, and they shared some of the catch with their enlisted men. When we returned to the lower forty-eight states, I was shocked at the price of salmon, and my memory would always return to those large salmon that were a gift.

Alaska is known as "The Land of the Midnight Sun," and the months of May, June, July, and August are the best time to enjoy twenty-four hours of sun. During these summer months, Fairbanks is home to a collegiate summer baseball team known as The Alaska Goldpanners of Fairbanks. We attended a few of the night games.

During one game, I had a person tap me on the shoulder. I turned around, and she said, "Hi, Gillian!" She was a dear friend of my mother's from Gunnison, Colorado. She and her husband were on vacation, traveling the Alcan Highway through Canada and Alaska. I was delighted to see them, and it was a little insight into how small our world can be.

Labor Day Weekend, we traveled in one van with two other couples to see the sights of Anchorage, Alaska. Located three hundred and fifty miles south of Fairbanks in south-central Alaska, Anchorage is Alaska's largest city and is one of the most beautiful cities I have ever seen. It is situated on the sea in a wide valley with high mountains to the east. We were able to secure rooms with kitchen privileges at the military base. We toured the city, visited an historic gold mine, and even tried our luck panning for gold along a nearby creek.

Leaving Anchorage, we traveled back along the beautiful scenic highway between Anchorage and Fairbanks, viewing majestic mountains and miles of forestland. Our weekend trip gave us an insight into Alaska's big city versus small-town community life.

## 7

When I resigned my teaching position in Texas, I thought I would be able to secure a teaching position in Fairbanks for the next school year. When I submitted my application, I was told there were about twenty-five applicants for every teaching position and a lot of hopeful teachers had secured jobs at banks and other businesses around town just waiting for a teaching position to open up because teacher salaries in Alaska were high compared to the lower forty-eight states. During my college years, I did some waitressing, so I spent several days trying to get a waitress position at the local cafes and restaurants but also without luck.

I came to realize the Fairbanks community was flooded with a workforce made up of not only locals but also military wives, college students, and personnel working to construct the Alaska Pipeline that would eventually convey crude oil from Prudhoe Bay in the north to Valdez, Alaska, in the south.

Living and exploring the Fairbanks community with friends was wonderful; however, it was also a very expensive place to live, even while shopping at the military base commissary. Fairbanks, being in Alaska's interior, required a large majority of supplies to be flown in, making items expensive. We were living on just our military pay which was low compared to the cost of living. I had some money saved from teaching in Texas, but it was quickly being depleted.

Since I couldn't find employment, we applied for assistance and were told we made one dollar too much (imagine that!). To make it month-to-month, we decided to reduce our rent by moving out-of-town to a lower income housing area. We moved into a small three-room apartment further into the forest. The rent was cheaper, but the electricity was higher, and we needed more money for gas. We saved a little with the move and learned to live on a tighter budget.

There were other military personnel living in the area, and it was fun making new friends.

In September, we received the first snowfall of the year, and along with it, I learned I was pregnant with my first child. We were delighted to learn we were going to be parents! Our families were happy for us, and my mom began sewing maternity clothes and sending them to me. It was fun receiving packages from home so far away.

Slowly, the snow increased, the days drew darker where we only saw the daylight about four hours a day, and the temperatures were far below zero. We had two unique experiences that happened to us during those winter months. The first one concerned our car. A Ford Fairlane is not a four-wheel drive and does not exactly belong in the bush of Alaska. When winter does come, a person needs to think about winterizing their car. To keep cars from freezing, every establishment in Fairbanks has a plug-in station receptacle, usually one to every parking lot. We did an oil change to heavier oil that handles the colder weather, changed the battery, and bought an engine block heater with an extension cord. The plugged-in heater keeps the engine warm to help ensure your car will start, and it also warms up the inside of the car faster.

One dark, cold morning, when the temperature was at sixty to seventy degrees below zero, Ricardo went out to start the car, and when he came back in, while it warmed up, I could tell something was wrong.

"Gillian, you're not going to believe what just happened. I just reached to and clicked the car door to open it, and all the glass on the driver's door of the car just shattered and fell out. There is glass on the inside and outside of the car to clean up. It's not going to be easy to clean up wearing parkas and gloves, so we'll vacuum the inside, and I will shovel what I can around the outside to get the worst of it cleaned up," replied Ricardo.

"Good idea. Let me get dressed and grab the vacuum so I can help you," I replied.

"We're going to need something like a piece of cardboard or small blanket to place in the window so I can get to base and hopefully get the window fixed today."

While I was vacuuming the car out, Ricardo tried shoveling up glass around the car. I found a box in the closet and cut a piece of cardboard off it. Together, we worked at fitting it into place, hoping it would stay.

Ricardo called later, saying he had found a window repair service that could fix the window that day but that he would be late getting home. The serviceman told Ricardo that it would be best if we purchased another heater for the interior of the car that ran at night. This would help to keep the windows expanded when the car was parked overnight. We followed through with getting the additional heater and had no further glass breakage.

Our second experience during the subzero weather was on a day Ricardo was returning home from his day at work. He got a flat tire that had to be changed, which he did, and made it home safely. That night, we had friends over to play cards. During the card game, we all began hearing a strange eerie sound outside.

We all stopped and looked at one another.

I said, "Do you all hear what I'm hearing?"

"Yeah, we do," everyone said.

Victoria replied, "It sounds like an animal dying."

Our friend, Kyle, said, "Maybe if we just sit here and not disturb it, it will quietly go away."

*My sentiments exactly*, I thought.

So we sat, and our eyes darted around the table, looking from one to another. As we sat there, the strange eerie sound continued its dying agony of death. We knew we were not going to be able to concentrate on the game until we discovered what was making that sound.

I said, "This is why we are married to strong army men. We know you are going to protect your lovely wives from all harm. Isn't that right, men?"

"Sure, it's why I joined the army," Ryan said, standing up. "Come on, men, let's see what is dying outside."

It was completely dark and very cold, and none of us were excited about venturing outside to the strange sound. But we couldn't just sit there and listen to the sound of death. So we ladies decided to join the men.

We all put our coats on and headed outside. With the lights from the apartment complex and two of our guys with flashlights, we ventured out, women behind the men. The closer we got to our car, the louder the sound became until we were all standing, looking at the trunk of our car.

"The sound is definitely coming from our car," Ricardo said. "I wonder if an animal jumped into the trunk while I was changing that tire on the way home."

Needless to say, none of us wanted to open that trunk! Slowly, Ricardo inserted the key and turned the lock. Us ladies yelled and hugged each other. When it opened, we all looked and saw a large tomcat freezing to death.

"Wow, would you look at that?" Ryan said.

"It's a large cat," I said.

Victoria said, "A large tomcat!"

Ryan said, "I bet you someone abandoned it, and when Ricardo changed the tire, it jumped in the trunk."

"Oh my gosh, what are we going to do?" I said. "We can't leave it here and just let it die."

"It's got to go inside, and we need to get some warm milk into it," replied Ryan.

Ryan picked up the cat and carried it into our bathroom. While I warmed up some milk, Victoria found a towel and laid it in the bathtub. Ryan put the cat on the towel and started rubbing its fur.

"Here's the milk, Ryan," I said.

"Thanks, I need to get some milk into its mouth. Maybe if I turn its head and he smells the milk, he will try licking some of it."

Ryan worked with the cat for a few minutes, rubbing its fur, and slowly, it tried some of the milk. We decided to leave the cat in the tub and see if it would make it through the night.

*****

The next morning, it was decided the cat would have to stay with me until Ricardo could return at lunchtime with a friend, and then take it to the Humane Society in town. The cat recovered nicely, and it was jumping off the bathroom walls while I was relieving myself during the frozen morning in the forest. I felt like it was the longest morning of my life. We never inquired or learned what happened to the cat.

Slowly, the dark days got shorter, and spring began to arrive in Fairbanks. During March, the darkness and daylight are about even with about twelve hours of both. April continues to bring warmer weather, and it is also the month the Nenana Ice Classic is held, which is an annual ice pool contest. This is a big charity event which involves the Tanana River. The river is over five hundred miles long and flows through Fairbanks, dividing the town. The subzero winter temperature freezes the river, and sometimes the ice can be over forty inches thick. People from the small town of Nenana, Alaska, located also along the river, plant a tripod with four supports that are securely frozen to the river three hundred feet from shore. A line is attached to the top of the tripod, and once that end is anchored, the other end is secured to the Ice Classic Tower nearby on the banks of the river. It's attached there to the clock inside the tower.

When the ice goes out and moves the tripod one hundred feet, the line breaks and stops the clock. The town of Nenana sells lottery tickets for people to guess the month, day, hour, and minute the ice on the river will break at Nenana. Ticket sales are worldwide and soar into the hundreds of thousands of dollars that support a prize pool and Nenana charitable organizations. The ice usually breaks between mid-April to mid-May.

**8**

Also during this time, the war in Vietnam began to de-escalate and the number of military personnel needed was reduced, and the draft was also reduced. It was Ricardo's dream to use his degree in history to teach at the high school and eventually the college level. Several times, he was given the opportunity to reup with bonus incentives. But his desire to return to Texas and begin a teaching career was more important. The final decision was made not to reup, so we received our notice that we would be discharged from the army in July 1972. Our time in Alaska was drawing short.

May brought the arrival of our beautiful daughter, Juliet. As a little girl, I loved playing with dolls. When I held Juliet for the first time, I thanked God for this real-live doll in my life. I spent three days at the military hospital in a ward with five other women learning to feed, bathe, and bond with my little girl. When I was to give her first bath, I spent time gently soaping, rinsing, and playing with her. When they came to get her, I hadn't even fed her. The nurse explained that babies don't need "that" big of a bath. I put it all down to being an excited new mother.

Ricardo came from a large family with several brothers and sisters. When he learned I was pregnant, he didn't care if it was a boy or a girl. However, several months before I was to give birth, Ricardo and his male friends would sit around and talk about babies and what a child brings to a marriage. Most of them agreed that it was important to have a boy to carry on the family name and the special bonding that can happen between fathers and sons.

With all this talk, my husband began wishing for a boy. When Juliet was born, his disappointment was evident. I arrived home to dishes in the sink, and he expected lunch and sat and ignored us. He felt trapped after having three days of freedom. I ignored his attitude, and slowly, the more time he spent alone with us, he bonded with Juliet and seemed to enjoy the family we had become.

Because we were leaving, we didn't purchase a lot of baby furniture, so Juliet's first bed was an orange box padded with baby blankets. We wanted to save most of our separation pay to begin our new life back in Texas. I really enjoyed being a mother. We were a happy family who enjoyed being alone or with friends, and those final weeks in the interior of Alaska with the days sunny and warm are wonderful memories in my mind.

# PART 3

## *Back to Texas*

## 9

The first week of July 1972, we said goodbye to our dear friends, promising them we would stay in touch. Our flight took some unusual maneuvers flying us over beautiful snow and ice-capped mountains before landing in Seattle, Washington, where we had shipped our belongings. We were one full day in Seattle, getting our items out of shipping and receiving and into a rental U-Haul to pull behind the car. Our destination was Dumas, Texas, where Ricardo had received an interview for a teaching position at the local high school.

It was a good feeling being back in the lower forty-eight states, and as we traveled through Washington, Idaho, and Utah, I started thinking about our families and getting together with them for the holidays. I mentioned it to Ricardo.

"Ricardo, what do you think about the family getting together for Christmas this year? It will be our first Christmas back and Juliet's first Christmas with grandparents, uncles, aunts, and cousins."

"I'm all for families getting together for the holidays, Gillian. But you're getting a little ahead of yourself. Right now, I haven't secured the position in Dumas, and we really don't know where we will be living," Ricardo replied.

"I'm just excited to see my parents and have everyone meet Juliet."

"I am, too, but we need to get settled first and find out how things go for us before we start making Christmas plans."

My mom and dad were living in a camper trailer in northern Colorado where my dad was working for a construction company repairing roads. As we approached the camper, my mom came out, waved, and greeted us.

"It is wonderful to see you!" Mom said.

"Oh, Momma, it is so good to see you and be hugged by you."

"Now, where is that grandchild of mine? I can't wait another minute to see her and hold her!"

I took Juliet out of her car seat, raised her up, and placed her in Mama's arms.

"Wow, she is such a pretty baby! She has dark hair like her father's along with a light skin tone like yours, Gillian. It's wonderful to see you and Ricardo, but I've been so excited to meet my first grandchild. I wished you could stay a few days. You've been gone over a year, and you're only giving us tonight to hear all about Alaska," Mom commented.

"We can only stay overnight, Mrs. Wilson," replied Ricardo. "I need to be in Dumas, Texas, by next week for my interview with the school district. I'm hoping to secure a position in their history department at the high school level."

"Robert and I are also excited about that for you, Ricardo, and I understand traveling with a baby will take you longer than usual. I just needed to ask," Mom said.

"Thanks for understanding our situation at this time," Ricardo replied.

"Mom, Ricardo and I talked on the way down here that as soon as we know where we will be living and get settled, we will make plans for the family to get together. We were thinking possibly this Christmas season when Logan and Nathan's colleges close for the winter break."

"Well, it is certainly something to think and talk about. It will depend on your dad's work also," Mom replied.

As we sat there, talking, I heard Dad's truck drive up. I was excited to see him but nervous also. He wasn't happy about me being married to Ricardo, and now I had Juliet, and I wasn't sure how he would respond to her. Dad opened the camper door and entered.

"Well, hello," he said.

I went over and gave him a big hug and told him it was good to see him and be back in Colorado.

"Good to see you too," he said.

Ricardo said, "Hello, Mr. Wilson."

Dad replied, "Hello. Give me a minute to wash up and get ready for supper, and then we can talk."

When Dad came out of the bathroom, I had Juliet lying on the camper bed and said, "Dad, this is Juliet."

"She's a little thing! Pretty too!" he replied.

Then, to my surprise, Dad lay down on the bed beside her and began talking and playing with her. He was even trying to get her to smile. My dad was the oldest of ten children, and when his brothers or sisters visited us, they always said what a great big brother my dad was. My heart was overjoyed with the affection and love both my mom and dad had shown to her.

We had a good visit over supper that night. They were very interested in the long dark winter days, the extreme cold temperatures that we survived in, and then the continuous sunlight during summer. That night, we found a room at a motel in town, and the next morning, we said goodbye after an early morning breakfast before Dad went to work.

*****

Our next stop was Amarillo, Texas, where Ricardo grew up, and we had a good visit with his mother and a few of his siblings. Mrs. Ramirez already had several grandchildren and a great-grandchild, but when she saw Juliet, she clapped her hands together and gave a big smile as I placed her in her arms.

"Ricardo, Gillian, beautiful baby!" she said.

Ricardo went over, sat beside her, and started telling her about Juliet and our trip down to Texas.

She asked, "Gillian, your parents are well, I pray?"

"They are very well and living in a small camper in northern Colorado near Dad's work. Thank you for asking," I replied.

The house began to fill up with siblings, the conversation turned to Spanish, which I didn't understand, and Juliet was passed around where she received a lot of hugs and kisses. Everyone was happy to see us, the food was delicious, and it was good catching up on the events in their lives. We stayed with them a few days so Ricardo could go to his interview in Dumas about forty miles north of Amarillo. He received a teaching position in the history department, and we were happy that things were working out the way we hoped. Within the week, we had secured a furnished apartment, bought some baby furniture, and were ready to begin our new life.

*****

Once settled, we began looking for a church in the community, and Ricardo also began looking for a second job. He wanted Juliet raised inside our home with her mother, like he and his siblings were raised. At church, we met a middle-aged couple that had a well-drilling business and needed help. Ricardo was hired, and we struck up a good friendship with them, and several times, we were invited to dinners in their home.

In December of 1972, we invited my family to come for Christmas. Dad and Mom along with my two brothers, Logan and Nathan, who were on winter break from the colleges they were attending, were excited to visit Texas and have the family all together. Dad and Mom were wonderful grandparents and were happy to spend time with Juliet who was now sitting up and had two teeth. I remember Logan was working on his master's degree at the University of Colorado in Boulder, and he brought several books with him that he needed to study, so I put him in the guest bedroom during the day.

Coming from the mountains of Colorado, Dad's main comment was, "This is the flattest land I have ever seen!"

They enjoyed seeing the oil pumps pumping up and down and learning about the well-drilling business in the area. Ricardo contacted his well-drilling boss and arranged to have Dad and my brothers visit one of the sites he was working on. Dad appreciated the extra attention, and Mom and I enjoyed some time together while they were away for a few hours.

As much as we were enjoying our life in Dumas, managing our money continued to be a problem, and we needed to reduce our expenses once again. Ricardo was also struggling adjusting to civilian life. He missed the life we had in Alaska and the daily camaraderie between friends and officers. He still wanted to follow his dream to teach at the college level, so we talked about moving to Amarillo, Texas, where he could attend the local college and work on his master's degree.

He applied at the Amarillo School District and was hired to teach in the history department at one of the local high schools for the next school year.

During the summer, we moved to Amarillo and found housing in a low-income housing area near the school where he would be teaching. He applied to Amarillo College master's program and was accepted into the fall term. He was happier in Amarillo. We were making new friends, invited to barbecues and weddings, and found a church to attend. Our lives improved, and after attending a wedding of a friend, he held my hand and said how much he loved me and our life together with Juliet.

As we drove up and parked in the driveway, his older brother, Carlos, was sitting on our doorstep. This was the beginning of the end of our lives together.

# PART 4

## *Carlos*

## 10

Ricardo was raised in a very large family with several brothers and sisters. When I met Mrs. Ramirez, she was a widow running her own Mexican restaurant in the family hometown of Amarillo, Texas. Many of the older brothers and sisters had left home, were married, and were raising families. Several had established businesses, earned college degrees, and were awarded honors in their selected fields. The brother Ricardo had the closest relationship with was Carlos who was eleven months older than him. Ricardo just enjoyed being around Carlos because he could tell events and stories in a unique way that made you laugh, and you wanted to hear more.

The one major difference between the two boys was Ricardo was strong in academics, achieved high marks, and was motivated with goals and dreams. Carlos, in many ways, was considered the black sheep of the family. He had no interest in doing well in school and tried to find the easy way out of most situations. It was hard for him to hold down a job. Stealing became easy for him, and he could talk his way out of most situations.

The day he arrived on our doorstep, he was running from authorities. They believed him to be an illegal immigrant. He had been taken to the border three times before he found his way to our doorstep. He was dirty, tired, hungry, and was asking for help.

As I was fixing breakfast the next morning, Ricardo approached me and wanted to discuss Carlos.

"Gillian, I want to try and help Carlos. He is my brother, and he is asking for my help. I want to know what you think about him staying here with us for a while."

"Ricardo, I'm all for helping a person in need. I know he's your brother, one you're very close to, and you haven't seen him in a long time. He just doesn't have a very good reputation of being dependable or trustworthy. We're barely making it ourselves. Do you really think it is a good idea?" I stressed.

"I'll help him find work, and maybe he can help us while we are helping him. I just can't say no to him when he is in such a bad way. We could a least try, and if it doesn't work out, he can go, and we'll know we did the right thing," Ricardo replied.

"Well okay, as long as he finds work and contributes to buying groceries," I said.

"Great! You'll see. Us helping Carlos will help us too," Ricardo said.

"I am going to pray that's true," I replied. And some part of me was hoping it would help Ricardo have the camaraderie he had in Alaska. However, I will always regret not saying no and standing firm on that decision.

*****

When Carlos moved in, Ricardo started spending all his free time with him. He became that buddy he had back in college or Alaska. Carlos now had a place to live, access to a car, some money (the little we had), and a sister-in-law to cook and wash his clothes. He found work as a day laborer and bought groceries occasionally. All Carlos had to say was "*Vamonos*" to Ricardo, and Ricardo was up and out the door for a good time. We were not helping Carlos. Carlos was destroying us.

During the summer break from school, we decided that we would all try to find work to help with the household expenses. Ricardo and Carlos would work during the day, and I would try and find a part-time job in the evenings. I found employment at a nearby factory, making shutters for windows. I learned to place the wood in the correct position in the machine before clamping it altogether and snapping the control device in place. I had a certain quota I had to achieve each day.

Now the situation was they cared for Juliet, who was now walking, for a few hours during the day, and after I returned from my shift, Ricardo and Carlos went out. Ricardo would not say no to

Carlos. Occasionally, they would stay home and watch TV, especially Saturday and Sundays with the college and NFL football games. The only way I saw that Ricardo was helping Carlos was keeping him out of trouble with the authorities. Our time together was gone, Carlos had a nice little setup, and Ricardo refused to see what was happening.

The fall school year began, Ricardo was back to teaching, and he was now enrolled at Amarillo College, working on his masters. I continued with my part-time job while Carlos found occasional work.

One Sunday afternoon, I had been doing the wash while Ricardo and Carlos were watching football. Juliet was napping in her room. Ricardo and Carlos began arguing at Ricardo's reaction to a game play. I had just hung out some clothes on the clothesline to dry, came in, and sat on the arm of the couch, listening to their disagreement when I began to make a comment.

"Ricardo, Carlos is right, you do react that way," I said.

Ricardo turned and yelled at me, "Gillian, just shut up! You have no right to say anything like that to me!"

I reacted, "What in the world is the matter with you? I'm just agreeing with what Carlos said, and I think you should take it under consideration, that's all I'm saying."

Ricardo replied, "I don't want you listening into our conversations, and we would like to finish watching this game without you. So, now, leave!"

"So, Ricardo, you're telling me that Carlos can speak any way he likes to you, tell you anything, and you believe him, and I make one comment about what you're arguing about because it is what I see is true, and you get mad at me? What you're implying is you can't stand me anymore and want me to leave? I'm sick of both of you and will leave you to yourselves," I said and left the room.

I went to check on Juliet. She was still sleeping, so I went into the bathroom, filled the tub for a bath, and got in. I could hear Ricardo and Carlos talking but couldn't understand what was being said.

In a few minutes, Ricardo slowly entered the bathroom, walked over to the edge of the tub, and began to speak. "You will never, ever talk that way to me again. Do you understand?" he said in a very firm angry voice.

"Ricardo, get out of here, I want some peace and quiet," I said in a very calm voice.

Ricardo bent down and started beating me in the face as hard as he could. I couldn't stop the blows.

Carlos rushed in and yelled, "Stop, Ricardo! Stop, man, stop!" And he pulled Ricardo away.

I was now bloody and shaking badly. I grabbed the washcloth and started covering my face. I climbed out of the tub and wrapped myself in a towel. Holding up my hand. I began to beg, "Ricardo, please stay away from me!"

Ricardo gabbed me, hugged me to himself, and started apologizing, "Gillian, Gillian, I don't know what came over me!"

"Ricardo, please don't touch me! Please stay away from me. I don't think I can trust you anymore!" I cried as I continued to shake and hold a towel to my face. "If you truly don't want Juliet and me anymore, we'll leave. I just don't want you hitting me anymore!" I cried.

"Gillian, please don't think about leaving me. Please!"

"Ricardo, I want to go lie down in bed and I want you to stay away from me. Don't try to come in. I want to check on Juliet first, see that she is okay. Then you and Carlos can stay away from me. Do you understand?"

"Yes, I'll stay away tonight, and we'll talk in the morning," he said.

I went to bed, praying to God to help me and show me what to do. Ricardo was no longer the man I had fallen in love with and was becoming a stranger. I felt like he had finally released all the anger he had been storing up since he left Alaska. It seemed like Juliet and I were more of a burden than a blessing. I was always trying to please him and fulfill his dreams, but I think he quit dreaming a long time ago of what he really wanted. I knew one thing: I wanted to save my marriage and get back to what we had, to work on our goals and dreams.

I called Mrs. Ramirez and asked if she could come and help me get Carlos out of the house. She came with two of her daughters. Carlos said he wasn't going anywhere, and Ricardo sided with him against his family. He told me, "My brother has been with me longer than you have, and he will come before you."

Mrs. Ramirez advised me to leave for a while.

I stayed and continued to work at the shutter factory until the bruises were off my face. When my fellow workers saw me, they were shocked.

"What happened?" one woman asked.

"I ran into a pole," I said.

"Angry pole," another woman said.

When I was home, Ricardo and Carlos ignored me, and I stayed in Juliet's room or in my bedroom. I only took care of Juliet's and my needs. I decided Ricardo and Carlos could take care of themselves since that's all they cared about.

*****

With the damage done to my face now healed, I decided to go and see my parents in Colorado. One evening, after putting Juliet down for the night, I walked out and informed Ricardo and Carlos of my decision.

"Ricardo, I bought bus tickets to Colorado today for Juliet and me. We are going to go see my parents."

"How long will you be gone?" Ricardo asked.

"I asked them if it would be okay if we spent a week with them. Mom was very happy we were coming," I said.

"Okay, I will drive you to the bus station tomorrow, and call me when you plan on arriving back in town so I can pick you up," Ricardo said.

We traveled by bus to Silverthorne in northern Colorado where Dad was working with a construction company on the roads in that area. Mom and he were living in a park in the camper trailer. They were very happy to see us, loved having time with Juliet, and I acted like everything was fine, but Mom told me later she was suspicious about the visit and worried about me.

At the end of the week, I called Ricardo and told him the time I would be returning and asked him if he could meet us. He said he would, but upon our arrival, he wasn't there. I made several calls home, but there was no answer and no way to get in touch with him (this was the time before we owned cell phones).

After waiting an hour at the bus station, I called a cab and arrived home around eight o'clock. The house was a mess, and I had no idea where Ricardo and Carlos were. I put Juliet to bed, showered, and went to bed myself. I awoke during the night to the sound of them entering the house and decided to pretend to be asleep. Ricardo came in, never said a word, turned his back to me, and went to sleep.

*****

When I began to wake up, I said a prayer to God that he would help me talk to Ricardo.

"Ricardo, could we please talk and see if we can get back to what we had together?"

He just ignored me.

"Ricardo, please talk to me. I want to save what we had together," I pleaded.

"Gillian, just stop talking. Don't say anything," he said, speaking like he just couldn't stand me anymore.

"Ricardo, it can't continue like this. Things have got to change around here."

"Gillian, don't say another word or you will regret it," he said with his back still to me.

"Ricardo, all I want to do—"

That's when he turned over and slugged me in the face as hard as he could.

I was crying. I got up and told him, "I've had enough!" I got dressed, grabbed my purse, and ran. I left Juliet asleep in her room and ran to the nearest phone booth a few blocks away. I called the pastor from the church where we occasionally attended and told him I needed help. He came and got me. He asked me what happened and what I wanted to do. I told him I wanted to save my marriage and if he could please go into the house and see if Ricardo would come and talk with him and me at the church.

He took me home but had me stay in his car. He spent a few minutes inside, and upon returning to the car, he said Ricardo didn't want to talk. I knew then I had lost the life I had loved

The pastor went back into the house and explained the situation to Ricardo and Carlos.

"Gillian is coming into the house, packing clothes for her and Juliet, and I will be taking her to the airport to fly her home to her parents," he said.

He stood in the living room while Ricardo and Carlos sat in the kitchen in silence. Not a word was said as I walked in, packed one suitcase, and walked out with Juliet in my arms. I wrote a check at the airport for our fare and learned later that it had bounced, and Ricardo had to deal with that situation. The pastor helped us through the airport and saw us safely on the plane. I remember the airline attendants being very nice to me, and one commented, "You've had a hard time, but you're going to get better."

# PART 5

## *The Early Years*

**II**

I have many good memories of my life with my two brothers growing up in a small home filled with love from two special parents. Logan, Nathan, and I played a lot of board games together, rode bikes around the neighborhood, played with friends and cousins, and enjoyed exploring the new places where we lived. Church was a big part of our lives. We attended services Sunday (morning and evening) and prayer meetings on Wednesday night. We participated in all the different events in the life of the church. Growing up, I never realized we were not a wealthy family, but I felt so rich in the things you could not put a price on—values, beliefs, and respect for people, especially family.

When I was thirteen years old, my mother had a major heart attack while working in the school cafeteria. My dad took over the role of managing the operation of our home and us children. He was very good about cooking, washing, and even did the ironing. He also gave his three children chores to do every day, some of which had to be done before school began. My oldest brother was vacuuming the floor; I was washing breakfast dishes and making sure Nathan, age eight, was ready for school.

After school, there were more chores and homework. When Mom came home from the hospital, we devoted ourselves to seeing to her needs and helping her get well. I just fell into the role of serving in the home, and it has been my major role in life.

Our family's life consisted of loving each other, attending church, working toward a good education, and learning music. I felt loved by both my parents and two brothers, and my brothers were fun to be with. Going to church was easy for me. I liked all the Bible stories and different events the church offered. However, school was hard for me academically because I had poor comprehension, and with

Dad working in the construction industry, repairing and building roads, mainly around Colorado, we moved around a lot. By the time I graduated from high school, I would have attended nine schools. Some teachers even considered us migrant workers or Gypsies.

Both Logan and I were born in Boulder, Colorado, where I spent the first seven years of my life, and it would be the most stability I would know for several years to come. In the early 1950s, when I turned five, most kids my age started attending kindergarten. At that time, it was a play-based program that could help kids make a gradual transition from home life to the world of school. My father didn't see it as an academically good program, so I didn't attend. It was also the year my baby brother, Nathan, was born.

My introduction to school was first grade with a teacher named Mrs. Bull (I felt she was appropriately named!). She was constantly criticizing my work.

"Gillian, these are some of the worst formed letters I have ever seen," she said as she handed me back my paper.

"I'm trying to form them correctly, Mrs. Bull," I said.

"Well, it's not good enough. What you need is more practice. You will stay in at recess today and redo the paper," she said with a demanding voice.

Recess was when I had some of my best times at school, and I also felt ashamed that I was not doing well in school. I knew Daddy and Mommy wouldn't like that at all. So as the bell rang for recess break, I sat in my chair and began to cry.

Mrs. Bull said, "Gillian, crying is not going to make those letters any better. So spend this time focused on making your letters according to the examples and try to do a better job."

I slowed down and tried to make the curves better, but I continued to cry. That is when the tears fell on my paper, then I began to erase, and that tore a black hole in the paper. Now I had to ask for another worksheet.

"Mrs. Bull, I need another worksheet. I have a hole in this one now," I said.

"So is crying helping to make your work better?" she asked.

"No," I stammered as I started drying my eyes.

"Here's another worksheet. Now quit feeling sorry for yourself, go slow, and if you do the work correctly, you can go to recess tomorrow," she stressed.

I remember her sitting at her desk, not willing to give me extra help, and me crying holes into my paper. All I wanted to do was go home to my mommy.

In second grade, I had a nice teacher who took me under her wing, and school didn't seem so bad. It was also the year I became nearsighted, couldn't see the board, and began wearing glasses.

During my third-grade year, we moved three times. Each time I would start learning, make new friends, and then had leave to where Dad's work took him. There are three events from that third-grade year that are strong memories in my mind.

The summer before my third-grade year began, we moved to Granby, Colorado, a small mountain town close to Denver, high in the Rocky Mountains (elevation 7,935 feet) near Rocky Mountain National Park. We lived in a trailer court that had a circle drive with railroad tracks behind the trailer court. Mom was in her forties and had never learned to drive, so one day, while Dad was working, she decided that she was going to start learning how to drive a car.

"Logan and Gillian," she said, "today, our neighbor, Mrs. Stanns, is going to instruct me on how to drive a car. So get Nathan, and you three will ride in the back seat while Mrs. Stanns and I are in the front."

"Wow!" Logan said. "Does Dad know about you doing this, Mom?"

"No because I what to surprise him," she said.

"Oh, I think Dad will be surprised all right," I said.

In a few minutes, Mrs. Stanns was knocking on our door. Logan, Nathan, and I headed out the door to get into the back seat of our Desoto family car. Mom and Mrs. Stanns climbed in the front.

Mrs. Stanns said, "Now, Rebecca, all we are going to do today is see if you can back out onto the circle drive and then steer the car around the circle."

"Okay," Mom said, "are you kids ready?"

"Yes!" Logan and I said, being very excited to see what Mom would do. And this was in the days before seat belts were installed in cars and it was the law to wear them. So being ready was just sitting in the back seat.

Dad's Desoto had a stick shift on the steering wheel column, so the first thing Mrs. Stanns had Mom do was to learn what the letters stood for and how to move the stick shift into place. Mom was slow and easy about backing up, and then, with the car in drive, spent time driving our Desoto around and around and around the circle. It was just so much fun seeing Mom learning to maneuver the car around that big circle drive. Logan and I kept jumping up to look over the seat to see how Mom was doing. The neighbors came out and cheered Mom on.

That evening, when Dad came home, he was very surprised that Mom would be so bold, and he decided he would take over the schooling of the car with her.

The second event was also in Granby and concerned skunks. One thing fun about living in a trailer court, there were always a lot of kids to play with, and usually, several of the families working for the same construction company ended up in the same trailer court. There were two families that we became close friends with, and us kids enjoyed growing up together. The trailer court in Granby had older children as well, and my brother made good friends with one of these older boys. He was making extra money catching muskrats and selling the hides to make gloves. Logan started helping him making ten cents with each muskrat.

So the owner of the trailer court heard how successful Logan and his friend were at being able to catch muskrats, and he offered the two boys a job. He was having a problem with skunks behind the trash bins in the court. He offered to pay the boys twenty-five cents for each skunk disposed of.

One night, a skunk got caught in a trap and went under the trailer of one of the families we were good friends with. Logan and his friend found the skunk in the morning. His friend shot the skunk in the guts underneath the trailer, causing it to release itself all over the trailer.

Well, Dad and his friend didn't talk for about two months, and when they did, he complained about how every morning, when he drank his coffee, it smelled like skunk! Logan and his friend were out of the skunk business.

We said goodbye to Granby and spent two months in west Denver before heading to Laramie, Wyoming, where I would complete third grade. When I started going to school, Logan and I had always attended school within the same building, and during our days, we would see each other occasionally. Laramie was the first time we were in different buildings on a larger campus, and I felt isolated from him. My third-grade teacher was an older adult, the principal of the kindergarten through third grades. She did not take kindly to me, considered us a migrant family, and it was very hard for me to please her (my brother had this same problem in Granby during his fourth-grade year).

The first day in her class, I stood up on the wrong side of the desk to say the Pledge of Allegiance, and she screamed at me to get on the other side of the desk. One time, during art in class, we were making tulips, and she would walk around and show different students' work. When she came to me, she held mine up and said, "Now, class, this is not a tulip!"

Laramie, Wyoming, was known to have severe winters with heavy snow accumulations; however, most of the time, school was not cancelled, and if schools were opened, Dad expected us to be there. To get to school, Logan and I rode the school bus, and to get to our bus stop, we had to walk down a short county road. One winter morning, it was snowing heavily, and Mom sent us on our way to the bus stop. I was holding on tight to Logan, and he encouraged me to just keep going. It turned into a blizzard. We were caught in it, and we could hardly see our hands in front of our face. We made it to the bus stop, waited a few minutes for the bus, when Logan said, "We're going home!" All I can remember was holding on to Logan who felt his way along the ditch that ran beside that short county road. It was Logan's quick thinking that got us safely home.

Later that morning, the storm had passed, and blue skies were out, so Mom took us to school. All I remember my teacher saying to me was, "Gillian, you know the time the bus is there, and next time, you make sure you're on it!"

This was a time in America when children didn't complain to parents about how they were treated in a classroom. To my father, teachers were held in very high esteem, and I was not to cause any trouble. If I did, I would have been whipped with a razor strap at home. It wasn't until my mother attended my teacher-parent conference at the end of the year, and she told my mom the reason Gillian doesn't do well in school is because of her background. I guess Mom let her have it with both barrels. When Mom came home, she wanted to talk to me.

"You've been having a very hard time in school, haven't you?"

I said, "Yes," broke down, and cried, and I was glad I wasn't in trouble.

Fourth grade, we moved twice; first to Eckert, Colorado, and then to Palisade, Colorado, where both communities are known for their fruit orchards, especially peaches. I remember the teachers being nice. I started liking school and was bringing home better grades. In Palisade, I remember all the students standing outside the school buildings, saying the Pledge of Allegiance which was led by the principal before we entered the school. The school administrators were going to have a band program in the fall for interested families.

Dad and Mom were excited about us learning music. Logan got a clarinet, and I got a flute, and eventually, Nathan, when he was old enough, began learning the saxophone. Music became a big part of our lives. On Saturday nights, the family would gather around the television to watch the western, *Gunsmoke,* and the musical variety program, *The Lawrence Welk Show.*

I began fifth grade in Cedaredge, Colorado, a beautiful small town made up of cattle ranches and orchards where I remember having a lot of fun with other kids. The town celebrated "Huck Finn Day," and I won a fly rod for having the most freckles in town.

I ended fifth grade and began sixth grade in east Denver. We lived near Fitzsimons Hospital, and I remember large planes flying right over the trailer court. I finished sixth grade in Aurora, Colorado, having very good memories of my time there. At the end of the school year, I won the award for being the best athlete in the school (my brothers were embarrassed).

That summer, I attended my first Girl Scout Camp in the mountains near Denver. So I could take pictures of my trip, Dad and Mom bought me a Brownie camera for my birthday. There were six girls to a tent, and we slept in our sleeping bags on a wooden floor. There was a large log cabin that was in the center of the camp where the cafeteria and art classes were located. We went on hikes, had scavenger hunts, and rode horseback on the mountain trails around the camp. The experience was the highlight of my summer, and I was hoping I could attend the following year. However, before school started, Dad informed us we would be moving again.

Seventh grade, we moved back into the Denver area and moved into a trailer court where we had a beautiful fenced-in yard. Dad made sure the lush green grass was always cut once a week, and Mom planted beautiful flowers along the fence line. What I liked best about this school was it started square dance lessons for interested students on Friday nights, and I was excited about learning how to dance. Dad and Mom loved to dance, so they let Logan and I attend the program.

After several weeks of lessons, a special potluck was held so parents could see their students' progress. Boys were dressed in white shirts and jeans, and girls were in pastel-colored skirts with white shirts. It was a special evening for our family. I hoped to attend more lessons in the coming school year, but in August, before school started, Dad informed the family we would be moving once again.

# PART 6

## Gunnison

### A Place to Call Home

August 1, 1961, Dad moved the family to Gunnison, Colorado, a small community of ranchers, farmers, and miners where he would be working on a Bureau of Reclamation project for a few years. This move brought more stability to our lives and a place we would come to call home. Dad and Mom were happy with the education system, and us kids became involved in the music programs in the schools. We even got to take trips with the band to state competitions. However, once the project was completed, our lives changed another way.

Growing up, the family always moved to where Dad's work took him. Over the years, Dad bought newer and larger trailers, and we became very good at being able to pack and hook up the trailer and move on short notice.

I do remember a time in Denver when Dad wanted to buy a home for his family in the Denver area, and we spent several Sunday afternoons looking at open houses. Then, we got the news that Dad's work would be taking him to Gunnison for several years. Mom didn't want to be living in Denver without her husband, and us kids wanted to be together with Mom and Dad. So Dad bought a new trailer, and we stayed together, which was the right decision. However, Dad always regretted buying that trailer and not putting the money he saved into a home in Gunnison.

By 1964, Logan and I were in high school, Nathan was still in grade school, we were doing well in school, plus the whole family loved living in Gunnison and didn't want to move. So the decision was made to keep Mom and us kids in Gunnison, and Dad would travel and stay at the different jobsites.

I remember dad spending a winter in Santa Rosa, New Mexico, in a motel, and each week, we would write Dad a letter, keeping him informed of the events in our lives, and he and Mom would talk often on the phone. When we knew Dad was going to be coming home, Mom wanted to look especially pretty for him, and she said she needed my help.

"Gillian, if I want to look extra pretty for your father, I want to do something with my hair. I've heard that Clairol hair-coloring products are very popular with women, so I want you to help me color my hair a little darker brown."

"How are we going to know what color to get, Mom?" I asked.

"I'm going to call a beauty shop in town and see what they suggest," Mom explained.

"This is exciting, and I think it will be a great surprise for Dad!" I said.

Mom talked on the phone for several minutes to a beautician at one of the local beauty shops, and if was finally decided Mom should try the color sable brown as her new color. So, the next day, Mom purchased the product, and that afternoon, we started reading the directions and applying it to her hair. As she was waiting the required time for the color to work, I made a comment.

"Mom, this color looks really dark, almost black. I hope it washes out lighter," I said.

"Well, it's too late now, so what's done is done," she said.

As I started to wash the coloring out of her hair, it wasn't getting any lighter, and I was worried about this surprise for Dad.

Mom finally looked in the mirror and said in a worried voice, "Oh my gosh, Gillian, it's black! I look ridiculous! What is Robert going to say?" Mom asked.

"I'm not sure, Mom, but it just doesn't look like you. Let's curl it, and when it dries, see how the style looks. It could be really pretty," I said, trying to ease her fears.

Well, Mom now had black hair, didn't look like our mother, and Dad was one day away. When Dad walked in, I can say he was surprised but not happy about what she had done to her hair.

"You look ridiculous," he said.

*My thoughts exactly*, I thought.

I felt bad for mom because I helped her look that way when she only wanted to impress her man. She wore the color until it finally washed out and never tried to color her hair again. The one thing I learned is that my dad loved my mom for exactly who she was, and she didn't have to impress him any other way.

Another time, he worked in the Pagosa Springs, Colorado, area about a hundred and sixty-five miles south of Gunnison at the foot of Wolf Creek Pass. During the week, he stayed at the Pagosa Hotel and came home on Friday nights and left Sunday evenings. This worked out better because we got to see him more often. Eventually, Dad bought a camper trailer to live in, and Mom traveled with him.

In the fall of 1965, my brother, Logan, started his first year of college at Western State, a small college in Gunnison. It was my senior year at Gunnison High School, and I was hoping for some changes in my personal life. I was seventeen and still waiting to have my first date. Deep down, I really wanted a boyfriend to go to parties and dances with and to make me feel special. I had a couple of close girlfriends that I had fun with, but I wasn't popular or a part of the "in crowd" at school. Some of the very popular kids at school were a part of our youth group and were nice to me at our Sunday meeting and youth socials during the year but wouldn't acknowledge me at school.

To pass my foreign language requirement, I took one year of Latin and one year of French. Latin I took in my senior year, and the class wanted to have a fundraiser. It was decided we would all be auctioned off as "a slave for a day." Whoever bought you, you would be their slave for one day, carrying around their books.

Mom helped me make a costume, and I was excited to see who would buy me. The auction was set at lunchtime in front of the school. A lot of the popular boys and girls went for ten to twenty dollars, although many of our classmates went for one to five dollars. Time was running out, and the bell was going to ring, and I hadn't been given a chance yet to be someone's slave. Just before the bell rang, they called my name and started the bidding. The auctioneer went down to twenty-five cents, and then whoever made the bid said, "Forget it!" The auction was over. I was disappointed and had a good cry that night at home.

The last big hurt of my senior year was the prom. I really wanted to go, but in those days, you needed a date. When the time of the prom came, most all the senior girls were all excited about their dates, hair appointments, nails being done, and, of course, their very special dress that would match that special flower their special someone would be bringing to them. It was a hard day for me to get through, and when I went home, I cried again. Mom felt sorry for me and spent the evening trying to cheer me up.

What my parents didn't realize was in our youth group, former graduates would come home on holiday breaks and share their experiences at the colleges they were attending. Christmas break of my senior year, two former graduates who were attending Christian schools down in Texas told me what they were experiencing on their campuses. One was Hardin-Simmons University in Abilene, Texas; the other was Wayland in Plainview, Texas. Both were private Baptist schools.

Wayland was a smaller college, more affordable, and it sounded like the environment I was looking for. So I applied to Wayland and was accepted into the fall term.

*****

Going away to college, being a single teacher in San Antonio, Texas, marrying my college sweetheart, living in Alaska, and becoming a mother were some of the amazing personal changes I achieved. Now, after seven years, my daughter and I were on a plane back home to the place I had fought to leave because I wanted something more out of life. And I found it. It just wasn't going to last forever like I dreamed it would.

Dad and Mom were waiting for us at the airport in Pueblo, Colorado. Dad approached me with a stern face. "What are you fighting about?"

I could tell he was mad and upset. "Dad, I just don't want to be hit anymore," I replied.

He calmed down, got silent, and we drove to their camper, which was now parked in Trinidad, Colorado, about ninety miles away. There was now four of us living in a twenty-three-square-foot camper. Dad would go to work every morning while Mom and I spent quality time together with Juliet.

A couple days after I arrived, I went to the employment agency to find work. They said there was an opening for a desk clerk at the Ramada Inn in town, so I would try there first. They also sent me over to Social Services for they thought they could help me with my living arrangement. I first went to the Ramada Inn and was hired as a desk clerk on the morning shift from seven to three, five days a week, and I could begin right away.

A few days after, I arrived at Mom and Dad's place. I was walking home from work when I saw Juliet and Mom walking toward me. Juliet ran into my arms, I picked her up, felt her forehead, and discovered she had a fever. I went inside the camper, placed her on the bed, and started taking off her clothes when she suddenly started shaking. Her head went back, her eyes rolled back into their sockets, and her arms went stiff and straight.

Mom yelled, "She is having a seizure!"

I yelled, "Get us some help!"

I started to breathe into her mouth, holding down her tongue. We were without a vehicle. It was about 5:00 p.m. with heavy traffic around Trinidad. Mom ran over to a neighbor's camper and asked for help to get us to the hospital. The man said he could take us in his car. While the man drove, I just kept breathing into Juliet's mouth, asking her not to die on me. I didn't think we would ever get to that hospital.

Pulling into the emergency entrance, there was a team of medical personnel waiting for us. They took Juliet from me and had me wait outside one of the medical rooms. It seemed like forever before a doctor came and told me I had a very sick child, and she would have to stay in the hospital. They were working on reducing the fever to get her stabilized. Within a few days, my life was turned upside down, and I was in a nightmare that wouldn't end. All I could do was pray that God's healing hand would save my beloved Juliet.

That night, Dad and Mom came to the hospital, and Dad just held me.

"You've had a hard time of it, haven't you?"

"Yes, but I am so thankful for you being here for me."

I learned later from Mom that before they came to the hospital, Ricardo had called to talk to me and ended up talking to my dad. Mom wouldn't tell me what Dad said, except that it was a heated discussion. I only knew that my dad was there for me.

He said, "Gillian, if you don't go back, I will help you and Juliet all I can, but if you go back, I won't help you."

"Dad, I'm not going back. I'm too afraid to."

Juliet spent three days in the hospital often in ice baths, trying to keep her fever down. While I was at the hospital with Juliet those three days, Dad put the camper in storage and rented a nice three-bedroom apartment in Trinidad. Dad and Mom had a nice large bedroom. Juliet and I shared a room, and we had a guest bedroom, which my brother, Nathan, would use when he came to see us on weekends when he was in Alamosa for college.

When I brought Juliet home from the hospital and started her bath, she ran, screaming in fear, behind a chair, saying, "No, Mommy! No, Mommy!"

So I got in the bath and had her come to me to show her how nice the water was. It took her several minutes to come into the bathroom, and I kept encouraging her to come and feel the water. She finally came over and stood by the bathtub and slowly started to feel the water. When she found out how warm it was, she wanted to get in with me. However, to this day, she does not like baths.

We lived in that apartment for six months. Both my brothers came for Christmas, and Mom and Dad really enjoyed their time with Juliet. I was finding out my parents made terrific grandparents. Mom enjoyed baking with her, and Dad loved to read stories to her. I was truly grateful for their love and support. During that time, I was able to buy a used car that helped me get back and forth to work, especially when I was changed to the night shift which was from three to eleven.

A couple of times over the Christmas and New Year holidays, I was asked if I could help in the lounge after my shift ended at eleven.

I told my boss, "I've never worked in a lounge or carried drinks. I wouldn't know what to do."

He said, "Just write down the name of the drink, and Art, the bartender, will help you with the money situation."

Well, let me tell you, this new experience was an education in itself. I carried a little tip jar on a circular tray with a pad and pencil.

I thought, "Yeah, I'm sure that's going to be full!"

My first order was for a Black Russian.

I replied, "Are you sure you want one?"

The lady just looked at me and smiled.

The rest of the order was for a seven-and-seven, a screwdriver, and a beer. I couldn't wait to see what a Black Russian and screwdriver looked like in liquid form. People were very nice and patient with me, and when it came time to check out, the other girl was counting dollar after dollar of her tips while I was already done counting mine.

I asked her "How can you do so well?"

She said, "I never give back change."

I figured I wouldn't want to argue with her if I was her customer and asked for the change.

One night during the winter, I was in the Ramada Inn restaurant, having supper. As I was looking out the window, I saw Ricardo in the parking lot. He came into the restaurant.

"Hi, Gillian, can I join you?"

"What are you doing here, Ricardo? I don't want you to start any trouble in here."

"I'm not here to cause trouble. I was hoping you would see me and see if we could talk about our situation. May I sit down?"

"Yes, but only for a few minutes. My break is almost over."

"You look great! How is Juliet?"

"She was very sick and had a rough time. She is much better now. Mom and Dad are wonderful grandparents, and she enjoys being with them."

"That's great," he replied nervously. "Gillian, I would like to talk to you if you would be willing to meet with me."

"I will not meet with you alone. If you want to meet with me, it will be with a lawyer present."

"I understand and wouldn't blame you if you were scared, but if that's the only way you will meet with me, then I will find one tomorrow."

"It cannot be during my work schedule, so it will have to be a morning or early afternoon appointment. I have to get back to the desk, so I'll walk you out."

As Ricardo walked away, I knew that night that I would be saying a prayer to God to help me find the strength to keep my promise to my dad.

*****

The next day, I received a call from a lawyer in Trinidad, telling me that my husband was in his office, and he had spent time talking with him about our situation. He asked me if I would be willing to come down to his office, and the three of us could talk. I said I would go.

With the lawyer present, he began by asking Ricardo to tell me what it was he wanted me to know.

"Gillian, I first want to apologize for my behavior. I now realize what Carlos tried to do to us, and I am so sorry for what happened. Carlos is gone now. You did not deserve the kind of husband I became or the treatment you received. I'm asking if you can find a way to forgive me. I want us to be a family and would like you to return to Texas with me."

"Ricardo, I am too scared to be alone with you. I'm afraid for Juliet also. I would never have believed that you would turn against me or not want Juliet. Around Carlos, you became a completely different person, a person that wanted to be free from responsibilities and the struggles that it takes to be a family."

"Gillian, these hands of mine can give you the future you always wanted with me."

"Yes, Ricardo, that was true at one time, but I also know what those hands have done to me in a very violent way when I never deserved it."

He broke down and cried and asked for me to forgive him.

"You destroyed what I believed in you the day you sided with Carlos over Juliet and me. I'm not coming back."

Ricardo came one other time to try again before he arrived in May for our appointed for the divorce to become final. He was still asking if I would reconsider. He told me his mom, who I dearly loved, said I would be making a mistake if I didn't come back. But I knew I wasn't going to change my mind. The court awarded me one hundred dollars a month for child support. Over the years, he remained mostly faithful in sending it to me.

# PART 7

## *The Single Parent Years*

In June of 1974, Dad's job required for him and Mom to leave Trinidad. I decided I wanted to stay. I had a job I enjoyed, and I also liked the people I worked with. I wanted to see if I could make it on my own with Juliet who was now two years old.

Through Social Services, I found a small four-room furnished apartment on the ground level that was owned and managed by an older couple. They agreed to rent me the apartment as long as we were quiet. I was able to move my work schedule to the day shift and enrolled Juliet in a day care center. Juliet's day care expenses would be paid for under Social Services.

It was now just Juliet and me, and she became the delight of my life. When I was not working, I was caring for her. She was so beautiful, and it was sometimes unreal that a child so beautiful could belong to me. I read books to her, created and colored pictures for her, took her to the park, and sang her lullabies as she laid beside me in a big queen-sized bed, which I moved up against the wall to make sure she would not fall out of during the night. I felt I was on a good path and was doing the right things for Juliet.

The one area of my life where I now felt unworthy and not acceptable was to find a church where I could worship the God I loved. When I left home and wherever I lived, be it in Plainview, Fairbanks, or San Antonio, I always found a church where I could give thanks to God who I felt had done so much for me.

I was now a divorced woman with a rebel past, a woman that would do things her way. I had stood against my parents, instead of honoring them, with my desires to go away to college. I didn't honor them again when it came to whom I was going to date or listen to the advice from my dorm mom or girls in the dorm. I was going to hold on to Ricardo and didn't care what people thought or believed. Now that behavior seemed so ugly to me.

At night, while Juliet slept, I thought about how I dishonored my God. I remember praying to God about dating Ricardo, but I knew what my will wanted. I didn't once think about the special man he might have had waiting just for me if I would have just trusted him more with the details of my life. I was always told, as his child, that he only wanted the best for me. I wasn't willing to wait for him to move in his time for me. I wanted it in my time. Now I sat in the dark and was ashamed of who I was and what I had become. But I would be a good mother to Juliet, for she was my gift from him.

To help me stay in contact with God and his church, I began watching the Sunday morning church services on television while Juliet played on the floor beside the television. They were an hour long, the special music performances were excellent, and I found the sermons to be inspirational. I eventually settled on one service, and that was my Sabbath time with God each week.

Ever since Juliet was born, she had sucked the two middle fingers on her right hand. I tried several remedies to break her of this habit, especially now that she was a toddler and liked to play in the dirt. In July, Juliet became fussy, would cry at night, and it would take me longer to settle her down for the night. The owners complained about the crying. Shortly, she developed a fever, and I found blood in her stool. I became alarmed and called Social Services who referred me to a doctor.

The doctor sent me to a clinic just over the border in Raton, New Mexico, about twenty-five minutes away. The tests revealed Juliet had an inflammation in her gastrointestinal tract. I needed to change her diet to one higher in fiber with more vegetables and fruit. The more I tried to get Juliet to quick sucking her fingers, the more she cried. The owners asked us to leave.

The last thing I wanted to do was go home to Gunnison, divorced, and defeated by trying to make it on my own. But I now knew I had to go back if I was going to give Juliet and myself a better life with fewer hardships. So I called my brother, Logan, and asked if he could come and help us move back home. He said he would be glad to come on the weekend. Again, he was there for me to see me safely home.

As a young girl, my mother grew up on the plains of Wyoming where she enjoyed riding horses during the early morning hours and learned to put up hay. She hoped that one day, she and Dad could get the family out of town and into the countryside so us kids could experience country living. In the spring of 1965, Mom learned of an opportunity to move the family into the rural area around Gunnison.

A recently widowed lady from her Sunday School class at church wanted to rent a trailer spot she had on her property. Dad was working out of town in New Mexico and agreed to the move but couldn't get the time off to move us. Mom wanted to move the coming weekend before we had to pay another month's rent at the trailer court, and then, too, the widow lady had another interested party for the spot on her property. So Mom called Dad.

"Rebecca, I can't get the time off to come home and move us. Do you think if I found someone to help you move, you and the kids could make the move without me?" Dad asked.

"Robert, Logan has a lot of experience helping you hooking up and moving this trailer. I know we can do it if we could get someone with the right truck and some moving experience. Do you know of anybody we could ask?" Mom said.

"Yes, I do," Dad said. He mentioned a good friend from church.

Logan called him, and he agreed to help us. Not only did he agree to help, but his wife also joined in helping us, and she made a big casserole for everyone to enjoy later. So, on a Saturday morning, Logan led and guided our helpers in hooking up the trailer and saw it moved four miles from town to a spot on the banks of the Gunnison River. The hardest part of the move, which took the most time, was maneuvering it into place between two Spruce trees.

There was only one mishap the whole day. While Logan and his helpers were blocking up the trailer on blocks, Mom, Nathan, and I were inside, unpacking. Suddenly, the trailer fell, and Mom screamed!

"Where is Logan! Where's Logan! Oh my God, where is Logan and the helpers?"

She knew they were blocking up the trailer and thought someone might have been killed. I rushed around the house, looking out the windows, screaming, "Logan! Logan!" Then I saw him walking by.

He shouted, "Everyone is all right! Tell Mom everyone is all right!"

I ran to Mom and held her as she cried in my arms.

As Logan and our friends inspected the fall, they found that one of the jacks on the right front side slipped and went up into the trailer, creating a hole in the subfloor. We were lucky it didn't go all the way into the house, and Mom placed the desk over that spot.

When Dad was able to come home, he thanked Logan for doing a good job and wanted to start skirting the house. So Dad wouldn't find out about the trailer falling, I went outside to help him. When it came time to work on the right front jack that slipped, I went under the trailer first and shoved my head up in the hole so Dad wouldn't see it. When he climbed under, he never saw the hole. Many years later, he was working under the house and found the hole.

"Strange thing. I found a hole in the right side of the front trailer," he said with an inquiring voice."

"Yeah, about that hole," I said and proceeded to tell him what happened. He was grateful no one was hurt.

Dad and Mom transformed that spot on the side of the road to a beautiful place for us to live. We had a large green lawn bordered by rose bushes and flowering plants. Eventually, a living room and workshop area was added to the side of the house with a concrete patio and sidewalk. There was a big duck pond in front of the lawn, and to the north of the lawn, Dad planted raspberry bushes along the riverbank. They produced a lot of raspberries for eating at breakfast and making jam. When Juliet went to pick raspberries with her grandpa, she would put one in her mouth and one in the bucket. It was one of Grandpa's best times with her.

This is the home that Juliet and I returned to. By now, Logan had graduated college and had a good job with the highway department in town. He was a bachelor living at home and taking care of the place. Mom and Dad were away, living in the camper where Dad was working. It was time to start over again.

## 17

I spent a few days unpacking and walking the property with Juliet. It was a beautiful place to reflect and remember my final years of high school. It was also a place I felt safe with Juliet, and I looked forward to watching her curiosity as she explored her new environment. It was also good to spend time with Logan and to discover what his life was like after college. He was a bachelor, golfing several nights a week with friends after work, and occasionally dating.

Toward the end of our first week home, I decided it was time to stop hiding and begin to find a job and childcare for Juliet. I said a prayer to God that he would help me and went to the local employment agency in Gunnison. When they found out I had experience working the desk at the Ramada Inn in Trinidad, they knew right where to send me. The Holiday Inn in town needed desk help. I called Logan and asked if he could watch Juliet after work so I could go and apply for the job. He said, "Sure."

Approaching the Holiday Inn front desk, I said, "Hi, my name is Gillian, and I have an interview for a desk clerk job."

"Hi, my name is Robin. I was just told a lady was coming to apply for the position. Let me take you back and introduce you to our manager," she said in a friendly voice.

She led me around the front desk, then down a hall where we entered a large office area. I was introduced to the manager, and after the interview, which I thought went well, was offered a position on the evening shift from three to eleven. I liked the hours because I thought I could spend most of my days caring for Juliet. My only concern was finding childcare for that time of day. I thought I would talk to the girls at the front desk and inquire about childcare services in town. As I climbed down the staircase, I approach Robin about my situation.

"Hi, Robin! Thank you for introducing to the manager. I got the position, and I am happy I will be starting tomorrow night on the evening shift," I said.

"You're welcome, and welcome to the team," she said.

"Thank you. I like the hours because I have a two-year-old daughter and can spend most of the day with her before I come to work. Would you know of any childcare service that does evening hours?" I inquired.

"Not a childcare service, but I might know of someone who is looking to earn some extra money, and I think she would like to help you out," she said.

"Wow, that would be great! How do I get in touch with her?" I asked.

"It's me!" she said.

"You!" I exclaimed. "You're looking for a childcare opportunity?"

"Yes, I have a boy about your daughter's age, and he spends his days with his grandparents who live next door to us. I've been looking for someone that he could play with during a few hours in the evening," she said.

"Robin, you seem like a really nice person, and I am so grateful for your offer, but we don't know each other, and I will be working until eleven o'clock each night. I won't be picking her up until after that hour and wouldn't want to disturb your sleep each night," I said.

"Gillian, I'm going to be getting off in a few minutes, do you have the time this evening to come over to my house? You can see our home, meet my husband, and my boy, Tommy. We can all talk about the situation," she said.

"My brother, Logan, is watching Juliet for me, so I could come to this interview. Let me call him, inform him of the situation, and see if he's okay watching her for a little while longer," I said.

I called Logan, and he was glad to watch Juliet. He said he was having fun getting to know his niece. He was glad I got the job and hoped the childcare worked out for me also. I agreed with him.

Robin lived about a mile from the inn inside the town of Gunnison. She and her husband had a small home that was very nice and clean with a fenced-in backyard. I met their little boy, Tommy, who was playing on the floor with his dad. Robin's husband was happy about the possibility of a playmate for Tommy and didn't mind if I picked her up late. Robin said Juliet could sleep on the couch beside the door, and when I knocked, I could just pick her up and walk out. So we agreed on a trial basis.

Robin and I decided we would meet at her home on her lunch break the next day so Juliet could meet her and Tommy and become familiar with each other. I also met Tommy's grandparents who were caring for him. I felt good about the situation, so later, when I started my shift, I walked into the office, introduced Juliet to everyone, and explained I would be bringing her each day, and Robin would leave with her. The arrangement worked out very well until I was moved to the day shift. The widow's land we lived on had a daughter who lived just up the road, and she ran a day care in her home. I knew her, she was a member of our church, so I took Juliet to meet her, and she accepted Juliet into her day care program.

The area we lived in outside of town had been zoned for commercial use. Since I had been away, there was now a market and gas station that had been built just around the corner from where we lived. It was very convenient to shop there for small items, but when we needed more supplies, I had to go into Gunnison to the larger supermarkets. Now I needed to run that errand.

Since coming home, I had been spending most of my time working at the inn, going to Robin's house, or just staying home enjoying time with Juliet and Logan. I was carrying a lot of shame, and I wanted to avoid running into people I knew, especially members of our church. I was afraid of what they would say or think of me.

I drove to the supermarket parking lot, walked into the store, put Juliet in the basket seat, and was in the fruit and vegetable section when I heard someone say my name.

"Hello, Gillian. Do you remember me?" she asked.

"Why, hello, Mrs. Anderson. Yes, I sure do. You are a member of our church, and I believe you were in Mom's women's Bible study on Sunday mornings. How are you?" I responded.

"Fine. Is this your little girl, Juliet?" she asked.

"Yes, she is a little over two years old and the love of my life," I said.

"She is very pretty, Gillian. Your mom and dad are proud grandparents. Juliet has brought a lot of joy into their lives," she said.

"They have been great and so good to both of us," I said.

"Gillian, it would be good to see you back in church. Several people know you are back, and they would like to see you. Won't you come?" she asked.

"Oh, I don't think I belong in church, Mrs. Anderson," I said.

"Why do you say that, Gillian, or even think it?" she asked.

"Mrs. Anderson, I'm not the same person I was when I left. I made mistakes following my heart. Now I am now a divorced woman and a single parent. But, one thing I know, Juliet is not a mistake. She is God's gift to me, and I want to be the best parent I can be to her," I said, trying to defend myself.

"Gillian, I think you have the wrong idea about the members of our church and what God's church really is. There are still a lot of the old members you know, and you also know they are good people. We also now have a lot of college age students coming, and there are a few other divorced young people who are single parents coming with their kids. I think it is just the place for you and Juliet," she responded.

"Mrs. Anderson, thank you for remembering and speaking to me. But this is what I was afraid of, people recognizing me and me having to explain how I feel. I can't talk any longer about this. I need to get some groceries, get Juliet back home, and be ready for work this afternoon. I hope you have a nice day," I said, walking away.

I pushed the cart into another aisle, hoping I wouldn't bump into another person who would recognize me. I finished my grocery shopping, got Juliet buckled into her car seat, and the groceries loaded into the car. As I headed out of town, I couldn't wait to get home where I felt safe.

After putting the groceries away, I bathed Juliet and put her down for a nap. I started reflecting on how nervous I felt when I ran into Mrs. Anderson who had only been nice to me. I hadn't ended our conversation well, and she sure didn't deserve my abrupt departure.

I also thought about what she said. "There are other single parents coming to the services? Oh, God, is it true?" I said as I began to cry. My head fell in the palm of my hands, and I started talking to God. "God, I feel like such a sinner. I want Juliet to have a mother she can be proud of, not one running scared. I love her so much, and I love you so much. We need you in our lives. Help me to be the woman you created me to be. I also love your church, and deep in my heart, I know it is where I belong. Help me on Sunday to walk through those doors, and maybe in some small way, I can serve you. I want to raise Juliet there and pray she will grow up with a heart for you also."

I cried for a while, asking God to guide and direct my footsteps.

*****

As I prepared to go to work, I knew that on Sunday, I would be taking Juliet to church. That was a good thought. I also wanted to find Mrs. Anderson and apologize for my rudeness and possibly our next conversation would end in a much better way.

On Sunday morning, I decided I wouldn't go to the Sunday school hour, just do the worship service. Driving up to the church, I parked along one of the side streets around the church, retrieved Juliet from her car seat, picked up her bag and my purse, and walked the short distance to the side door of the church. A man I didn't know was handing out the service bulletins and welcoming people into the church.

"Hello," I said. "Is the nursery still just downstairs and around the corner?" I asked.

"Why, yes, it is. My name is Mr. Gray. Are you acquainted with our church?" he asked.

"Yes, I attended here with my family during my middle school and high school years. I moved back last month. This is my daughter, Juliet. I thought I would see how she does in the nursery today while I attend the service," I said.

"Welcome back! I'm glad you're here. Here's a bulletin of the service today, and there is also more information about upcoming events you may be interested in," he said.

"Thank you," I said as I walked through the door, went down the steps, and made the left turn and approached the nursery door. An older lady I didn't know walked up and introduced herself.

"Hi, I'm Mrs. Jenkins. I haven't seen you here before. Is this your first time here with your daughter.

"Yes, it is. However, I grew up in this church during my middle school and high school years and just moved back. This is my first Sunday back at church," I responded.

"Well, welcome, I'm glad you're here. How old is your daughter? She looks around two?" she asked.

"Yes, Juliet is a few months over two," I said.

"She will be in the toddler area. I need you to sign the register and fill out a name tag for her," she said. After following up with her request, and as I placed Juliet in Mrs. Jenkins' arms, she began to cry.

"Don't worry, she will stop crying as soon as we get her focused on some toys. Go and enjoy the service," Mrs. Jenkins said.

I walked back up the stairs and entered the sanctuary and started walking down the side aisle when I heard someone call my name.

"Gillian! It is you. It's good to see you. I heard you were back," said a girl from my high school youth group.

"Yes, I just moved back a few weeks ago. I'm working at the Holiday Inn north of town in the office as a desk clerk. It's nice to see you. How have you been?" I asked.

"I graduated from Western and got a job here in Gunnison at a real-estate firm. So I've hung around. Would you like to sit with me today?" she asked.

"Sure, that would be nice," I said.

Before the service began, a couple of other members of the church I had known for a long time came up to me, gave me a hug, and said they were happy to see me. I was beginning to feel good and not so nervous as the service began.

After the service, I spotted Mrs. Anderson and made my way over to her after greeting several other people I knew who all were very friendly to me.

"Hello, Mrs. Anderson," I said.

"Hi, Gillian, I noticed you were here today, and I am so glad you came. Did you enjoy the service?" she asked.

"Yes, I did. Everyone has made me feel very welcome. I want to apologize to you for my abruptness the other day when we met in the grocery store. You were very kind, and I'm sorry I was being defensive," I said.

"Gillian, it is so sweet of you to apologize, but I am glad I talked to you and invited you to come back to church because you're here today. I just want you to realize that God's church has a place just for you. Sometimes, life doesn't work out the way we hope it would. That's why God's church is important in this world. It's a place to worship God, but it is also a place to learn how to love the way Jesus loved, to encourage, build up, and share with fellow believers. It's all a process. It takes time to learn how to do it right, but it makes this journey called life easier. I hope you will come back next Sunday."

"I'll be back, Mrs. Anderson," I replied. "I was wrong about my feelings, and it was good to see so many people I knew. They were only friendly, and some people have invited me to attend their Sunday school classes next week."

"That's great, Gillian," she said. "We have several young adults coming, and the leadership committee is talking about starting a new class for college through thirty-five years of age. Right now, they are looking for a couple to lead it," she said.

"Well, I fit into that age group, so I will keep an eye out for it. I need to get Juliet. Thank you again for your kindness and encouragement. It was good to be here today. See you next week," I said.

"Bye, Gillian," she replied. Then she turned and walked away.

**20**

A few weeks later, during a morning worship service, a special announcement was made that a new Sunday school class would begin next Sunday for young single adults. A young couple in their thirties was introduced to the congregation as the leaders of the new class. The couple spoke for a few minutes about their past experiences. The husband had been divorced, now remarried, and they had a little girl. They welcomed anyone single working in the area, college students, and a divorced or widowed person with children.

Our first meeting was well attended. We introduced ourselves, told a little about our lives, and shared our expectations as a group. They also had some names of people who were coming to services who fit the criteria of the class and might not know about it. We planned an evening to go out in teams of two and extend an invitation to these people to come to our meetings. My brother, Nathan, who was away at college, had a friend who was a member of our group, and he asked me if I would like to go with him. I accepted, and one evening, we went into town to a downstairs basement apartment which had an entrance in the backyard. Knocking a few times, we found no one home, so we left an invitation note.

The following Sunday, a few new people attended the class and began to introduce themselves. The first one was a dark-haired lady with olive complexion and, I thought, a few years older than me.

"My name is Oliva. I'm employed at a local bank and have been coming to services here for a while where I have been attending the married couple's class. I am recently divorced and have a six-year-old daughter. Mr. Watkins of the church told me about this class, and I was also pleased to have been left a note on my door, inviting me to the group," she said.

I responded to her introduction, "Hi, my name is Gillian, and this is my friend, Randy, over there. We are the ones that came by to see you, and when we found no one home, we left the note. I am so glad you came today."

More introductions continued from a couple of college students, a single businessman who had been recently transferred to Gunnison by his company, and another lady, a beautician in town, divorced with two children. I was glad to see the class growing and wanted to talk more with Oliva before she left the church today. So I approached her when class was over.

"Oliva, it's good to meet you. I also am divorced and have a little girl who is a few months over two years of age. I have a job as a desk clerk at the Holiday Inn outside town," I said.

"Yes, nice to meet you also," she said.

"So what do you think about the group?" I asked her.

"I really like the diversity of people. Everyone seems easygoing and friendly. I also am excited to hear the leaders are going to start a Bible study in their home next week. Are you interested in the Bible study, Gillian?" she asked.

"Yes, I am. I like the idea of gathering outside the church in someone's home, and it's always good to be in God's Word," I responded.

"I can't stay long and visit today. I need to be somewhere shortly, but I look forward to coming to this class and will look at my schedule and arrange to attend the Bible study also. Thanks again for reaching out to me, and hopefully, I will see you next week," she said.

"I'll be here," I answered.

Oliva and I both attended the first Bible study. The leaders announced that the group would meet at their house each week, unless a member of the group would like to open their home or apartment to hosting it. Oliva offered to host next week's study in her home and made sure everyone present had her address. The leaders would announce the location in class on Sunday and then make needed phone calls.

Oliva's apartment had a good location in town with a wide-open floor plan of a living room, dining area, and kitchen with bedrooms along the east side. It was easy to fit the Bible study group of twelve to fifteen people inside her home. Her daughter, Stacey, was home, and it was nice to meet her. She was a friendly girl, slender, with brown hair, a big smile, and was holding her skateboard. She told the group it was how she got around town. After the study, Oliva asked if I could stay a few minutes so we could get better acquainted. I was delighted to do so.

That evening, we shared more of our lives, how we both had husbands that we loved but turned out not to be good husbands. Our daughters were the loves of our lives, and we both agreed we wanted them to grow up to know the Lord and have a heart for him. She liked me because of the heart I had for the Lord and asked if my daughter and I would like to do something with her and her daughter on the upcoming weekend. I told her I would love to have her as a friend, and I was anxious for Juliet and Stacey to meet. So began one of the dearest friendships I would ever know. We both felt God had brought us together and wanted us to know each other.

## 21

Oliva was so much fun to be around, and her daughter became a big sister to Juliet. Oliva was from an Italian background and loved to cook. And what was so amazing was how fast she could make so many different tasty dishes so fast. One weekday evening, Juliet and I were visiting Oliva and Stacey when Oliva decided to make bread.

"You're going to make bread now?" I said.

"Sure, it's not that late, and if I start now, we can all probably have a piece before you and Juliet leave," Oliva said.

"That's the most amazing thing I've ever heard. When I decide to make bread, I usually must plan several hours before it's out of the oven," I said.

"It will only take a few minutes to stir it up, and we can continue with our visit," she said.

It turned out to be an enjoyable evening, and true to her word, all four of us shared a hot slice of bread before Juliet and I left.

Other times, I just enjoyed watching Oliva cook. She would take vegetables, scramble them with eggs, put garlic salt on them, and that was another delicious treat. She introduced me to garlic, something my mother never cooked with, but I found out it was the leading ingredients used in Italian dishes.

Shortly after we became friends, Oliva took me upstairs to meet her grandmother. I was to learn that the apartment where Oliva and Stacy lived was in the lower level of her grandmother's home. She was a lovely elderly Italian lady who had a pot cooking on the stove.

"Grandma, I would like for you to meet my friend, Gillian," Oliva said.

"It's lovely to meet you, and I see you like to cook also," I said.

She responded in Italian and just smiled.

"Grandma, what are you cooking on the stove?" Oliva asked.

Her grandmother responded in Italian.

Oliva just smiled and then asked me in a sly voice, "Gillian, would you like to guess what my grandmother is cooking?"

"I bet it's something Italian and something good," I said. "Could it be a special soup she might like?"

"No, it's kidneys! She's boiling the piss out of them," Jenna said and then started laughing.

"Kidneys!" I exclaimed. "Who eats kidneys?" I said.

"My grandmother loves them and considers them a delicacy," she said.

"Really! I've never heard of anyone eating kidneys!"

"Gillian, what kinds of Italian foods have you eaten?" Oliva asked me.

"I suppose spaghetti and meatballs plus lasagna are the two dishes Mom would fix," I said.

"My grandmother was a young girl when she came to America as a mail-order bride from Italy. She's a very good cook and cooks a variety of Italian dishes."

"That's great! My mom is a good cook also. She took cooking classes when my dad was overseas during WWII. We ate a lot of basic American foods like meat, potatoes, and vegetable dishes, and she enjoyed making different desserts my father liked. But we never did get into a lot of different cultural foods. I'm sure enjoying learning about your cultural heritage," I said.

We went back downstairs, and as we were talking, a girl I had known in high school walked into Oliva's apartment.

She looked at me and said, "I know you!"

"I know you too!" I said in agreement. "You're Maria, and you and I were in the same chemistry class in high school. We were lab partners."

"Gillian, this is my sister, Maria," she said.

"Maria is your sister?" I said to Oliva, so surprised. "I had the best time with Maria in chemistry during labs. Our teacher put us together as lab partners. She was so much fun to be around. She would tell about what she did on the weekends with her boyfriend and where she would hang out at nights during the week. All I could do was just listen and laugh," I said.

"Yes, I did have some amazing stories to tell," Maria said. "So, Gillian, how do you know my sister, Oliva?"

"Our church formed a new young adult Sunday school class, and I invited Oliva. I had no idea Oliva and you were related. It is sure good to see you again. You could take a situation and make it funny. Even our science teacher would stop at our lab section and enjoyed talking with you."

"Gillian, I used to do everything I could to get out of school," she said.

"I know. I remember the time when you came to school with your hair in big curlers, a short skirt, and spaghetti top and wanted to be kicked out of school so you could go to Ouray with your boy-friend. But the principal made you report to every class that day dressed like that. Maria, that took real guts to do that!" I said.

"Gillian, didn't you have a brother, Logan, who went to Gunnison High School also?" she asked.

Yes, Logan graduated in 1965, went to Western State, and now has a good job working for the Highway Department in town. So, Maria, what do you do in Gunnison?" I asked.

"I own and operate a beauty shop in town. Oliva should bring you by sometime," she said.

"Thanks for the invite," I said.

"Maria has a good mind for business ventures, and the ladies love coming to Maria's shop to hear the stories she tells. You not only get your hair done, but you also get entertainment," Oliva said.

Before Maria left, she had a brief conversation with Oliva, said goodbye, and as she walked away, I knew I would be hearing some of her funny stories another time.

## 22

The fall of 1974, Mom and Dad returned to Gunnison. They were excited to be back home, to have their children to talk to, and to be a part of Juliet's life. Dad retired the following spring in April of 1975, and they eventually became Juliet's caregivers while I worked. With Grandma, she baked cookies, made donuts, picked berries, and worked in the garden. With Grandpa, she went fishing in Grandpa's boat on mountain lakes, worked in the garden, and read books. When Juliet turned four, Grandpa bought her a pony she named Smokey. He taught her how to ride and even made her get back up when she was bucked off.

When I came home after work, I would take Juliet on a walk with Smokey up a country lane, just across the bridge from where we lived. It was great coming home to her and seeing the great childhood she was having with two very special people.

In the spring of 1976, my mom planned a trip with her sisters where they all would meet in Reno, Nevada, for a reunion. Mom was excited to be going, but she was having an issue with one of her breasts and said she was going to have her sister, Roberta, who was a nurse, look at it. Roberta knew right away there was a hard lump and told Mom to be sure and see her doctor when she got home.

The four sisters had a great time, and she was always glad she went on that trip. When Mom returned home, she did see her doctor, and the biopsy confirmed breast cancer, and the breast was removed. This was the beginning of many medical visits for chemotherapy and radiation treatments with my mom being very sick and Dad and I caring for her.

My brother, Logan, loved his family and was a big help to me with Juliet and spent about a year with us all living back home. But, for six years, he had lived the life of a bachelor and was seeking to return to that life. So, in the fall of 1975, he began looking at property for sale in Gunnison, and on December 1, 1975, moved into his own home. He was happy, and we were all very proud of him.

For a while, a friend of his from high school rented a room from him. Then, in July 1976, Logan married the love of his life, Lucia. They have raised two boys, Matt and Andy, and have been married for forty-five years.

After working at the Holiday Inn as a desk clerk and sometimes as a night auditor, I found a job as a bookkeeper, doing accounts receivable and payroll for a steel fabrication company in the industrial area of Gunnison. It was a step up in pay and responsibilities. I was learning a lot about the different trades of blue-collar workers. I came to respect their skills in engineering, drafting, welding, and machining. I was amazed at what started as an idea on paper and what the finished product looked like as it was loaded on to delivery trucks.

I eventually was promoted to office manager while continuing with payroll, accounts receivable, and payable transactions. At the end of each month, I submitted reports to the company's accounting firm. I loved the job and looked forward to going to work every morning.

## 23

Oliva and I enjoyed being actively involved in the young adult group and especially enjoyed the social activities that children were invited to. In the summer of 1976, a camping trip was planned into the San Juan Mountains north of Durango, Colorado, over rocky roads that connected Silverton, Telluride, Ouray, and Lake City, Colorado. I bought a two-man tent for Juliet and me to sleep in and packed a duffel bag of warm clothes and toiletries. Oliva's aunt offered her jeep for Oliva, Stacey, Juliet, and I to use on the trip. On a Saturday morning, there were about twenty of us that met in the valley north of Durango.

Heading north, the road begins to curve and climb in elevation along breathtaking mountain and valley views. At times, the road parallels the Durango and Silverton Narrow Gauge Railroad train tracks that run between Durango and Silverton, and tourists can stop along the road and wave at the passengers on the train.

Our first stop was Silverton, Colorado, a former silver mining camp with an elevation of ninety-three hundred feet, surrounded by thirteen-thousand-foot peaks. It is now a national historic landmark. We spent time sightseeing and having lunch in Silverton before we entered the San Juan National Forest and made camp in a beautiful meadow that stretched with green grassland and wildflowers surrounded by huge pine trees and majestic mountains. Juliet enjoyed helping me put up our tent and getting our sleeping bags rolled out.

One of the girls in our group had purchased the food, organized our group into teams, and made schedules of who would be cooking the different meals each day. Meals were cooked over open campfires and served on metal dishes that were washed from water from a nearby mountain river.

While we were at the river that first night, two girls decided to wash their hair, using water from that cold mountain stream. Oliva and I looked at each other and thought they were crazy. That night under a starry sky and around the campfire, we worshipped and sang praise songs. It was great to be enjoying God's creation with friends.

The next morning, Stacey took Juliet exploring while Oliva and I helped cook breakfast. Talking and laughing with friends while you're cooking bacon, eggs, coffee, and hot chocolate over a campfire makes a meal extra special. Being a Sunday morning, and before leaving the meadow, we held a worship service, and we said an extra thank you prayer to our Lord for making this time possible in our lives.

Emerging from our campsite, we began driving on a section of road known as the Million-Dollar Highway. It is twelve mile of road that runs north between Silverton and Ouray, Colorado. Legend has it the highway was named so because it cost a million dollars a mile to build. The road winds and clings to the mountain through a deep gorge with steep cliffs, narrow lanes, no guardrails, and hosts majestic views.

Five miles up the Million-Dollar Highway from Silverton is the entrance to a gravel road known as Ophir Pass Road that connects Red Mountain Pass to Telluride, Colorado. This would be our main venue today, and one of the men in our group would be driving our jeep. Ophir Pass is a very narrow road that hugs the side of the mountain as it curves and ascends to an elevation of twelve thousand feet. There are numerous breathtaking views with the road becoming very narrow and rocky in spots. Descending from the summit, we went into the San Juan Forest and made camp for the night.

We were deeper into the forest with tall pine trees and less sunlight. We were a tired group around the campfire that night, and as we were finishing our evening service, dark clouds began to form, and it began to rain. Breaking camp, we entered our tents, and as Juliet and I became snuggled in our sleeping bags, we listened to the rain pelt our tent.

As I drifted off to sleep, I prayed the tent would keep us dry. Waking up in the morning, we found our tent soaking wet with our sleeping bags surrounded by water. As we emerged from the tent, we discovered some of the men had already started a fire with coffee and hot chocolate brewing. There is nothing like the smell of clean woodsy air with the damp earth as you sit and drink a warm beverage around a friendly fire.

Since this would be the last morning of the camping trip, we lingered a while longer around the morning campfire, sharing memories of our time together. Favorite times were being in a convoy over the mountains, food cooking on an open fire, worship services in the mountains, and deciding who had more stamina overall: the men or the women.

Packing up and heading out of our campsite, our destination today was to visit the historic towns of Telluride and Ouray, Colorado, high in the San Juan mountains of southwest Colorado. In the late 1800s, these towns were inundated with prospectors seeking their fortune in the gold and silver discoveries. Over the years, Telluride has gone from a few hundred miners to over five thousand to a few hundred again, depending on the price of the ore. In the 1970s, the town's image changed to a world-class ski resort in the winter, and during the other seasons, it hosts music festivals and cultural events.

The quaint town of Ouray was named after a Ute Indian chief, and today, the town has restored many of its original buildings. It is surrounded with majestic peaks and canyons, rushing waterfalls, and has a large open healing hot spring that the locals and tourists enjoy. Before Oliva, I, and the girls left Ouray, we found a place that offered hot showers for one dollar each. It was thoroughly a revitalizing experience after camping for three days.

Our camping trip was over. As we headed back home through the San Juan mountains, over the Million-Dollar Highway, and into the Animas Valley, Oliva, the girls, and I laughed, sang songs, and praised God for the rich friendship we had found with each other and our church group.

## 24

In the fall, our church was planning on establishing a mission church in the valley and planned on renting a Grange Hall as a place to hold the services. Dad and Mom enjoyed belonging to the Grange and enjoyed the different meetings and socials that were held there. Now, they were excited about the church using it for its mission outreach program.

The pastor wanted to be able to offer the valley people a worship service and Sunday School classes each week. He called Oliva and I and asked if we would attend this week's meeting. We agreed to come and wondered what he could be asking us to do. He asked people to be praying about what God would have them do in helping to establish the church and see who might be led to teach some of the Sunday School classes. After the meeting, a casual social was held, and the pastor's wife approached Oliva and I with a question.

"Oliva, Gillian, the pastor and I were wondering if you two would consider teaching the children's Sunday School class at the Grange on Sunday mornings?"

"Wow!" I said. "You do know that we are divorced women. Do you want us in that role?" I asked.

"Gillian, what we've noticed is you both have hearts for the Lord, and we think God can use you in spreading the Gospel," she said.

"You don't know what that means to me. Thank you," I said. "I've helped in vacation Bible schools during the summertime, but I've never been a lead teacher before. What do you think about the idea, Oliva?" I asked.

"I'm humbled you would ask me. But I'm just learning about the Bible myself and certainly wouldn't do it without Gillian's help and guidance," she said.

"I would like for both of you to pray about it and see if God is leading you in that direction. You can talk about it this week and let us know."

"What would you want us to teach?" I asked.

"The church has some curriculum you could use, but you can also come up with your own ideas and see where God leads you," she said.

"Where would we be holding the class? Is the Grange really that big to hold both adult and children's classes?" I inquired.

"We've looked at the space and thought you both could hold the children's class around the tables in the kitchen, and the adults could use the main meeting area. If we grow in numbers, we will cross that bridge later," she explained.

Oliva was always up for a new adventure, and I was excited that I could be teaching children again. The following week, we prayed about God showing us if he wanted us to do this ministry for him and talked about the different talents we had to offer between us.

"I'm excited about this new opportunity, Oliva. I was thinking we should start the class with a song or two," I said.

"I play a little guitar, so if you know some simple songs with three or four chords, you could lead, and I could accompany you," Oliva said.

"That's great, Oliva!!" I said. "I never knew you played the guitar! It is one of my favorite instruments, and I hope to learn how to play it someday." I do know a couple of simple songs we could start with, and I already have an idea about what our first lesson could be—one on the seven days of creation. We could have an art project to go along with it," I explained.

"Wow, look at us," Oliva exclaimed. "We are already on our way to being Sunday School teachers. I think God wants us to do this. Don't you think so, too, Gillian?" she asked.

"I love teaching children, Oliva, and if we can teach them God's Word, that is a double blessing for us. So I think we should call the pastor and tell him of our decision," I said.

"Oh, good," Oliva said. "A new adventure begins again for us!"

Our first Sunday, a couple of members from the church with children decided they would support the mission ministry by attending Sunday services at the mission church. This added to the number of children attending each week, so Oliva and I prepared music sheets and an art project for twelve, and our numbers usually fluctuated from week to week.

Since our focus was on creation, we began teaching them "The Butterfly Song" with an array of hand positions to illustrate the different animals in the song. The song teaches that just as God made each animal with different characteristics, he also made each person unique with a heart and a smile but also gave us Jesus, and we are thanking him for making us who we are. The kids loved singing the song, and we were asked to be the special music at one of the worship services.

Oliva and I enjoyed serving in this ministry for a little over a year before our lives changed. The church also struggled with increasing membership, and eventually, the mission church in the valley closed.

Our church also had a Bible camp with a lodge and cabins. Once again, the pastor's wife asked if Oliva and I would consider helping in the kitchen during one of the weekend camps. We were delighted to be asked and thought it would be a good way to spend a weekend. We imagined we would cook a little, help clean up, and then we would have plenty of time to ourselves to relax or go hiking around the campgrounds. Well, little did we know, we hardly ever got out of the kitchen the whole time. Just as we finished one shift and were cleaning up, the pastor's wife started having us prepare for the next meal.

When the evening meals were served, and the kitchen was cleaned up, we joined all the campers in the main lodge for an evening meeting which was fun to attend, but we were exhausted instead of being relaxed and refreshed. It's an experience we still laugh about today.

**25**

Christmas of 1976, Juliet and I were at Oliva's, decorating her and Stacy's tree, when Oliva and I got into a conversation of where we had spent our past vacations.

"Gillian, have you ever been to Mexico?" Oliva asked.

"No, I haven't, have you?" I inquired.

"Yes, my husband and I spent a week in Mazatlán. It is a resort town along the Pacific Ocean, and it's a fun place to spend a vacation," she said.

"How did you and your husband do sightseeing and shopping around Mazatlán? Can you speak Spanish?" I asked.

"I took a couple of years of Spanish in high school, so I did okay with the exchange of money and purchases, and I could also converse some in the restaurants ordering meals. But most all the major hotels and restaurants hire people that can speak English well so that it's not a problem for tourists," she explained. "It's the open markets along the street that we will need to be aware of with quick exchanges and prices."

"Oliva, are you thinking of taking a trip back to Mexico?" I asked.

"I'm thinking that you and I should take Stacey and Juliet to Mazatlán for a vacation this coming year, "she said.

"Oliva, I don't have the money for that kind of trip," I said.

"Me either, Stacey, and I struggle month to month as it is. But Mexico is one of the cheaper places Americans can vacation because of the exchange rate of the different currency. I think if we start planning and saving now, we could possibly go next summer," she explained.

"As long as it's next summer, I can start saving for the trip now and probably come up with the money for the trip," I said.

"My husband and I stayed at a very nice hotel, right on the beach, and it wasn't that expensive. The one thing I could do this week is call that hotel and see what a one room with two queen-sized beds would cost and possibly get our reservation made. Then we can start planning and saving for the trip. What do you think?" she asked.

"Juliet and I are in, and you already have me excited about going! My brother, Logan, has been a couple of times and has a few favorite places he loves to visit. I've experienced Alaska. It would be great to experience Mexico. Alaska was expensive, so it's nice Mexico will be more affordable," I explained.

Oliva called that same week and was able to reserve us the room we wanted with an ocean view for the middle of June which was off-season rates. I was surprised how affordable it was and was so excited about the plans we would be making, and it was good to know that Oliva had been there and she would know her way around.

The next time we were together, Oliva explained how we could save money by not flying to Mazatlán. Instead, we would drive to the border and ride the train that runs through Mexico the rest of the way. She said it would be best if we left at night, drive through the deserts of New Mexico and Arizona while the girls sleep, and be at the border town of Nogales, Arizona, to catch the morning train from Nogales to Mazatlán. On the train, we could have sleeping car accommodations so we could catch up on our sleep and rest, and then, when the train pulled into Mazatlán, we would be ready to "hit the beach!" So, for six months, Oliva and I began to tighten our belts, and we saved every extra penny for our Mexico trip.

In March, Oliva called me and said she had been talking a lot about our trip at the bank and had a coworker that was asking if it would be possible for her and her two children to join us on our Mexico vacation.

"Gillian, I'm sorry, I talked so much about our trip. I hope you're not too upset with me about possibly including another family?" she asked.

"Oliva, I have no problem with it as long as you know her and think we will all be able to get along together. How old are her kids?" I inquired.

"Middle school age," she said. "Gillian, her name is Cindy, and she is a lovely person to work with. I haven't met her children, but I think you would like her too," she said.

"It's fine, Oliva, as they say: the more, the merrier. I would like to meet her and get acquainted with her and her children before we begin the trip. She will also need to see if she can still get a reservation at the same hotel," I said.

"Gillian, you are right about the reservation, and I think all three families will need to meet a couple of times before this vacation begins. So, you are okay with saying yes to her and her kids coming along?" she asked.

"Absolutely fine with me. I trust your judgment, Oliva," I said.

Then, in April, Oliva called me again and needed to ask me another question.

"Gillian, you're not going to believe this, and I'm not sure how to ask you either," Oliva said hesitantly.

"Oliva, the best thing is to just ask me. I can't imagine I would get upset with you about anything. I'm not that hard to talk to, am I?" I said cautiously.

"No, you're not. Well, I was talking with Ruth whose kids come to our Sunday School class in the valley, and she called me and wanted to know if she and her two children could come along also?"

"Wow, this is now becoming a small group vacation." I said. "I've met Ruth and visited with her a couple of times. Her kids are great, too, but doesn't she have health issues? And is she really strong enough to make the trip?" I asked.

"Well, I asked her about that, and she assured me her health is better and she is quite capable of making the trip. I told her I would need to ask you again," she stressed.

"Oliva, I can't turn them down. But I do think for you and me to really enjoy ourselves on this vacation, we shouldn't take anyone else on board. We are all going to be looking at you for guidance, and I want you to enjoy this trip," I said.

"I agree, Gillian. If anyone else asks, I definitely am saying no!" she said as we both started laughing. "Oh brother, Gillian, I'm not sure what we've gotten ourselves into," Oliva said.

"Oliva, let's start praying about the trip. We need to pray for everyone's safety and about the new friendships we will establish with these mothers and their children," I said.

"Definitely," Oliva said.

There were now four women and five children that would traveling to Mexico for a summer vacation. We had two meetings, one at Oliva's home where we all got better acquainted and shared our traveling experiences. The kids seemed to get along well together, so Oliva and I were encouraged with how the trip was shaping up. The second meeting was held at Cindy's home, and her husband wanted to talk to us about important things to think about when crossing a desert. He especially stressed the need to carry extra water, wanted Cindy and I to have our cars inspected by a competent mechanic, and possibly carry extra belts and hoses.

Oliva spoke up and said, "Ladies, he's right. One time, Stacey and I were traveling to Texas when the fan belt broke on my car. We were out in the middle of nowhere in New Mexico, so I took the hose off my douche bag, cut the end off, and made it work until I could get to the next town to get it fixed."

"A douche bag hose!" I exclaimed as we all began to laugh. "Oliva, you are one clever lady for sure. That's why you're riding in my car!"

Oliva and I told Cindy and Ruth that on the Friday, we planned to leave and we wanted to sleep a few hours after work and depart Gunnison around nine o'clock. At the time, that was a good idea with them, but when that Friday came, Cindy and Ruth decided they wanted to leave right after work. Oliva and I didn't agree with leaving at that time, so we told them to go ahead, and we would meet them at the train station in New Nogales at eight o'clock Saturday morning.

Juliet and I picked up Oliva and Stacey at eight-thirty Friday evening. We were on our way and so excited the day had finally arrived. We had no trouble the whole way to New Nogales and arrived at the train station about seven forty-five Saturday morning. However, Cindy, Ruth, and the kids were not there. Oliva went ahead and got us our sleeping compartments on the nine o'clock train leaving for Mazatlán. Eight-thirty came, and they still weren't there. Oliva and I were worried something happened to them. We never saw them along the road and never intended to run into them because they had at least a three-to-four-hour head start. At eight forty-five, they came dragging in, exhausted, and told about their night on the road.

They left Gunnison about five-thirty and got fifty miles down the road when they were stopped by a police barricade for over an hour because a truck hauling gas spilled on the highway. Then in the middle of the night, their car broke down, Cindy didn't have it inspected, and they waited a long time before a trucker came by who was willing to tow them into the next town where it could be fixed. By the time Oliva and I went the same route, the spill was all cleaned up, and we never saw them on the road because they had been towed to a repair shop in a nearby town.

Oliva hurried to get Cindy and Ruth's tickets for the train. By the time they got there, the sleeping compartments had all been taken, and the only remaining seats left were the ones where passengers would be sitting up the whole way. Ruth and Cindy were tired and unhappy with their accommodations. There were only a few minutes before the train was ready to pull out, so Oliva hurried to get them all a cold bottled drink. As she was passing them out, one bottle fell and spilled all over a couple of them. It was the icing on the cake to a very bad night, and all Oliva could do was say sorry and walk away. From the section of the train they were on and where our compartments were, we never saw them until the next day when we pulled into Mazatlán and departed from the train.

We took taxis from the train station to the hotel. Our route took us through the poorer sections of the town, and it was a sharp contrast to the fancy hotels that lined the cost of Mazatlán's beach front property. I also remember looking out our train window and seeing how the people lived in the towns we passed through. The people lived in very tough conditions, and I thanked God for allowing me to be born in America.

When we got to the hotel and were checking in, Ruth and Cindy found that their rooms were on the other side of the hotel from ours and we would be separated by quite a distance. They thought it would be better if we were all in the same section of the hotel for security reasons. Oliva talked a while with the desk clerk, and the only way we could all be together was if Oliva and I gave up our ocean view room. There was another room by Laurel and Donna's area. So to keep the peace and make everyone happy, that is what we did. We told them we would see them on the beach. Now when we emerged from our room, we were overlooking an alley with dumpsters.

As soon as we got into our room, we just threw the suitcases on the bed, found our beach clothes, changed, and went and sat on the beach. We were where we had dreamed of being six months ago. Oliva and I made our first purchase, which were long Mexican dresses locals were selling on the beach.

Being June and hot, we soon moved to one of the hotel pools. Oliva and I enjoyed lounging by the pool, sipping a cold beverage while we watched our daughters play in the pool. Juliet was five and hadn't had swimming lessons yet, so Stacey was very patient with her and showed her how she could move herself through the water. The pool became Juliet's favorite place, and by the end of our stay, she had made a lot of progress with her breathing, floating, and kicking skills.

As we sat there by the pool, Cindy and her kids joined us. As Cindy walked up, she looked like a model in beautiful swim wear attire and with high heels. Oliva and I thought we could sure take some lessons from her. Shortly afterward, Ruth and her kids arrived. We all were beginning to relax and enjoy our arrival. We stayed by the pool until we went and prepared for dinner in the hotel dining room.

For Oliva and me to make our money stretch, we bought food to eat in the room for breakfast and snacking. For lunch, we ate from the different marketplaces we visited and shopped at. This way, we could save to go out to a nice restaurant each night in the city of Mazatlán. Two of our favorite places were one that served large fried shrimp and French fries in a bucket while island music was played, and the other was a restaurant on the ocean, and as you ate dinner, you could watch the sun go down.

Each week, the hotel put on a fiesta dinner with Mariachi musicians and Spanish dancers. We all signed up for the special night, and Oliva and I bought Mexican dresses for the girls to wear. It was a delightful evening experiencing the Mexican culture. Afterward, outside the hotel, a band played while guests danced under the stars, listening to the ocean roll onto the shore. Oliva was asked to dance, and we both laughed because the gentleman was a head shorter than her, and she kept rubbing her chin on the top of his slicked down greased hair.

Our time in Mazatlán was over, and it was a magical experience. Going back on the train, we all had a sleeping compartment close to each other. We had several hours to sit, laugh, and share our best times as we watched the Mexico landscape pass by. Reaching the town of Nogales, I found my car with a flat tire in the car lot where it had been safely locked up behind a high fence. I paid for it to be changed and fixed.

Oliva, I, and our girls said goodbye to Cindy, Ruth, and their kids. They were headed back to Gunnison, and I had planned to visit and introduce Oliva and Stacey to some good friends I knew in Alaska that now lived in Phoenix. They invited us to spend an evening with them. It was also the city where Juliet's father lived, and I promised him he could see her while we were in town.

Sunday morning, we said goodbye and headed to Gunnison. I dropped Oliva and Stacey off at their apartment and told Oliva I would see her at Bible study this week. I also thanked Stacey for being such a great big sister to Juliet on our trip. As I entered our driveway, I found Mom alone, and she was happy to see us. She asked me how our trip was, and I told her it was magical.

"Mom, where's Dad?" I asked.

"Gillian, he is in the hospital. He had a heart attack while we were fishing up at Rainbow Lake near Baldwin, Colorado. We got the camper set up and the boat on the lake. We made our first casts, and that's when it hit him," she told me.

"How bad is it, Mom?"

"The lower part of his heart is not fully working. He will be able to live that way for a while and will also continue to take his meds. The doctor said one day, he will be doing something, and his heart will stop, and he will go down. For now, he is alive, and he was hoping to see you and Juliet today," she said.

As soon as I got the car unpacked, we headed back into town. When Juliet and I walked into his hospital room, Dad was sitting up, ready to hear about our trip. Juliet was so happy to be back with her grandparents and was sad that her grandpa was sick.

As I went to sleep that night, I thanked my God for making it possible for Juliet and I to go to Mexico and see more of his creation. I also knew Mom was fighting breast cancer, and now Dad's heart was not functioning well. I prayed for my parents and knew our time together was getting shorter.

Oliva's cousin, Debbie, was dating a man named George who had a masonry business in Gunnison. During the winter months, he was also on a man's city league basketball team which traveled the area playing the different city league teams. February of 1978, Frank's cousin, Dan, a dairy farmer from Nebraska, came to visit George, and the two planned on doing some skiing around Colorado. Before leaving on their skiing trip, George had a basketball game to play in Silverton, Colorado.

Debbie and George introduced Dan—who had a long beard and looked like a member of The Brethren Faith—to Oliva and invited her to go to the game with them. George was hoping Dan and Oliva would establish a relationship.

The next day, Oliva made homemade soup for everyone and invited me to the dinner so I could meet Dan. He was a kind man, rather quiet with a deep voice, and from his outlook, I believed him to be a man of faith. What I also noticed was he enjoyed watching Oliva's magnetic personality while interacting with her friends and family.

That evening, Dan asked Oliva and Stacey to go watch the ski jumps at a nearby ski resort. While watching the skiers jump, Oliva had a serious talk about God with Dan and wanted him to know how important God was in her life. Oliva found out that God was just as important in Dan's life a well. When it came time to leave the ski area, Oliva and Stacey also noticed two qualities about Dan. First, instead of Oliva and Stacey walking all the way to where the car was parked, Dan had them wait in the resort area; he would go get the car and pick them up. Second, his car had intermediate wipers when Oliva's car only had one speed. Oliva and Stacey were impressed!

George and Dan left on their ski vacation and headed to Steamboat Ski Resort, a major ski area in northwest, Colorado. While there, Dan wrote Oliva a letter declaring his intent on dating her. When Dan returned to Gunnison, Oliva wanted to make sure Dan knew all about her. So she told him of her past with her husband and that she couldn't have children. Dan's response surprised Oliva.

"My folks helped me to learn to get the second half out of things," he said.

So began a period of letter writing and phone calls between Oliva and Dan. During the summertime, he returned to Gunnison, proposed to Oliva, and she accepted.

At the end of October, a bridal shower was held for Oliva, and she beamed with happiness at the new life she would be living. A week before the wedding, she put all her bridal shower gifts in her car and headed to Nebraska by herself, something she still enjoys today, heading out on the open road by herself to family. She was going to be meeting Dan's family, and it would be her first look at the dairy farm which would become her and Stacey's new home.

Dan and his family were busy with the fall harvest. Oliva saw Dan milking the cows, putting up silage, and how it was stored on the property. Dan enjoyed introducing Oliva to his world. What fun it was for her to ride on a hay wagon, see the beauty of a Nebraskan evening sky, and tour the white two-story home that they would be living in.

When it was time to return to Gunnison, Oliva left her car in Nebraska, and Dan and she drove one of Dan's big farm trucks back to Gunnison. It would be used to pack up Oliva's and Stacey's furniture, household items, and belongings. The three of them would drive it back to Nebraska after the wedding which was next Saturday.

**27**

The Spring of 1978, Mom's cancer had spread into her bones, and she was undergoing a series of chemotherapy and radiation treatments. The doctors encouraged Dad to take Mom to Albuquerque, New Mexico, for more intense treatments. While in Albuquerque, Dad rented an apartment not far from the hospital to make their stay more comfortable. When they returned, I could tell Mom was very weak, suffering more, and would be mostly in bed now. When I wasn't working, I was staying close to home, caring for Mom, being with Juliet, and helping Dad. I will always remember the night I called Oliva for help.

"Hi, Oliva. How was your day at work?" I asked.

"It was fine. How are things going for you tonight?" she asked.

"Well, Oliva, that is why I called. I need some help. I'm exhausted. Dad is with Mom, and the house is a mess. I need to get it cleaned up tonight, but right now, I just don't have the energy. Do you think you could come over to my house tonight and help me clean house? I think between the two of us, we could get it done in a little over an hour," I explained.

"Gillian, give me half an hour, and I will be on my way," she said.

While waiting for Oliva, I cooked supper and got the cleaning supplies ready to use. When Oliva arrived, she had a smile on her face, a bucket, and rubber gloves ready to go and the best attitude a friend could ever have.

"Gillian, where do I begin?" she asked.

"Oliva, you are the best. If you take the kitchen and living room, I'll take the bathroom and bedrooms. With both of us working, we should be done in a little over an hour," I said.

And we were. It was the lift I needed, and we shared a cup of tea before she left. It was one of the greatest examples of friendship I would ever receive from Oliva.

Shortly after Dad and Mom returned from Albuquerque, Mom's youngest sister, Roberta, who was a registered nurse and lived in Montrose, Colorado, called and asked if she could be a part of Mom's caregiving. I was delighted she wanted to come be with Mom and help with her care. So, each week, Roberta would ride the bus for two hours. Then it would stop and drop her off close to our house before going on into Gunnison. There was a loving relationship between the two sisters, and I will always be grateful to Aunt Roberta for those weekly visits.

In November, the week of Thanksgiving, Dad took Mom for her radiation treatment Monday morning. The doctors informed him Mom would not live to the end of the week. Dad called me and gave me the news and said Mom would be dying at home. I told my boss, and he gave me the week off. We called Logan, Lucia, and the boys, and they came and stayed at the house for the week. Dad called Nathan, who was at seminary school in Denver, and he made it home through a bad snowstorm across Colorado and entered the house with a cast on his foot which was supposed to be removed before he came home for Thanksgiving. We had all gathered to surround a beloved wife and mother with our love for her and to say goodbye.

People from church brought us Thanksgiving dishes to eat while we took turns sitting at mom's bedside. Tuesday night, Mom went into a coma and died on Thanksgiving Day at two o'clock in the morning. We called the mortuary. They came and put her in a plastic bag, zipped it up, loaded her into their car, and drove away.

Dad hung his head and said, "I can't believe she is gone." We mostly sat around, numb, and knew Mom was now in heaven with Jesus and with her new body. Thanksgiving Day, we sat around, sharing memories of Mom, and Logan and I helped saw off Nathan's cast, and we began to laugh and feel again.

Saturday, Juliet and I attended Dan and Oliva's wedding. To my big surprise, the groom, Dan, at the front of the church, was a changed man. The last time I saw Dan, he still had his beard. Now he was clean-shaven, and there stood this very good-looking man with a great smile. Stacey was her maid of honor. Oliva was truly radiant walking in with a ring of wildflowers in her hair and a bouquet in her hand. After Dan and Oliva said their vows, Dan then turned to the people attending the wedding and read a vow that he was making to them. His oath was to the kind of husband he planned to be to Oliva and the father he would be to Stacey. With the extra vow made, I knew Oliva had found a special love with a man after God's own heart. Before we said our goodbyes, I had one last question for Oliva.

"When and why did Dan shave his beard? He looks terrific without it," I said.

She said, "One week before the wedding, he wanted me to know what I was getting into!"

I was so happy for Dan, Oliva, and Stacey and the new life God had given them. They invited Juliet and I to Nebraska when Juliet had her spring break from school. It was a trip I was looking forward to.

Tuesday, we held Mom's funeral at the church she was a member of for twenty-eight years. Roberta attended, and she noticed the peace that seemed to surround us with Mom's passing and asked me how I could be at such peace.

I told her, "Mom is with Jesus and is not suffering anymore. God is also with us as we are going through this valley of our lives. The peace we feel is the peace only God can give when you are his child."

Within three days, I said goodbye to two women I really loved. God had closed two doors in my life. Within a few months, he would be opening a new door that would give Juliet and I a new life.

## 28

In December, I pulled the Christmas decorations out and started to bring the holiday season into our home. Mom and Dad always loved this time of year and enjoyed all the festivities that went along with the spirit of the season. I knew Mom would want that same spirit to continue in her home. So, the first weekend after Mom's funeral, Juliet and I listened to Christmas music as we filled the tree with ornaments and displayed decorations around the house. The next weekend, we baked. Dad especially enjoyed all the extra baking of holiday desserts, so we began baking some of his favorites.

During the holidays, it was always a delight to go to Logan and Lucia's home. Lucia was famous for filling their tree with beautiful homemade crafts, and they always had special cookies that were a delight to eat with a cup of their special hot chocolate. We spent Christmas and New Year's Day at their home, stuffing ourselves with the different holiday dishes and watching the special events on television. Nathan was home for his winter break from seminary, and it was fun having him play the piano while we sang Christmas carols together. We all missed Mom a lot that first Christmas without her, but I believed she would have been proud of us for how we celebrated one of her favorite holidays.

January and February brought good snowstorms to the Gunnison's ski resort. Saturdays, Juliet and I would pack a lunch and head up the mountain for a day of skiing. We stayed on the easy runs as we slowly made our way down the mountain. While skiing, memories of Oliva and I skiing with the girls flooded my mind. Most of the times, when we skied with the girls, the days were warm, the skies were a beautiful blue above, and snow-covered mountains were our paths. We brought sack lunches and ate them outside at the lodge halfway down the mountain.

I especially remember one day Oliva and I were skiing, and we were coming onto the chairlifts to be taken back up the mountain. The lift we were using required skiers to be in pairs when they caught the chair. One time, Oliva was a little ahead of me coming into the lift, so instead of yelling out "Single" so she could pair up with another single person, she yelled out, "Divorced! Abandoned!" She could always make people laugh.

Spring arrived in the Rocky Mountains, and that meant spring break from school was just around the corner for us. It also meant that Juliet and I would be going on a nine-day vacation to Nebraska to see Oliva and Stacey and visit the farm. It was good to be out on the open road, and it would be our first time traveling along the upper part of the state of Kansas which was a straight road with miles of wheat fields on both sides. On the far east side of Kansas, we turned north into the eastern part of Nebraska. At the end of two days, Oliva and Stacey met us just outside their town, and we followed them down country roads to the farm.

We were so happy to be together again, and Dan proved to be a wonderful host showing us around the farm. We met Dan's brother, Phil, and watched how the two of them ran their operation of milking the cows. We had a visit from Dan's dad who stopped in to say hello, met a younger brother who was practicing his golf swing, and a younger sister also. Oliva and I spent a lot of time in the kitchen, preparing meals, talking about our lives, walking the country roads, and did whatever Oliva needed to do to keep the operation running smoothly. Stacey once again became Juliet's big sister, and she enjoyed showing Juliet around the farm. Evening meals were especially fun with us sitting around talking and laughing about old times. It was time to say goodbye to our dear friends and a place I knew we would be returning to someday.

In late spring, I read in the *Gunnison Herald* that the city league softball teams were going to be holding their first meeting at City Hall in the coming week, and interested people in playing the sport were invited to attend the meeting and join a team. Softball is the one sport I enjoyed playing during my grade school and middle school years. I played the game well and thought it would be a way I could meet new people.

I went to the meeting, found a women's team that still needed players, and signed up to play with them. The drugstore in Gunnison was going to be our sponsor. It was a good choice in my life. I met an amazing group of women who were fun to be around, and we became a force to be reckoned with on the field. It was fun having Dad and Juliet at our games.

**29**

After spring break of 1980, when I returned to work following a vacation to Nebraska, it was time to do the payroll for the crew. After handing out the payroll checks, one of the new men who had worked for the steel fabrication company for a couple of months came into my office on his break and said he needed to talk to me.

"Hi, Gillian, I'm Josh. I think you made a mistake on my check. I turned in more hours than you reported on the check."

"Oh, let me look and see what I have recorded," I said.

After checking over the figures, I had made a mistake.

"Josh, you're right. I'm sorry. Will it be okay if I put the additional hours on your next paycheck?" I asked.

"Yeah, sure. That will be fine," he said and walked out of my office.

The next day, on Josh's morning break, he came into my office again and asked if I had a moment to talk.

"Sure, Josh, what did you want to talk about?" I asked.

"I would like to ask you if you're married?" he inquired.

"No, I'm not married. I'm divorced and have a daughter. Why do you ask?" I said.

"I would like to ask you out and wondered if you would like to go out to supper with me this coming Friday after work?" he said.

"Josh, are you married or are you dating anyone serious?" I asked.

"No, I was married for five years, but I'm divorced now and am not dating anyone serious," he said.

"Well, it's very nice to be asked out, and I will accept your invitation to dinner on Friday," I said.

Josh said, "I'm off at three-thirty, so I'll go home, freshen up, and we'll meet back here at five when you get off. Will that work for you?"

"Yes, I'll make arrangements with my dad to see if he can watch my daughter while we're out," I said.

"Good, see you Friday," Josh said.

My dad was happy for me that I had been asked out and was wondering where all the single men were in town.

True to his word, Josh was back at the shop on Friday night, and we were ready for our date. We decided on a popular Mexican restaurant in town, and we agreed we would both drive our cars into town and park near the restaurant.

When we sat down and placed our orders, Josh wanted us to get better acquainted.

"Gillian, tell me where you went to high school?" he asked.

"Gunnison High School," I said.

"You did? So did I!" he said. "When did you graduate?" he asked.

"1966," was my reply.

"You did? So did I!" he said again.

"I don't remember you, Josh. I was not popular, so I didn't get acquainted with all the kids in our class," I replied.

"Gillian, did you play in the band? I think I remember you coming out of the band room one time," he asked.

"Yes, I was in the band. I played the flute. Both my brother and I were in the high school band. Did you know my brother, Logan?" I asked.

"No, I didn't know him, but I think we have a lot we can talk about over dinner tonight," he said. "One thing I would like for you to know about me, Gillian, is that I lost my right eye in a car accident in 1965. So, since then, I've worn a glass eye in that socket. Does that disturb you in any way?" he asked.

"No, not at all. My brother, Logan, also lost his right eye when he was three years old in a knife accident. So I know all about glass eyes and the situation of depth perception that comes with that condition. I always made sure when I served him any food or a drink, especially, he always had a good hold on the container or dish before I released it to him. He's done quite well in life with just the one eye. It's really all he has known. How has it been for you?" I asked.

"Well, I was eighteen and enjoyed looking at the girls. I had a complex about being disfigured for a while and mostly stayed on the ranch. The loss of my depth perception was a big thing to overcome. I was a month late beginning my senior year of high school. My best friend and his girlfriend also died in the accident," he said.

"I'm sorry for your loss. I think you have healed very well, and I don't think you are disfigured at all," I said.

"Well, it took me a while to get my confidence back and begin to ask girls out again," Josh said.

"You mentioned a ranch. Tell me about that," I asked.

"My family had owned and operated a cattle ranch outside of Gunnison, about seven miles from town. We sold it last year. Now I am living in a trailer on my cousin's property until I figure out what I want to do with the next part of my life," Josh explained.

"Did you enjoy your life on the ranch?" I asked.

"Absolutely! I loved everything about it. I didn't want to sell it. I wanted to increase the herd and continue the operation. The best time of year was when school was out, and I hated it when school began again. I also wanted to get forty acres of the ranch so I would have my own land and possibly start my own herd. But the buyer wanted all or nothing," he explained.

We shared a very nice evening talking about our high school years and what we had been doing since that time. When we left the restaurant, we stood by our cars, talking about the different sports we liked and played in our lives.

"Gillian, I don't want to possess you right off, but I would like to see you again. Would you like to go out with me again next week sometime?" he asked.

"Yes, I'd like that. Thanks for asking me. It's been a fun evening, but I should get home. I want to see Juliet before she goes to bed," I said.

"Goodnight, Gillian."

"Goodnight, Josh."

After our first date, Josh would regularly come into my office on his breaks, and we would talk. I learned he was a cousin to a wife of one of the owners of the company we worked for. It was their property he was living on, and when he went over to pay his rent, he told his cousin that he needed to find a job and if she would know where he might find one. She told him they were hiring welders at their business and encouraged him to try there first. He was hired and said he started noticing me when I walked around the shop and on his breaks. It wasn't long before everyone in the company knew we were dating, and they seemed to be happy for us.

I invited Josh to supper one evening so he could meet my dad and Juliet. I felt the evening had gone well, and before he left, I told him I had joined a women's softball team and invited him to my next game, and he accepted the invitation.

He invited me to go horseback riding with him above the ski resort area. He showed me the cabin that his grandfather, his dad, and he built on the grazing permit they had in that area. He explained to me they built the cabin, but it belonged to the Forest Service, and whoever had the grazing permit had use of the cabin. He showed me his favorite area to ride, and as we rode, he would tell me stories of how they rounded up the cattle each year and how they were brought back by trucks to the ranch for the winter and spring months.

There were times during the summer months that Josh, Juliet, and I would fish along mountain streams, catch small minnows, and then fry them over a campfire. I knew very little about the agriculture industry, especially ranching and cattle operations. I loved learning about Josh's life and was beginning to understand what losing the ranch and its way of life meant to him.

Another weekend we enjoyed was when the owners of the company we worked for and their wives, who I had become friends with, invited Josh, Juliet, and I to join them for a day of fishing at a former owner's cabin on a private lake above Gunnison. It was a very relaxing day. We enjoyed boating around the lake, catching fish, and then we all had a big fish fry which included favorite side dishes people had brought.

For our next date, Josh wanted to cook me dinner, so he invited me out to his trailer. I remember Oliva had a serious talk about God with Dan and wanted him to know how important God was in her life. I decided I wanted to have the same talk with Josh. While he finished the final preparation of a spaghetti and sausage dish with a side salad, I enjoyed setting the table for our dinner. After sharing our favorite foods, I decided it was time for a discussion of where God was at in our lives.

"Josh, I enjoy being with you a lot and want to be honest with you about something that is very important in my life," I said.

"Sounds like this could be a serious conversation," he replied.

"I want to talk to you about God, where he is in my life, and I would like to know where he is in your life. I've accepted God's Son, Jesus Christ, as my Savior. Since I have put my faith in him and follow his teachings, I consider myself to be a Christian and am trying to live a life that is pleasing to him. I like going to church, studying his word, the Bible, being in small group Bible studies, and serving in his church. All those things help me to have a relationship with Jesus. I'm a sinner, saved by his grace, and I need him in my life to help me live the best life I can on this earth. I haven't always followed his commandments, and I have made some poor choices, but he doesn't give up on me, and I know obeying him is my key to a better life in his world," I said.

"Gillian, why are you telling me all this?" Josh asked.

"Because the man I want in my life needs to be a Christian. I want him to believe the same things about God, Jesus, the Holy Spirit, the Bible, and his church the way I do or we're just not going to be compatible, and I couldn't marry a man that is not a Christian. Do you have a faith, Josh?" I asked.

"I was raised in a different faith and have just had a bad experience with church in general. I suffered with nightmares under religious teaching. I was really glad when Mom enrolled my sister and I in the public-school system," he said.

"Josh, I had some bad experiences with teachers in the public-school system, and they gave me nightmares too. So we share something in common with our early school experiences. Do you like going to church and practicing your faith, Josh?" I asked.

"I believe in God, Jesus Christ, and the Holy Spirit. I've never studied the Bible. And I haven't been inside a church in a very long time," he said.

"You sound bitter toward the church. Are you?" I asked.

"I definitely am," he replied.

"Can you tell me why?" I asked.

"My mom was always attending church. During the week, she enjoyed helping in different areas to see that things were ready for every Sunday service. She entered a period of depression, didn't come out of it, and committed suicide. We had to beg them to hold her service. I walked away from the church ten years ago and haven't been back.

"That must have been a terrible time for you and your family. I'm so sorry for how you lost your mother," I said.

"My mother and I were never close. The truth is I spent more time with my grandparents and were raised more by them than I was by my mom and dad. I felt loved by them, and that is where I wanted to spend my time," Josh said.

"Josh, you've had a lot of loss in your life. You've lost an eye, your mother, good friends, and the ranch you loved. How have you been able to cope with all that in your life?" I asked.

"Gillian, there were a lot of family problems on the ranch between different members of my family, and the best way I was able to handle it all was to go out and be among the cattle, be with my grandfather, and be in the mountains where we had the grazing permit. I'm now looking for a new life and have no idea where that life is," Josh said.

"You told me you walked away from the church. Did you walk away from God also?" I asked.

"Like I said, I haven't thought much about it in the last ten years until now when I met a certain red-haired girl," he said, smiling.

"Josh, I was raised in a Christian home by two very special parents who worshiped in church on Sundays and raised their kids in the church. I accepted Jesus Christ as my Savior when I was ten at a Bible camp above Denver. I told God that I was a sinner and needed a Savior. The Savior God gave to me was his Son, Jesus Christ. Jesus and studying the Bible has been an important part of my life ever since that day. He's been a faithful friend who brings peace to my life, and I trust him more each day. God can do the same for you if you let him," I said.

"Gillian, God doesn't need me to tell him I'm a sinner. He already knows that," he said.

"Yes, he does know you are a sinner, but he wants to hear you tell him you are so you and God will agree about the sin in your life. It's the first step on the road to reconciliation with God and a new life that could be waiting for you," I said.

"Gillian, do you believe I'm a Christian?" Josh asked.

"I believe you had a church experience and not a good one. A Christian needs fellowship, a relationship with God and his Son, Jesus Christ, and from what you've told me, you don't have one."

The next time I saw Josh, he told me he had a talk with God, told him he was a sinner, and that he needed him in his life. When Josh told me that, I felt God wanted us to be together. He started going to church with me on Sundays, but he didn't want to be pressured into attending the young adult weekly Bible study or attending a Sunday School class; however, he would come with me to the social events the church offered.

One Sunday afternoon, the church was holding a barbecue and games up at the church camp. I invited Josh, and we had a good time playing horseshoes and socializing with the people. While Josh was talking with some men, the pastor came over and asked how it was going with Josh and me.

"Gillian, it is good to see Josh coming to church with you and to our social events. How is it going so far?" he asked.

"Pastor, we enjoy our times together, and a couple of weeks ago, we shared an evening of where God was at in our lives," I said.

"That is always a good thing to do when couples date. It's a good foundation for a dating relationship," he replied.

"Pastor, I told Josh how important being with a Christian man was in my life and that I couldn't marry a man if he wasn't a Christian," I explained.

"What did Josh say to that Gillian?" he asked.

"He explained how he was raised in a different faith, the experiences he had, which weren't good, but he does believe in the Trinity. He hasn't had much to do with God, Jesus, or the church for ten years. It's just since meeting me that he's even considered it all again. He asked me if I thought he was a Christian, and I told him I didn't think so. A few nights after that talk, he told me he talked to God, told him he was a sinner, and that he needed him in his life. When he told me that, I believe God wants us to be together," I said.

"Gillian, it's good you are stepping out and sharing your faith with others. But one thing I must explain to you is when you told Josh he wasn't a Christian, you were putting yourself in God's position. He is the only one who has the right to judge another person, no one else. God doesn't need your help."

"But, Pastor, I want to be honest with Josh," I said.

"Gillian, it is one thing to share your faith and lead a person to Christ. That's very commendable, but in doing so, you cannot stand in judgment against them, just because they are not living the way you want them to. If Josh made a true confession to God, the Holy Spirit would enter his life, and you will see the fruits of the Spirit as he works in his life. Those fruits are love, joy, peace, patience, kindness, goodness, faithfulness, gentleness, and self-control. That is what you can discern about Josh and base your relationship with him on that," he explained.

On the way down the mountain from the camp, I told Josh what the pastor and I talked about. I also apologized for judging him and said I was sorry. I told him judging people and situations has been one of my biggest faults and struggles in life and has caused me to have regrets. It's a constant battle that I fight within myself every day.

"Gillian, I accept your apology and can also relate to judging other people. I'm bad at it, especially since I lost my eye. I think everyone does it to some extent. Some are just more open about it than others," he said. "Gillian, how long do you think we should date if we think this relationship could become something more?" he asked.

"Josh, we started dating in March. That's been three months. You know what I desire for a man to be in my life. I've fallen in love with you. But you also must know, if you want me, you are accepting Juliet also. I think you should know by October, that's another three months, if you want to continue this relationship or not," I said.

"So you're putting a time limit on our relationship now?" he asked.

"You asked me how long we should date. I'm just giving you my answer. If Juliet and I aren't what you want in the new life you are seeking, then I don't see any reason why we should continue seeing one another. Josh, you're the one that asked the question, how long do you think we should date?"

"Well, let's see where we are at in another three months," Josh replied.

During those last three months, there was one incident with Juliet when I told Josh I was breaking up with him. We had traveled over into the center valley to look at farm equipment. We stayed overnight with a friend, and the next morning, while we were waiting for the family to wake up, Juliet told me she was hungry. Josh said she could wait until the family woke up and we would all have breakfast together. He walked outside to spend time inspecting the equipment. A half-hour later, we were still waiting, so I fixed Juliet a bowl of cereal to eat. She was eating it at the table when Josh walked in.

Later, when we were headed home, he was silent in the car, and I could tell he was upset. As I started to talk to him about the cereal, Juliet asked me a question. "Mom, can I play when I get home?" she asked.

Suddenly, Josh turned around and with a mean face and said, "Juliet, you be quiet, and don't you say anything! You will learn to do what you are told!"

"Josh, that's it!" I said. "You are not going to talk to Juliet that way! We're through! You're not going to treat her that way!"

"No, we're not through. We are going down here into the next town and go to a restaurant, settle down, and talk this out," he said in a firm voice.

Seated inside the restaurant, he began to speak and apologize. "Gillian, I'm sorry I yelled at Juliet and you also. I probably overreacted to the situation," he said.

"Josh, when you walked out the door, we still waited for the family to wake up. My child was hungry, and I didn't think a simple bowl of cereal would matter until we had breakfast. You haven't been a parent with a hungry child. I have, and when she is hungry, I will feed her. Do not talk to her that way again."

"Like I said, I'm sorry for blowing up. Sometimes I just spark like that. But I want us to be together and don't want to lose what we have together," he said.

"You are going to have to show me that you want the three of us together. Not just you and me," I said.

When he dropped us off at the house, I knew this was a big red flag warning me. But I also didn't want to lose what we had, and it was why I was willing to give him another chance.

After this incident, Josh was the man I enjoyed being around. He included Juliet when we went places and spoke kindly to her. In October, Josh asked me to marry him, and I accepted his proposal. We planned to be married on Valentine's Day, 1981. Everyone was happy or us, and I felt blessed again by God.

Josh decided he wanted to buy a home in Gunnison for us to live in when we married. His cousin agreed that Josh could leave the trailer on their property and he could rent it out. We spent our weekends looking at properties for sale, and in December, we decided on a three-bedroom home with a den and attached garage a few blocks from the elementary school Juliet was attending.

Before the closing date, Josh wanted to have a talk with me about our financial situation and especially his money. He wanted me to sign a prenuptial agreement stating that the money he had before our marriage would be his money and whatever property he bought with his money would belong to him. I agreed it was his money to use as he wished. I had a new love, a home we were establishing for the three of us, and I dreamed we were going to have a wonderful life together. My parents fought over money, and I didn't want fighting over money to be a part of my marriage. So it was easy for me to sign the prenuptial agreement.

In January, Josh took Juliet and I to Denver, Colorado, to select bedroom furniture and a dining room set for our home. Juliet could pick out her own bedroom set, and she choose a pretty yellow princess style that was a perfect fit for her room. Josh's aunt and uncle gave us a loveseat and couch set for our living room. We also hung new drapes on the windows and had the placed furnished with kitchen and bathroom items. We planned on doing some remodeling later, but for now, the house was ready for us to live in when we returned home from our honeymoon.

For our honeymoon, Josh surprised me with a trip to Hawaii. We spent three days on the big island of Oahu. We toured The Polynesian Cultural Center, spent a day at Pearl Harbor, and a day visiting the local shops. We then island hopped by plane to the island of Kauai. It was a quieter island than Hawaii with breathtakingly beautiful mountains and valleys. We rented a car and drove around the island, stopping and looking at the dramatic waterfalls that were unique to the island. The last night on the island, we attended a Luau and enjoyed learning how to do the Hawaiian Hula dance.

There was only one time during our time in Hawaii that Josh became upset with me. We were in a restaurant, sitting at a bar, waiting for our table in the dining room, and I was watching a girl work the bar and how efficient she was at her job. When she served us our drinks, I asked Josh if he would tip her a couple of dollars. He said no, and I let it go. After dinner, and when we got back to our room, Josh turned on me and said, "You understand right now. Don't you ever tell me how to spend my money!"

"I'm sorry if it upset you," I said. "It's only a couple of dollars we're talking about."

"I don't care if it was fifty cents. If we're going to get along in this marriage, you will not tell me how to spend my money."

"Okay, I got it. It's your money, and you will spend it how you want," I replied.

I wasn't going to let this upset the magical time we had. So we started talking about how beautifully unique the Hawaiian Islands were. Tomorrow, we would be heading back home and to our new life.

# PART 8

## My Second Marriage

When we arrived in Gunnison, we went to see my dad and get Juliet. I was so happy to see her, and Dad had her packed and ready for us to take her to her new home. I gave my dad a big hug and thanked him for all he had done for us. I told him we would have him over for dinner soon, and I would also be seeing him at church.

The other new member of our family was Chico. Chico was an Australian Shepherd and was Josh's dog on the ranch. The first time I met Chico was at Josh's trailer when he cooked supper for me. I could tell he was a one-person dog and very devoted to Josh. Chico would lower his head and growl when I approached Josh or sat beside him. I wasn't afraid because I had been raised around dogs due to my father's love for the animal. We always had a dog as a family pet, and there were several different breeds my brothers and I cared for while growing up.

Because of my dad, I understood the bond between Josh and Chico. I did wonder how Chico would adjust from being a dog raised in the country to one confined to a backyard in town. It took Chico a while to accept his new home, and as Juliet and I gave him treats by hand, he became more accepting of us.

Josh decided before we were married that it probably wouldn't be a good idea if we both worked at the same place, so he quit the fabrication steel company. He was excited about his new home and enjoyed working around the place while I worked, and Juliet was in school.

Eventually, Josh decided he needed more structure to his day and found employment in the maintenance department at a condo resort twenty minutes from Gunnison and near the ski area. He enjoyed this job a lot more than when he worked at the fabrication steel plant because he was outside, working around red cliffs, tall pines, and aspen trees.

Within a month, I received a support check from Ricardo for Juliet. I asked Josh how he wanted me to manage this money. I was surprised by what he told me.

"Gillian, I don't want the money. I want you to put the money in a separate account to be used for Juliet's education. I don't believe it is my responsibly to give her a college education. That will be up to you and Ricardo," he said.

"Okay, I'll go to the bank and set up an account for her this week," I replied.

I was beginning to wonder what kind of stepfather Josh was going to be for Juliet. When we started living together, Josh started taking more of a firm hand with her. Like the first night she slept in her new room, she was afraid and came into our bedroom, asking for me. Josh said he would address this now.

"Juliet, you will go to your room and sleep in your own bed tonight. You won't be coming in here asking for your mommy anytime you want to. So go back to your bed and stay there now," he said very sternly.

"Josh, she's scared, and this is her first night in a strange place. We need to give her a chance to get use to the change," I said.

"Gillian, don't question my authority. She's old enough to stay in her room. We're not that far from her," he said.

Juliet complied and stayed the night in her bed. I was hoping he would see what a good girl she was and would come to appreciate her in his life. So, already, I was trying to make peace with the situation.

At the end of March, school was out for spring break, and Josh said he would take us to Nebraska. He looked forward to meeting the close friends I talked a lot about, and plus, having an agricultural background, he was also interested in seeing their farm. It was a fun trip. At nine years old, Josh gave Juliet her first driving lesson on a Kansas road, and at the farm, she enjoyed learning to ride a small motorcycle. She was a quick learner and always said yes when she was given the chance to drive any motor vehicle. Dan showed Josh a couple of farms for sale, but Josh said he had been in Gunnison all his life and didn't feel comfortable moving to Nebraska.

Living in our new home, we spent most of our time in the kitchen, dining room, living room, and bedroom areas of the house. We spent very little time in the den. Josh had an idea of turning the den and two-car garage into a small rental that would make the mortgage payment on the house. I liked the idea, and before long, Josh had hired a contractor, and construction was underway for a two-bedroom, one bath small apartment. We decided it would rent better if we furnished it.

Our first renter was a divorced man that worked twelve-hour days out-of-town and said it would be an ideal place for him. He paid the rent, and we hardly ever saw him. Between Josh's trailer and the small apartment behind our house, we were in the rental business, and I learned how to keep the books for our taxes.

Within three years, Josh bought a duplex across the street from our home and another home in the north section of town. We rented mostly to college students and a few families. He eventually bought a one-acre parcel of land west of town where he moved his trailer off his cousin's place. Josh was a good landlord, always keeping the properties well-maintained, and he enjoyed visiting with his tenants.

When tenants did move out, the three of us worked at getting them ready for the new renters. Josh painted and did the repairs while Juliet and I worked on the kitchens, bathrooms, floors, and painted the baseboards and trim. Weekends, I would work on updating the books for our personal taxes and our rental business. It was an exciting time in our lives, and I was learning how to manage my time wisely to keep up with all the responsibilities this new life had given me.

A few months after we were married, Josh came home from work and wanted to talk to me. He said he had something he wanted to say and he didn't know how I was going to take it, but he wanted me to know how he felt.

"Gillian, this isn't easy for me to tell you this, but I resent Juliet being in our lives and I don't know what you are going to do about it," he said.

"Why would you say such a thing? Where did this come from?" I asked, trying to believe what I heard. "Josh, Juliet has had some adjustments to make, leaving a grandfather she loves, coming to a new home, and now living with a stepfather that doesn't seem to want to have a relationship with her. I think she has been doing quite well with the adjustment so far. You need to give Juliet a chance in your life. You need to try and include her into your life. She's a smart girl, and you could teach her so many things. Is it the attention I'm giving her when we're together that has you upset?"

"Gillian, I don't think she needs the extra attention you're giving her. I'm telling you how I feel, and you will just have to figure it out," he said.

"Josh, she is a nine-year-old girl that needs her mother's attention daily. I love her deeply, love doing things with her and for her. I also love you, enjoy working beside you, and building this home we're establishing. I hope I am showing you that love every day. But you can't have all my attention because Juliet is in my life and now. She is in your life too. You knew that when we married Juliet came with me. You need to figure out how you can build a relationship with her."

The next night, as I was getting ready for bed, Josh said he didn't want me taking anymore birth control pills.

"Gillian, if I have to raise Juliet, I am going to raise one of my own," he said.

Lying in bed that night, I was thinking about what Josh's father, Leo, told me when Josh and I became engaged. "Gillian, you think you know Josh, but you don't really know him at all. Growing up as a little boy and young teenager, Josh was a nice kid and easy to be around. Since he lost his eye, his personality has changed. Now he can go from nice to mean in seconds."

Lying there in the dark, I decided Leo was probably right. There was so much about Josh I didn't really know.

Before Josh and I were married, we talked about the family we wanted.

"Gillian, how do you feel about having more children?" Josh asked.

"I always thought that if I married again and the man had children, I wouldn't have anymore. But if I married a man that never had children and he wanted them, I wouldn't deny him children. I will be happy to have children with you," I said.

"Gillian, when we are married, I would like to have one child, and I hope that child could be a boy. I would like to carry on my family's name through that son," he said.

"Well, you know, don't you, that the man determines the sex of the baby?" I asked him.

"Yes, I know that," he said, "and I will hope for a boy."

"Josh, when I became pregnant with Juliet, Ricardo didn't care if it was a boy or a girl. The more he talked with his friends and the importance a boy means to a man, Ricardo was disappointed when Juliet was born, and she isn't a boy. However, it wasn't long for him to fall in love with her. I don't want to go through that again with you. If our first child isn't a boy, you will have to consider having more children, and I'm willing to do that for you."

"That's what we will consider if it comes to that," he said.

## 34

My father-in-law's name was Lorenzo. People called him Leo. He was a friendly man, and since selling the ranch, he loved to sit and talk with people. When I met him, he was living with his girlfriend who owned and operated a beauty salon in Gunnison. He spent part of his day around the beauty salon, listening to the gossip, and the other part of his day at the Community Center in town.

When Josh and I were dating, Josh told me he didn't have a good relationship with his father. There had been disagreements between them while working on the ranch, but now, the main reason he was further estranged from him was the woman he had chosen to date and live with. With all the women Leo could have picked to date after his wife died, he picked the one woman who had a bad history with Leo's family. She had an affair with a close relative. The family dynamics became even more complicated.

In August of 1981, Leo walked into my office at work and said he needed to talk to me. His girlfriend had thrown him out and he needed a place to stay. He asked if he could come and live with us for a while. I told him it was okay with me, but it had to be okay with Josh also. I wanted Josh's approval with the arrangement. Josh agreed to help his dad but wanted him to be looking for a place of his own.

Leo moved into our spare bedroom. He spent his days around the house or at the Community Center. In some small way, I was hoping I could help them heal their relationship, but Leo living with us put more of a strain on our marriage. Many of their conversations would end up in arguments with Josh speaking very disrespectfully to Leo. When I tried to talk to Josh about how he spoke to his dad, he turned his disrespect on me.

I enjoyed visiting with Leo. He would tell me stories about him growing up in Gunnison and how all the Reynolds were related. Several times, we would invite Josh's aunt, uncle, and grandmother over to a Sunday gathering, and the stories got even better. I really loved the good times we had when we were all together.

## 35

In September of 1982, I was pregnant with my second child who was to be born in late April 1983. Josh was happy to learn he was going to be a father. I felt blessed by God, and Juliet was so excited to learn she was going to have a little brother or sister to play with. My father was happy to hear he would have another grandchild. This would be Leo's first grandchild, and he, too, was hoping for a boy. We told Leo that we would be turning the guest bedroom into a nursery, and he would need his own place by early spring.

It wasn't long before Leo brought home a new lady for us to meet whom he had met at the Community Center in town. Her name was Eleanor, but most people called her Elly. She had moved from Texas to Gunnison a couple of months ago to be closer to her sister whom she was living with in Gunnison and played the piano at the Center.

Elly became Leo's new girlfriend, She was a woman who had a big heart, was easy to like, always had a joke to tell, and was free to enjoy her days with Leo. They both looked forward to the special lunch and dance on Friday afternoons at the Center or the special dances held at the Elks Lodge during the month. It was easy for me to love Elly, and we became close friends.

October 1, 1982, I received a call at work concerning my father.

"Gillian, this is Mrs. Ann Morris. My husband and I live across the street from your brother, Logan."

"Yes, I remember you, Mrs. Morris. You and your husband operated a small business in town. How can I help you?"

"Gillian, you need to come to your brother's house right away. Your father has collapsed in Logan's driveway. There is an ambulance there at this time," she said.

"Oh my, it's happened!" I replied. "Thank you so much for calling me. I will let my boss know and be right there," I said.

"You're welcome, Gillian."

I went and informed my boss of my father's situation, and as I was walking out the door, the company's front desk clerk said my brother was on the phone and needed to talk to me.

"Gillian, Dad's had a heart attack. He is in the ambulance, and we are all on the way to the hospital. Meet us there at the emergency room," he explained.

"Okay, Logan, I'm on my way."

When I got to the emergency room, Logan and Lucia were there to meet me. We hugged each other, and I could see the worry in their eyes.

"What happened, Logan?" I asked.

"Dad was picking apples off the trees in his backyard. He drove into town and drove up into our driveway. He got out the truck, reached into the back on the truck to get the sack of apples he was bringing to us, and collapsed in the driveway. Lucia was walking out to meet him, saw him collapse, and began CPR on him. The Morris's across the street saw him collapse, too, and Lucia helping him, and they called the ambulance. He was still alive when he arrived here at the emergency room. They are working on him now," he said.

We just stood there in silence. I could see through the emergency room door window his feet coming off the table, so I knew they were using the heart defibrillator paddles to revive him. We stood there for ten to fifteen minutes before a doctor came out to talk to us.

"I'm sorry, folks, we tried to revive him, but he never regained consciousness," the doctor said.

I put my hand over my mouth and started to cry. There were tears running down my brother's face as he held Lucia. My father was dead, and I knew he was now in heaven with Mom, his beloved wife.

The doctor said, "In a few minutes, you will be able to go in and see him. The team just needs a few minutes before you enter. Again, I am sorry for your loss." And then he walked away.

In a few minutes, a nurse came and said we could see him now. Walking in, my father was lying on a table with a sheet up to his neck. I reached out and touched his forehead. It was ice cold. I leaned down and gave him a kiss. The man who had been my father and grandfather to my daughter was gone.

We went back to Logan and Lucia's home. Logan called Nathan at Hotchkiss, Colorado, where he was serving as minister at the Community Church. He came down to Gunnison the next day. We then began to remember the man who led our family for over forty years.

"Logan, I know since Dad retired, he enjoyed calling you every evening, and you shared your day with each other. He enjoyed those calls very much. You worked for the Highway Department, and he spent half of his life building and repairing roads around Colorado and the nearby states. I know you are going to miss those calls."

"Yes," he said. "I am. It was a nice way to share my day with him," he said as tears rolled down his cheeks.

We started mentioning people in the church whom my father admired a lot and knew we would like for them to either sing or speak at his funeral. Time passed as we reminisced about the life Dad led, the love Mom and Dad had for each other, and the grandfather he was to our children, a role we felt he was born for. It was now time for me to leave and be home when Juliet came home from school.

When Juliet entered the house, she was excited to tell me about her day. I also told her I needed to tell her about my day and that I had bad news for her.

"I received a call at work today that your grandfather drove into town and parked in Uncle Logan's driveway. He got out of his truck and was getting ready to grab a sack of apples he had picked to give to Uncle Logan's family when he collapsed in the driveway. Juliet, he had a heart attack, was taken to the hospital where they tried to save him, but they couldn't. Honey, your grandfather died today," I said.

"Oh, Mama, Mama, no, no," she cried as I held her. "I loved him so much, Mama," she cried.

"I know, dear, he was such a good grandfather to you. Taught you to fish, ride a horse, and you spent so many wonderful hours with him and Grandma around their home, in their garden, and among the flowers. It will all be wonderful memories for you to keep alive in your heart," I said.

To Juliet, my dad was not only her grandfather, but she has always considered him to be her father also. She knew he loved her. Today, she still holds a deep love in her heart for him.

My father was not a wealthy man, but there were possessions he valued and wanted to pass on to his children. Several years before he died, he made a will. At the time he made it, he looked at where each one of his children were in their lives. Logan was married, had a home, and was raising a family. He willed to Logan his truck and boat. Nathan needed help with furthering his education, so he willed to him his savings account. To me, he willed the trailer because when he made his will, Juliet and I were living with Dad and Mom when we needed a home. I was able to rent it for a while and then I eventually sold it to a young couple just married and starting out in life. I put the money from the sale of the home into Juliet's education fund.

During those fall months, Josh was helping a dairy farmer put up silage for the fall harvest. He learned about a forty-acre parcel of land that was for sale on the mesa area west of Gunnison. The day he stopped and looked at the land before coming home is the night, we talked about purchasing the it.

"Gillian, I stopped and looked at that forty-acres today, and it's a nice piece of land that lays well for raising hay and possibly running a few cows on," he said.

"Josh, I know ranching and working the land is in your blood, and we've talked about us owning land someday, so do you think this is the opportunity you have been waiting for?" I asked.

"Gillian, buying this home in Gunnison and establishing the rental business has given us a good start, but I don't want to be just a landlord. I've dreamed about returning to the life I enjoyed in my youth. I would begin raising hay, pasturing a few cows, and eventually build a home on it," he said.

"Josh, you are working at the Resort which is one direction, and the land is in the opposite direction. Are you still planning on working at the resort?" I asked.

"Yes, for a while. I like working up there, especially in the summertime. It will be a lot of driving for a while. But when the land starts producing, I'll probably quit. If I buy it now, we can plan on starting to make improvements to it in the spring. I can start getting water on the land and check the property lines. So what do you think?" he said.

"I think you are very excited about it, and as long as you can handle the driving, I think it's the beginning of a new venture for us. Let's do it!" I said.

The following March, Josh and I signed up for a Lamaze class. We enjoyed meeting other expectant parents and having them share their individual stories and hopes for their families. This was going to be a new experience because I never went through the class when I was expecting Juliet and I don't remember even being told about these classes being offered. I do, however, remember the pain I experienced with labor having Juliet and was excited to learn about some breathing and relaxation treatments to help cope with the birthing process.

The first of April, I gave my notice at work. It was a sad day for me. I really loved my job and had only respect for the men I worked with, all the while admiring their abilities and skills with the fabrication of steel. I wasn't an employee; I was family. I had come to know many of their wives and children and enjoyed every Christmas planning the company Christmas party, buying and wrapping the toys to be handed out by Santa. I had worked their seven years and had learned a lot about the bookkeeping and accounting process.

May 5, 1983, Luke Jameson Reynolds was born and joined our family. God had blessed me with a boy. When the nurses brought him to me, I held him to my heart and thanked God for this amazing gift. Josh and Leo were very happy. They had their heir, and Juliet was delighted to have a little brother whom she started calling her "buddy."

Leo was still living with us, so we bought a cradle for Luke to sleep in beside our bed. Leo knew it was time for him to find a place of his own. He purchased a two-bedroom trailer and had it set up in a trailer park outside of Gunnison. He enjoyed having Elly as his girlfriend, and when the trailer was ready, they began living together. They would usually stop by a couple of times a week to say hi and chat. Occasionally, we would be enjoying a meal together at either home. Elly was a good cook, and it was a treat to be invited over for a dinner.

The spring and summer of 1983, Josh began making improvements to the land he now owned. He first checked the property lines and improved the fences. On weekends, I would pack a lunch, and the kids and I would join him for a few hours. It was nice to be out of town, in the country, and I was able to help him with some of the fencing improvements. He next focused on getting the ditches ready for the irrigation water. Josh was raised with a shovel in his hand, and he was very good at knowing how to use the shovel to guide the water throughout the lay of the land which improved his hay production. Once the water was in the ditches, he was driving out to the property every day to change the water and move it around the land.

During the summer, when it wouldn't get dark until around nine o'clock, he worked at the resort during the day, stopped at the house for dinner, and then would drive to the land to change water. The major project Josh began that summer was obtaining a permit to build a shed on the land to have a shop area and to be able to store the bales of hay when they were brought in from the field. His dad helped him with the planning, layout, and some of the construction. When he received his permit, he gave his notice at the resort and now was able to devote full days to the building project.

By the fall, Josh had a nice shop area to work in and a place to get in out of the sun. The shed was full of hay from two cuttings, and I was now learning how to do another set of books to keep income from the hay operation separate from our rental and personal income.

In March 1984, I learned I was pregnant with my third child. Josh wasn't happy about the pregnancy and accused me of getting pregnant on purpose so Luke wouldn't have the yearning for a brother or sister like Juliet did. It wasn't true. After Luke was born, I didn't want to take the pill because I didn't like taking pills, so I had an IUD inserted to prevent another pregnancy. When I found out I was pregnant, I told Josh I needed to have the IUD removed to prevent a miscarriage.

When I went to the doctor, he said it wasn't there. I was stunned. How could I not feel its expulsion? I heard theories about the IUD sometimes being expelled during heavy periods or being very athletic and exerting oneself. None of it made any sense to me. It wasn't until 2001 when I had a hysterectomy that the doctor called and said he had news for me.

"Gillian, I wanted to let you know that the biopsy on your uterus came back and it was benign."

"That's good news, Doctor, I'm glad to hear it."

"But, Gillian, I also wanted you to know that they found an IUD attached to it upon its removal."

"What!" I said in a shocked voice. "That is unbelievable and such good news for me to hear," I said. Then I explained about having it inserted in 1983, found myself pregnant in 1984, went to have it removed, and found it wasn't attached like it should have been. The mystery in my mind had been solved, and I was excited to tell Josh about it.

All he said was, "Really? Well, now you know."

At least I had proof I didn't get pregnant on purpose like he said I did.

I was so happy with my new baby girl. Once Pilar was born, Josh loved being her daddy. He especially like to hold her on his chest. Eventually, they would both fall to sleep in Josh's recliner, and even today, it is a favorite picture of them together in my mind.

For the next seven years, Josh enjoyed attending the different farm auctions held in Gunnison and the surrounding areas. He purchased tractors and hay-cutting equipment so he wouldn't have to depend on others when he wanted to harvest his crop. He eventually taught Juliet and Luke how to drive a tractor, and I was learning to "buck bales of hay onto a wagon." We even attended the large farm auction in Montrose, Colorado, held in February each year. We would make a weekend out of it, staying overnight, and I would take the kids roller-skating, bowling, or to the movies while Josh attended the auction.

During the summers, Josh would rotor-till an area of the land near the shed where I could raise a garden. I taught my children about planting seeds, watering, weeding, and harvesting the different crops. When Josh went out to change his water, the kids and I would join him so we could work in the garden. If there was still time, I started teaching them about a bat and ball and how they connected.

When the last cutting of hay for the year was completed, Josh purchased a few mother cows to graze on the land. We built a corral behind the hay shed, and in the spring, when new calves were born, Juliet and I started learning about branding, ear tagging, inoculations, and banding steers. One year, he purchased a horse he named Misty, and eventually, she gave birth to a foal we named Prada.

Other improvement Josh made was having a well dug, electricity brought to the shed, and a rental space where a family could put their trailer if they wanted to live on the land and watch things for us. A young married couple answered our ad in the paper and lived there for two years before leaving the area. The last improvement he made was buying forty little starter trees from the forest service to create a windbreak.

With all the good things this piece of land brought into our lives, there was one major problem. The last couple of years he owned the land, Josh would move and reset his water each night, and then when he went back the next day to move it again, the water had been taken and diverted back into the main ditch which flowed to other land. Someone was stealing our water. Josh worked with the situation for two years and decided he would look for another piece of property that had a home and better water rights.

## 37

In the fall of 1984, Juliet was a sixth grader and in her first year of middle school. She proved to be a good student, earning high marks. Luke was sixteen months old and was a joy to have in our lives. Juliet looked forward to coming home from school and playing with her little "buddy." In two months, she would also have a new baby sister to play with we would be calling Pilar.

One day, my good friend, Patricia, stopped by for a visit with her baby girl, Emma, who was born in February 1983, three months before Luke. Patricia and her husband, Joe, both worked at the steel fabrication during the last years when Josh and I worked there. The four of us had established a good friendship, and we continued to see each other on a regular basis. Today, Patricia had a question for me.

"Gillian, you know I have been working the night audit at the Holiday Inn since going back to work after Emma was weaned. Yesterday, I was able to secure a position on the day shift, working seven to three. Joe and I are now in need of childcare. We were wondering since you are home caring for Luke if you would be willing to also care for Emma?" she asked. "Of course, we would be willing to pay you," she added.

"Patricia, you know I love Emma, and I'm willing to help you and Joe with your childcare situation. I would just like to talk to Josh about it tonight. Can call you tomorrow with our decision?" I replied.

"That would be great!" she said.

During supper that night, I told Josh about Joe and Patricia's situation and what he thought about me caring for Emma.

"It's fine with me, but I do think they should pay you for caring for her. Even though we're friends, I think it would keep everybody responsible," Josh said.

"I agree, and it would be fun for Luke to have a playmate. Emma is a loveable child and easy to care for," I said.

"So, what do you think you will charge them?" Josh asked.

"Since we are friends, I was thinking a dollar an hour would be fair, and I could save the money for extra expenses Juliet will have in middle school being on the different sport teams. What do you think?" I asked.

"I agree. It holds them accountable and doesn't take advantage of you," Josh said.

I called Patricia the next morning and told her Josh was in favor of the situation if I was paid. I told her the amount I would be charging, and she offered me more, but I wouldn't accept it because the friendship meant more to me than the money did.

This was the beginning of caring for children outside my family. I never raised my rate, it felt good helping families I personally selected, and my own kids learned how to play with other children.

## 38

In middle school, Juliet joined the volleyball team. She could just stay after school and then walk home. Her freshman year of high school, she joined the basketball team and continued walking home after practice. At the end of her freshman year, she was fifteen years old, and we talked about her getting a summer job. Gunnison was a popular tourist town with numerous motels and restaurants and managers that hired teenagers as part of their work force. We lived just off Main Street and only two blocks from the Dairy Queen, so Juliet applied and was hired. She worked there all summer, started dating her first boyfriend who she met through the drive-up, and continued to work there in the evenings when school started. She quit when the basketball season began in November. That month, she also received her permit to drive.

When Juliet was a little girl, she complained about pain in her right foot, especially when she wore her ski boots. I took her to the doctor, had her foot x-rayed, and we learned that she was born with an extra bone in her right ankle. The bone wasn't causing any additional problems, only when she wore her ski boots. The doctor informed me it wasn't necessary to remove the bone at this time, but if she went into sports, it could cause a problem, and surgery would need to be considered.

May 16, 1988, Juliet turned sixteen. She was in her PE class playing softball when her right foot entered a small hole, causing her to twist the ankle which ripped the ligaments around it. We celebrated her sixteenth birthday in the backyard around the picnic table with her foot in a cast. Surgery was now needed to repair the ligaments, and it was also decided to remove the extra bone at the same time.

The one thing our family didn't have was major medical insurance. Josh didn't like insurance companies and wouldn't pay for it. The medical insurance I carried on Juliet was the insurance the schools offered, and that did not cover surgeries. When I was referred to an orthopedic surgeon, I explained I didn't have insurance but I would sign a promissory note paying one hundred dollars a month. Since I would be paying cash with a promissory note attached, he reduced his fee to fifteen hundred dollars and agreed to do the surgery.

I asked Josh if he would help me with this medical bill. He said Juliet was mine and Ricardo's responsibility. I called Ricardo; he had no money to give me. My friend, Patricia, told me the Holiday Inn needed a relief night auditor, so I applied and was hired to work Friday and Saturday nights. Josh agreed to the arrangement if Juliet would be watching Luke and Pilar during the day so I could get some sleep.

The last few weeks of Juliet's Sophomore year, she attended school with her foot in the cast. Even though she would be able to play basketball next year, her coaches approached her about a way she could participate in the different sport programs by becoming a student trainer. She would learn to do athletic taping, especially on ankles.

One evening, Juliet talked to Josh and me about the program.

"Josh, Mom, the coaches at school want me to consider becoming a student trainer for their sports programs," Juliet said.

"What would you be learning?" Josh asked.

"I would be learning medical terminology associated with athletic taping, especially ankles and wrists," she said.

"And how would you learn all this?" Josh asked.

"There is a student trainer program that is being held this summer at the University of Greely in Northern Colorado (UNC). If I could attend that program and learn to do athletic taping, I could be an asset to the different sport programs at the high school."

"How do you plan on getting there and paying for it?" Josh asked.

"The school will pay for the training program. I just need travel expenses to and from Greeley. I saved all my money that I earned working at Dairy Queen, so I believe I would have enough to fly round trip. I just need a ride from the airport to the school. I thought Mom might call Uncle Nathan and see if he would meet me at the airport and take me to UNC," she explained.

"It sounds like a wonderful opportunity for you, Juliet. What do you think, Josh?"

"It sounds like you would be learning some valuable skills. If the school and you can do it yourself, it's okay with me," he said.

Juliet was able to have the surgery and the cast removed before the student trainer program began. She used her Dairy Queen money for the travel expenses, and Uncle Nathan drove her to and from the airport. When school began in the fall, she was the student trainer for the football team, a position she thoroughly enjoyed.

During that same summer, Juliet was experiencing pain with her wisdom teeth. We made an appointment with the oral surgeon in town, and x-rays showed she had two impacted wisdom teeth and needed surgery to remove them. I asked if I could sign a promissory note, paying twenty-five dollars a week, and he agreed. I thanked God for helping me find the job at the Holiday Inn.

In 1977, when Juliet was five, and I started my new job with the steel fabrication company, I bought a brand-new car. It was a silver Subaru with blue interior and had the special feature of being two-wheel drive or four-wheel drive (a heavenly feature for sure after using chains on the old car to get around in the snow). I paid five hundred dollars for the old car I was driving, and it was needing repairs weekly. I needed something more reliable and safer. I felt like a queen driving that new car off the sales lot. It was fully paid for before I married Josh.

When I did marry Josh, he had a beautiful new truck and a used VW bug to drive around. He also occasionally purchased cars and trucks to work on as a hobby when he was around the house and time allowed. Josh even gave Juliet driving lessons to drive a stick shift in his VW bug when we were out in the country on private land.

In the fall of 1988, Juliet began her junior year of high school by joining the swim team. Practice was to be in the mornings before school began at the college swimming pool in town. She now left the house at five o'clock in the morning, drove over to Western State, and swam for two hours before attending classes beginning at eight o'clock. After school, she was the trainer on the football team and didn't get in until seven o'clock at night. When football ended, she still planned on joining the basketball team. She made a schedule for herself that would keep her away from home as long as possible while continuing to achieve a high grade point average. So for her to attend all the different activities she wanted to be involved in, I gave her my car to drive. This only infuriated Josh.

"Where do you get off giving your daughter a car to drive?" he said bitterly.

"What's wrong with giving her my car to drive around for all her school activities? It will make things a lot easier for her and me."

"That girl has no business having a car of her own to drive. Did you even plan on discussing it with me before you just gave her your car?" he said, becoming even more angry about the situation.

"No, I didn't. Lately, you seem to disapprove about any decision I make about Juliet. You have three, sometimes four cars around here to drive. I didn't think we needed mine to get around, and Juliet really needs it now. It allows me to be here more in the evenings to care for Luke and Pilar," I explained. "I just thought it was a good idea," I said.

"Gillian, you don't know what a good idea is. I never got to have a car when I was sixteen, and I really wanted one. But my parents couldn't agree, so I wasn't allowed one. Now she turns sixteen, and you just hand yours over to her. It's unbelievable, Gillian!" he yelled.

"I can't change what your parents did or didn't do for you at sixteen, Josh. I'm not giving her the car, Josh. The car will stay in my name. She is just going to use it while she attends high school," I explained.

"The high school is only four blocks away, and she can get a ride with other students with the sports she's in, Gillian. She can walk!" he yelled.

"I'm not having her walk to and from school with books and sports gear when she can use my car, especially since it can get dark early with the time change," I stressed.

"So you think you can trust her with the responsibilities and freedom that car is going to give her?" he asked.

"Josh, I do trust Juliet. You've already seen the responsibility she takes around this home being a big sister to Luke and Pilar. The last time we went to the land to work, we left them with her. She not only cared for them but had supper on the table for us as well. Her last report card, she brought home straight As. You said you would buy her whatever she wanted within reason. She asked for a new pair of jeans. She is motivated to be a trainer for the high school, participate on a sport team, and tutors students with their geometry homework. Juliet is a good kid, and you need to give her a chance and trust her also," I said.

He walked away and out of the house.

One evening, after supper, and as I was clearing the table, Josh told me I wasn't going to be doing the supper dishes in the evenings. Juliet was going to be doing them after she ate when she got home from her sport activities. He also wasn't going to pay for electricity after nine o'clock at night. Juliet would just have to get her homework done by then. Tension in the home was high, and Juliet and I were walking on eggshells.

A few days later, a Saturday morning, I just returned home from working at the Holiday Inn. Juliet, Luke, and Pilar were in the living room watching television. Josh was sitting at the table, drinking coffee. I got a cup of coffee and sat down to talk with Josh when Juliet asked me a question.

"Mom, tonight there is no game scheduled, and some of the girls and I were wanting to know if we could go out," she asked.

"It's all right with me. I just want to know the details of who you will be with and what you plan on doing," I said.

Josh got up from his chair. "You just can't say no to that girl, can you?" he said in a disgusted tone. "When are you going to get some backbone and stand up to her?" he asked.

"Josh, what's wrong with her going out on a Saturday night with some of her friends?" I asked.

"She can stay home! She doesn't need to be running all over the place!" he yelled.

Juliet got up off the couch and said, "Josh, why don't you just leave her alone?"

Josh started for Juliet, and I could tell he was going to try and slap her face. I jumped in front of Juliet and said, "Josh, you are not going to hit her, now just calm down!" I yelled.

That's when Josh started slapping me and said, "You will not talk to me that way!"

I pushed him away and said, "Get out of this house! Just go!" I yelled.

He grabbed his hat and keys and walked out of the house. He was headed for his land.

I looked around, and Juliet was gone. I discovered she ran across the street to a friend's house, and later, she went to stay with another friend across town.

Luke and Pilar were crying. I walked over to where Luke and Pilar were, knelt, and hugged them.

"I told myself I can't live like this. I won't have him striking out at one of my children." I needed to call a friend and get some advice and help.

I sat down at the kitchen table and cried. Josh's anger, jealousy, and bitterness had only gotten worse, not better. Why couldn't he see the beautiful family he had and all God had blessed us with. Juliet and I helped him with his rentals when they needed painting and cleaning. We helped him at his land with his hay and cattle. We tried to show our appreciation for the home and life we had. But he only seemed to show contempt for us. I needed help and advice and called the one lady I knew would tell me the right thing to do. She helped me when my mom died, and now she would be helping me again.

I called my friend who was able to come right over and see me. When she found out Josh had tried to hit Juliet and did hit me, she advised me to go to a safe house in town. I packed bags with clothes and necessities for a few days for each of my children and left. After being checked into the safe house, I contacted Juliet and made sure she was safe and okay. She assured me she was. I made arrangements with my friend to take Juliet into her home until I found a place for us to live.

We could live at the safe house for a month, so I needed to be looking for other living quarters. I had some money with an insurance company that I had been paying ten dollars a month into and hadn't touched it for several years. I took it out when Juliet was a baby and just paid the ten dollars into it each month. I contacted the company, and they said I had over three thousand dollars in the account that I could take out. I asked them to send me the funds.

The first of November, I signed a three-month lease at an apartment complex in town and rented a two-bedroom apartment. The apartment was furnished and came with four twin beds. Juliet and I shared a bedroom. Luke and Pilar shared the other bedroom.

Josh was furious that I had left and taken his children.

"Gillian, if there is one way you could get back at me, it would be to take my children away from me," he said.

"Josh, you need some help, and we could use counseling as a family. I will not have you trying to hit one of my children," I said.

"I want to know when I can see Luke and Pilar," he asked.

"After you have gotten some counseling and I know that I can trust you with them," I said.

Over the months, Josh calmed down, complied with my wishes, sought counseling, and always asked when he could see his children. I slowly let him have them for a few hours during the day. He would play with them, feed them supper, and I would pick them up. He never came around the apartment or forcibly sought his way about anything. We slowly began having dinner together at different restaurants in town, and we talked about getting the family back together.

I was a woman with one divorce behind me, and I knew what it was like being a single mother raising one child. I didn't want to be a woman with two divorces and three children to care for as a single mother. I really thought Josh was trying to improve his behavior and attitude, and he did want his family back. I wanted to try and save my marriage, but I also wanted to find a safe place for Juliet to take some of the stress off her. I was also running out of money.

I went and talked to my pastor at church about my situation, and he told me about a family in church, Bill and Denise Edwards, who had taken children in difficult situations into their home and thought it might be a good situation for Juliet while our family continued to heal.

The pastor had spoken to the Edwards about my situation, and they agreed to take Juliet. They had raised two boys of their own and were excited to have a girl. I called them, introduced myself, and arranged a time to meet them. They had a lovely home a few miles outside Gunnison, and I felt the arrangement would work. Driving away from that meeting, I wasn't sure about anything or if I was doing the right thing. I just knew I had to forgive and try and save the life we had worked so hard for the last six years.

When I told Juliet about going back to Josh and the family I had found for her to live with for a while, she was very sad and wondered what she had ever done to create this situation. I told her nothing was her fault, and my heart broke for her, but I wanted to protect her and thought this was the only way I could and save my marriage at the same time. The new arrangement seemed to help the family to continue to heal. Josh was a lot nicer to be around, and Luke and Pilar were happy to be back home. They did miss Juliet and were always asking when they would see her.

The Edwards came to love Juliet and shared their interests with her. Bill had a career in radio broadcasting, and Denise was a quilter and seamstress. I would visit Juliet during the week and on weekends, and I always enjoyed seeing what Denise was making. The Edwards, who were friendly and easy to talk to, brought a sense of peace to Juliet's life, but she felt like she had lost her home and she especially missed Luke and Pilar. She deeply loved them and wanted to be a part of their lives.

When school ended in May, Juliet got a job in the café at the bowling alley in Gunnison. She liked waitressing and made good tips, which helped her with gas and spending money. During that summer, she went to visit her dad and his family in Arizona. While there, she attended an advanced trainer course at ASU which furthered her skills. When school started in the fall, she was back on the swim team and the trainer for the football team. A boy named Ethan on the team asked her out, and they started dating. Ethan was good to Juliet, and he brought a lot of happiness into her life.

The basketball season began in November. The team traveled to Montrose, Colorado, to play one of the beginning games of the season. Juliet was running down the court when a girl from the oppos-

161

ing team ran into her, causing Juliet to twist her knee and tearing the ACL in the left leg. Surgery was needed to repair the leg. It was time to bring Juliet home. I wanted Juliet home and wanted to take care of her.

"Josh, with the surgery and recovery process Juliet is going to need me to take care of her, this is not a situation for the Edwards to handle. I want to bring her home," I explained.

"I agree. You should care for her, and it is also time to bring her home," he said.

"Thank you, Josh."

When Juliet came home from the hospital, she had different machines to help maneuver the leg. Luke and Pilar were so happy to have her home and very anxious to help her. My heart was filled with joy as we helped her get her mobility back. At the end of the basketball season, Juliet was hired at City Market, the local grocery store in town. She began sacking groceries and working the carts. Not long after she was hired, they moved her into the seafood department and eventually the deli, an area she enjoyed.

**41**

In the spring of 1990, Juliet and I were making the final decisions on where she would attend college.

"Juliet, I want you to know that with the money your dad has sent me over the years that I was able to save ten thousand dollars to give you for your college education."

"Wow, Mom, that's wonderful! I didn't know you had been putting money into a savings account for me."

"What you need to understand is that if you go to Western State here in Gunnison, I will probably be able to pay for the four years you attend. But if you choose to attend the University of Colorado (CU) in Boulder, which will be a lot more expensive, I will send you the money you need each semester, but when the ten thousand is gone, I won't have any more money to give you."

"Mom, my heart is set on attending CU in Boulder. CU is offering me an academic scholarship and I can also apply for grants. If I keep up my grades, I can probably receive additional scholarships as well."

"I remember when I wanted to go away to college. I wanted to experience dorm life and all that came with living on a college campus. Those were four of the most wonderful years of my life. I want you to have the same experience if that is what you want. In my heart, I know it is time for you to be set free, and you deserve all that is being offered to you."

In June, Juliet and I were expected to attend orientation for incoming freshman. We needed to travel to Boulder, stay a couple of days to participate in orientation, and return home. The Subaru Juliet had been using through her junior and senior year of high school was burning oil badly, and Juliet was putting in a quart of oil a week just to get through her senior year. We needed a better car for our road trip.

I approached Josh about using the family car for our road trip.

"Josh, Juliet and I need to go to Boulder to attend orientation for incoming freshmen. Can we use our car?" I asked.

"Absolutely not. You're not using my car for anything like that. It's not my problem," he said definitely.

So here was the old Josh coming back. I wondered where this was attitude coming from. I just couldn't understand why he wanted to be so belligerent about helping Juliet. It's like he wanted her to fail. All she did was excel, achieve, and work toward her goals, supporting herself in the process, and not once could he offer any form of kindness to her. And he still expected her to help with his rentals and out at the land. It was time for Juliet to be free of his madness.

I went and asked my brother, Logan, and his wife, Lucia, if I could borrow their car for the trip. There was no problem with us using their car, and we all were once again amazed at how Josh was treating us. Again, we all wondered, "Why? What had we personally done to him for him to treat us this way?"

Juliet and I had a wonderful trip up the state of Colorado to the beautiful campus of CU in Boulder, Colorado, the town that my brother and I were born in. I knew Juliet was going to be happy there, and I was going to pray to God that she would be able to attend all four years there.

In August of 1990, with her bags packed and scared to leave, Juliet said goodbye to Luke, Pilar, and me. Ethan and his family wanted to take her to the airport outside Gunnison for her flight to Denver. Uncle Nathan would be meeting her in Denver to take her to her dorm on the CU campus. Ethan and Juliet were going to try a long-distance relationship. I absolutely adored her, would miss her terribly, but I would be extremely happy for her at the same time. It was time for her to use her wings and soar wherever God would take her.

**42**

In the fall of 1990, with the second cutting of hay completed and the auction over, Josh started looking for a forty-acre property around Gunnison. In November, he came home and was excited about a property for sale on the edge of Gunnison County.

"Gillian, there is a forty-acre parcel of land that has a nice two-story, three-bedrooms, two-and-a-half bath barn-style home already constructed on it."

"What do you mean 'barn-style' home?" I asked.

"The home is built in the shape of a barn, and the roof is a gambrel shape. Our shed in the back yard is gambrel-shaped. This style increases height which gives more space to store items. When this design is used in building homes, it makes the second story have more livable space."

"Do you like the inside floor plan? Is it rustic or modern?"

"Oh, it's very modern with an open floor plan. I think you will really like it. There isn't a garage, so that will be one of the first additions I would like to add to the north side of the house, and we will need to build a corral also to manage the cattle."

"Are there any other buildings on the property?" I asked.

"Just a tall narrow storage shed that could be used as a tack room."

"What about your shop area?"

"I was thinking I could extend the width of the garage and add a shop area along one of the sides."

"This is the first piece of property I've seen you excited about since you began your search. It sounds like this property has a lot of potential for us."

"It is a lot nicer piece of property than what we have now on the mesa. There are several areas of natural pine, spruce, and oak trees that landscape the property which make for good windbreaks. There is one other benefit and it's even better. The water rights are a lot better, giving us more water for irrigating."

"Well, that's a very good benefit and the one you're most concerned about. Are you planning on walking the acreage soon to get the lay of the land?"

"Yes, I'm hoping to meet the realtor on Saturday. I wanted you and the kids to come along. They can run and play while we walk and get an overall feeling for the land. You will also be able to see the inside of the house and will have a better understanding of a barn-style home."

"Okay. I think I will make a picnic lunch to take along to make our time a little more fun."

"Sounds good," Josh said.

Driving out to the property on Saturday, I was excited about our day. If we were going to be moving, I wanted us to be able to live on the land where Josh would be spending his time doing what he loved, and he was good at it. All the driving back and forth would be over.

Entering the land, we drove up a long-graveled road, fenced on both sizes, ending with a circle driveway in the front of the house. I was delighted to see that the house was tucked away from the county road, giving the two-story barn-style home a feeling of privacy. It was also landscaped with a wooden, rustic, split-rail fence surrounding a lush green grass lawn and tall spruce trees. We began walking the property just north of the house down a well-established winding dirt road which ran though some more tall spruce trees, ending just before the south property line. Large open grass fields laid on both sides of the tree line and dirt road.

Luke and Pilar ran up the dirt road, among the trees, ran up on a rock pile, and then along the ditch banks in the fields. I was so happy to see them outside, running free and enjoying themselves. The west property line had a row of smaller oak trees growing along the fence line, giving us even more privacy. We found the land to be rockier than the mesa property, but Josh still saw its potential to raise hay and graze cows.

We entered the house through the laundry room that led into an office area and stairs leading to the upper floor. The living room and dining room were open areas together with a roomy kitchen on the side that had a counter that could be used for an eating area also. A woodburning fireplace was on the south side of the living room which would be the main heat source for the home. Panoramic views of the valley could be seen through the living room and dining room windows. Upstairs were nice-sized bedrooms and two full baths. There was even a hidden roomy L-shaped storage area attached to one of the bedrooms, which I thought was a unique architectural design.

Both Josh and I felt very optimistic about the property, and I really liked the barn-style design of the house. We thought it was just what we were looking for, so Josh purchased it in December.

In the spring of 1991, when the snow melted and the land was dry, Josh began spending his days walking the property lines and making improvements on the fences. We moved a few pieces of furniture into the house to make it more comfortable for him when he was there or when we joined him on weekends. In May of 1991, when school finished in Gunnison, we moved to begin our new life on the new property. The home we were leaving would become another rental.

**43**

The first summer in our new place seemed like a magical time to me. The weather was beautiful with the big blue sky overhead, summer breezes blowing, and extended daylight to enjoy evenings on the front porch which viewed our circle driveway with its tall pine trees and two front pastures. We would reminisce about our day with a cool refreshing drink while making plans for what we would be doing the next day.

Luke and Pilar weren't interested in the television being hooked up. They wanted to be outside, exploring their new world, especially the trails that wound around the different grooves of trees that landscaped the property. During the day, all four of us were outside working as a family, clearing the area under and around the trees that had broken branches under them. We also spent time gathering the smaller pieces of aged wood that covered the land which could be used as kindling to start the fires we would be building in our wood-burning stove.

Luke loved driving the tractor. He would drive it up to an area being worked, Josh would load the larger branches on the loader above the bucket, while Pilar and I would gather the smaller pieces of wood, throwing them into the bucket. Then the loads were dumped at a designated area where we spent time cutting and stacking. The time spent doing this gave us a good start on the much-needed supply of wood we would need when the colder weather arrived.

Josh was also happy. The many long hours of driving back and forth to a piece of land where dreams slowly faded away were over. He now had a home and his family with him on the land where he was making new dreams. This year, those dreams included a corral for the cattle and a garage/shop area added to the north side of the house. It wasn't long before an opportunity arose for us to get lumber for the garage. We were in town at the co-op when an elderly gentleman approached Josh with a job he needed help with. Josh visited with the man for a few minutes and then, on our way home, told me about their conversation.

"Gillian, that elderly gentleman and his wife have cleared some land on their property, and they have about twenty logs ready to go to a sawmill. If he can find someone who has a trailer that will haul the logs to the sawmill, he will give them half the lumber."

"Wow, that sounds like what we are looking for to begin the garage. What did you tell him?"

"I told him I would be interested in the lumber, but I first wanted to see the logs and look over the situation. He also said he had a hired hand at his property that could help with the loading of the logs onto our trailer."

"Did you plan a time to go over to their place and evaluate the situation?"

"Yes, today, he has more errands to do, but they will be home all day tomorrow, and we could go by then."

"I'm looking forward to meeting them. This could be quite the adventure for us."

The next morning, we were driving down a country road landscaped with tall pine trees, a river flowing by, with squirrels and chipmunks running across the road. There were several farms located along the road which seemed to have been established there for many years. The elderly couple's property was beautifully located at the end of the road, nestled inside a cove of the forest. It was at the log site that Josh introduced me and kids to the elderly couple.

After meeting, Josh and the elderly gentleman started walking over to where the logs were piled up. I could see there were about twenty to thirty nice-sized logs in an organized pile. The elderly gentleman's wife was very friendly and asked if the children and I would like to walk the property while the men talked about the logs. We were very happy to accept her invitation. I believed her to be in her eighties. She had a small frame and carried a walking stick. Luke and Pilar listened to her intently and enjoyed running along the different paths she took us along. I was worried about how fragile she might be, but she seemed secure with her walking stick, so I quit worrying.

I saw how much she enjoyed sharing her memories of different events she had experienced on the land. She explained about the flood of 1926 and the damage it had done to the property and the severe winter of 1969 when the snow was so deep they never got far from the house. Returning to the log site, I was sorry our time together had ended.

Josh and her husband shook hands on us taking the logs to the sawmill, so I knew I would be seeing his wife again. It was now time for Josh to visit the sawmill and arrange for delivery of the logs. Conveniently, there was a small private sawmill on the county road we lived on, just down the road from our house.

Josh took the kids and me home and then went to the sawmill. He was gone for a couple of hours, and when he came back, he said the owner of the mill was a very friendly man, loved to talk, which Josh liked to do also, and was happy to help with the milling of our logs.

So began our new adventure of seeing logs loaded, hauled, and milled at a sawmill. For several days, and when it was convenient for the elderly couple, we were at the log site, getting the lumber for our future garage. Some days, we watched Josh and the hired man load and secure the logs on the trailer. Other days, Luke, Pilar, and I were walking with the wife, listening to more stories about life on her land. The last time I saw her was a few years later when she appeared as the Grand Marshall in the Fourth of July parade in a small town near Gunnison.

## 44

After the logs were milled and construction on the garage began, Josh laid out his plans for the large corral that would be built north of the garage and circle drive. It would be concreted and welded into place. Josh would be teaching Luke, Pilar, and I how to mix the right amounts of cement, sand, gravel, and water into a cement mixer. Once mixed, Josh poured a measured amount into a hole which had a round pipe in it. I worked with a level, making sure the pipe was level vertically while Josh worked the cement into place. Once the cement had dried and the posts were secured, we then measured and worked at placing long sucker rods horizontally into place with a twisted wire. When the last sucker rod was wired on, Josh hired a welder to secure all the rods to the pipe. We now had a large area to corral our cattle, a holding pen to work with small numbers of cows or calves, and a runway to run the cows into a chute where we could work on them individually.

The new corral was a good addition to our place. We now knew that this coming fall, we had an enclosed area to run the cows into so we could separate the mother cow from her calf and the steers from the heifers. It would also be easier to load the calves when the fall buyers came around. Over the years, we added another pipe corral on the east side of the first one, mainly for the horses. And, eventually, a large barn was built on the north side of the corrals which had opened stalls to work with a mother cow and her calf and to hold the hay that was grown in the fields.

Sometimes, Josh would hire different people and equipment to help us with these different projects, but mainly, it was the four of us working side by side until they were completed.

The corral also made a good place to work when branding time would roll around in late spring. We would start having our first calves by the end of February into the first week of March. When the calves arrived on the land, it was always fun loading up the tractor with hay to take it out to the fields where the cows and their claves were bedded down. The little calves would get so excited running around, kicking up their heels, then they would push the hay with their noses trying to discover what it was we were throwing out to them. However, they usually ended up lying on it.

By the end of May, first part of June, we started to schedule a Saturday where we would spend a full day branding, ear tagging, and inoculating the herd. Once all the cows and calves were in the corral, we began separating the mother cow from her calf. Once separated, Luke would maneuver each cow into a narrow runway leading to a large cow chute. I would operate the tailgate, letting the cow into the chute. Josh would trap their heads and Pilar would be ready to hand Josh the different needles and knives for their ear tagging and inoculations.

For the calves, Josh bought a smaller calf chute which was secured in front of the larger cow one. Luke would run them through the large cow chute, then into the smaller chute. Once caught, the chute would be turned on its side, and now the calf was in place for me to secure their feet. I oversaw the rope that would be formed into a circle eight, then slipped on the calf's feet and pulled tight around a pipe so the calf would be stretched out so a nice brand could be marked on. There were many times I would get looks from Josh or an "Oh Mom!" and laughs from the kids when I didn't have the rope just right and a calf's foot would come loose, kicking Josh in the stomach. He certainly didn't think it was very funny and gave me looks that I wasn't doing my job well. During those times, I did not look in his direction.

Luke had strong hands, and he was good at holding the calf's head still while being ear tagged. The process worked well for us, and at day's end, we were all tired but very happy with a successful band- ing season accomplished.

The first few years we lived on the new place, we hired day laborers to help us with our hay season. It was hard holding Luke back when he also wanted to work with the laborers to buck the bales of hay. By the time he was thirteen, he was not only working along-side our day laborers but was running all the hay equipment and the different tractors Josh was buying. Working alongside his dad, Luke proved to be very mechanically inclined, and he thrived on the work around our place. And he was especially excited when Josh would turn him loose to rake the hay all by himself or drive the stack wagon. When Luke did operate the stack wagon, Pilar would ride along with him to help turn a bale if it was not laying correctly.

As the years went by, Luke and Pilar would work together bringing the hay in from the fields with a 105-bale stack wagon. They would dump the load by an elevator and head back out for another load. I would take a bale, place it on the elevator, and then Josh would take if from the elevator and work, building the top of the stacks closer to the roof of the barn. It usually took us twenty minutes to work the 105 bales.

Within a couple of years after buying the forty acres we lived on, another forty acres came up for sale that was right next to our land, so Josh purchased it. We now had different pastures for grazing the cattle and increasing our hay production. Some years, the hay fields produced so well that we had stacks of hay coming out the barn and going down the road that wound through the property. It was during these years you could find us at the sale barn, buying mother cows to increase the herd.

45

In the middle of the year, I had a chance for a part-time job in Gunnison. I would be learning to run a computer while entering data into the system. It was for a bookkeeping service, and the hours would be from twenty to twenty-five a week with the possibility of becoming fulltime. I could set my own hours when I wanted to go into work and get off. I was excited to further my bookkeeping skills with computer data entry programs. The hours also worked in well with my family and other responsibilities. It wasn't long after I applied and was interviewed that I received the position.

That summer, Josh and my roles seemed to have reversed. I was the one driving to work, and Josh was at home with Luke and Pilar. I didn't mind the drive because I was able to listen to my favorite Christian radio station. While driving, I would sing along with the music and then listen to the program that gave helpful ideas about living better. Some were about being a better parent, improving your marriage, but most were about not only having a religion but learning how to have a relationship with Jesus. It didn't matter what I listened to because when I arrived home, I was able to take on whatever came my way with a positive attitude.

Both Luke and Pilar enjoyed their new home. Luke loved having the land to roam and explore. He built himself a fort and considered it his little piece of heaven on earth. He and Pilar would ride the three-wheeler or the horses, and sometimes, Luke would spend time learning how to lasso a piece of pipe in the corral while Pilar played with her kittens. They always had chores to do and books to read. As the years went along, I worked with them on their numbers, reading and writing, and even added scholastic worksheets to their daily activities, which Pilar enjoyed and Luke found no fun doing, but he always had it done when it was time for me to inspect their work.

As good as Luke and Pilar could get along, they mostly disagreed on how they were going to do things. And it became the main issue that Josh and I had to deal with daily. When school was in session, times were better because they were involved with their studies or after-school activities. But when school was out, the battle lines were drawn. Luke wanted Pilar to play with him. Pilar wanted to play, but if she did, Luke made up all these rules Pilar had to follow if she was going to play. So Pilar didn't play. Luke was yelling, "Quitter! Quitter!"

All solutions to help resolve their differences never seemed to work. So Josh had enough and said he was taking them to counseling. To avoid that, they came up with an idea that might help both of them. They listed what each one was doing wrong and came up with their own consequences. They are as follows:

| | | |
|---|---|---|
| 1. | Flipping the bird | Pick up wood fifteen minutes |
| 2. | Talking dirty | Sweep out vehicle |
| 3. | Name calling | Write word 100 times |
| 4. | Dirty looks | Sweep floor |
| 5. | Hitting or pushing | Read half hour out loud |
| 6. | Intrusion of privacy | Nose in the corner fifteen minutes |
| 7. | Lying | Write fifty times. |

When this solution was first implemented, Pilar was writing "Jerk" and "Dork" a hundred times each, and Luke was writing "Sucker" one hundred times, and we could find him sweeping out the vehicles. These consequences worked for less than two weeks, and then they decided it was best to just ignore each other. And that also didn't work very well, so the battle lines continued to be drawn.

## 46

Besides raising kids, cattle, and collecting hay on our small farm, we also had a variety of animals. Josh was a dog lover, so we had a dog as our family pet, and Checkers held that place of honor. She was a close companion of Josh's during the day as he walked the land as he was checking fences and changed the irrigation water. She did prove to be a good kid's dog. Once Luke and Pilar started catching the bus for school, Checkers would walk with them down the gravel dirt road to our gate and wait with them until the bus came. In the afternoons, she could hear the bus coming, even when it was still out of sight, then she would begin to walk down the road to the gate and be there when Luke and Pilar got off the bus, always walking with them up the road to home. She was very friendly when people came by, so we didn't trust her to be a good watchdog, thinking she would probably invite the thieves in, wag her tail, and want to play with them as they left with all the goods.

They say mothers need to experience everything with their children, and sitting at the mall with a "Free Puppy" sign on a box is one of those experiences I've had a couple of times. Before we had Checkers spayed, she had a couple of litters of puppies. It was so much fun watching her lay on the lawn and seeing her pups climb all over her. They were also very cute, charging across the front porch to their bowl of food, which sometimes they stood in while eating. With the different litters of pups, there would always come a day when Josh would announce they were going to have to choose between Checkers or the puppies. They both chose Checkers, and as Pilar said, "She belongs here!"

There were a couple of horses to help round up the cattle and for pleasure riding. Josh's horse was named Misty, and a couple times, he had her bred to a donkey which gave us a couple of mules on our place. The kids loved them. Luke claimed the larger mule and named it Samson. Pilar rode the smaller one and called it Molly.

Pilar was a cat lover, so there were a couple of cats that lived around the barn and roamed the place at night. I'll never forget the day we came home from town and discovered Checkers had killed one of Pilar's kittens. Pilar cried a lot, and it wasn't long before we discovered Luke and Pilar burying the kitten. After the burial, Luke had a ceremony for it like preachers do during a funeral service.

One year, we tried raising pigs and rabbits but decided we didn't want to put the time into them, and Luke and Pilar were not interested in raising 4H animals. Josh was disappointed they didn't want to be active in the local 4H program. He had great memories as a boy growing up and attending the local County Fair, its rodeo, and seeing all the 4H animals. He was hoping to see his kids riding in the parade down Main Street and showing off their special animals. It was just something they weren't interested in putting their time into.

The animals we looked forward to purchasing every year were the cute baby chicks at the local feed store meant to be replacement egg-layers. About six weeks before we could put them outside, we started planning for the arrival of our baby chicks. Warmer temperatures do not arrive in the Rocky Mountains until late May to early June, so it is usually six weeks between May and into June that we would plan on keeping the chicks inside to better monitor them. In April, Josh would want us to think about the preparations for their arrival.

"Gillian, when you and the kids go into town today, I have some supplies I need picked up at the feed store, and it would be a good time to start looking behind the department stores for a discarded refrigerator-sized box. If we start looking now, we should be able to have one by the first of May," he said.

"Do you also want me to pick up the bedding for the box while I'm at the feed store?" I asked.

"Yes, it won't hurt to have it ready when the chicks are here."

When we found the right-sized box, we would take it home, cut one of the longer sides off, placed several layers of newspaper on the bottom, added some bedding, attached a warming light the chicks could huddle under, and placed a water and a feed container inside the box also.

When the chicks arrived on the farm, Luke and Pilar were good about checking their feed, water, and changing the paper daily.

"Mom, it's fun watching them grow, seeing their feathers come in," Pilar would say.

"I like watching and their daily activity of eating, drinking, picking, and sleeping," Luke said.

When the warmer weather arrived, we moved them to their new outside environment. Josh had built a special area near the house and by the corral where some hay was stacked that also protected the area. Placed inside this area was a special enclosure which had a door opened on the side and a small fenced-in yard, so the chicks could run around. The enclosure was closed at night to protect them from cooler temperatures and predators.

Over the weeks, as the chicks grew older and when Josh was working around the corral, he would often open their fenced in area and let them explore further out. The chicks lived in this setup until they went into the chicken coop.

This routine worked well for several years, all except the year a fast-moving whirlwind went through the farm. The day started off sunny and bright. I had washing hung out on the clothes lines. That afternoon, while I brought in the washing, I let the little chickens out to run around the area near the corral.

Suddenly, it became windy and within seconds, the winds turned into a rushing whirlwind around the house. I hurried to get the remaining wash off the lines and then ran to close up the chicks. When I got to their area there wasn't a chick in sight. I ran around the corral and found one little chick running around the side. I will always remember how she looked trying to run through that wind. She was in a state of confusion with her head up, pushing against the wind, trying to get to her place of safety. I thought she was amazing! I ran to her, guided her into the enclosed area, and shut the door. I had one chick and started looking for more. Within minutes, the winds died down. I resumed my search, but I couldn't find a chick or even a feather anywhere.

I sent Pilar and Luke to look for the chicks in the nearby fields while I got in the car and drove around the side ditches and properties near ours. Luke and Pilar even scouted the outer fields. There wasn't a chicken or feather to be found. Only one survived the whirlwind. Now I was the one that was in a state of confusion. Like, what just happened?

Where did the chicks go to? I have no idea. I decided the fast-moving whirlwind carried them all away to a neighbor's property, predators could have gotten them, or some farmer down in a nearby county was wondering how new little chickens got on his property.

I was lying in bed in the camper. It was 7:15 a.m., and the "hunters" (Josh and Luke along with a couple of friends) were out in the forest, going to bring home the meat. This was the biggest joke of a hunting trip there ever was.

It all started out last May when Josh, his friend, Joe, and Joe's brother, Marvin, from Lincoln, Nebraska, decided the three of them would go deer hunting "the Davy Crocket way" during muzzle-loading rifle season in Colorado, which starts on September eleventh.

In June, Josh learned from Joe that Marvin wanted to bring his wife, Ava, along on the trip who could do the cooking. Joe had rented an old forest service cabin that was up near Crested Butte, Colorado. Josh was really excited it was going to be three guys in a hunting camp having male camaraderie. Now instead of Joe, Josh and Marvin having the cabin, it was going to be Marvin and Ava in the cabin, and Joe and Josh would pitch a tent. To say the least, Josh was not happy.

Since June, that was all we knew about the trip. In September, with the time approaching to leave on the hunting trip, Josh called Joe and asked what he should bring and when to meet. Guess what Joe said? He was going to be taking Patricia, his wife, and daughter, Emma, along, and the three of them would stay in the camper on his pickup, and they would bring a tent along for Josh. But Joe told Josh, "Why not bring Gillian and the kids along? They would probably have a great time!" It is not even printable what Josh said after he hung up the phone so we will continue with the story.

I told Josh I didn't want to go. This was supposed to be his hunting trip, and now it was becoming a *Lampoon's Vacation*. Josh didn't even want to go now unless I went along.

He said, "How is it going to look with two guys and their wives and kids, and I pitched in a tent outside? Talk about odd man out!"

So now we had two days to prepare the camper, buy food, ask someone to take care of the animals, and get a family ready to go hunting. I also had two full days at work to put in, and there were hay bales lying in the fields. Nevertheless, by Friday, at five o'clock, we were ready to pull out. Josh was mad at everyone. Luke was extremely happy he was going to get to go hunting. Pilar was my organizer and excited to play "house" in the camper, and I was exhausted and had lost my mind.

The story got even better. Joe said to wait at our house for a phone call from him, and we would meet at the Conoco in Gunnison. Marvin and Ava were going up early Friday and set up camp and would have a roast beef dinner waiting for us around 7:00 p.m. that night. We wanted to get up there and set up the camper before dark, which was 8:00 p.m. By 6:30 p.m., we were still at home, waiting for Joe's call to leave. So I called Patricia to see if they were ready, and she said Joe was finally ready. Patricia explained the locker plant that processed their meat called and said it was ready to be picked up. Joe wanted to get it before leaving. He was also late getting the camper ready and needed a shower. Now Josh was ready to explode again!

We met at the Conoco at 6:45 p.m., and Joe said he had four dogs along with him and needed to stop at Almont and drop off three of the dogs at his mother's so we should go on ahead, and we would meet them just outside of Crested Butte since Joe knew the way up the forest service road. He said he would be five minutes. He was half an hour at his mother's because she wanted him to take a few minutes and change the filter on her water system. Can you believe it?

It was now 8:45 p.m., very dark, and we are sitting just outside Crested Butte, hungry, and Joe finally arrived to show us the way up the mountain, which was eight miles up a narrow winding rocky dirt road. Josh wasn't even talking English or Italian by this time. We arrived at the camp at 9:30 p.m. The roast beef dinner tasted wonderful through Ava's efforts of trying to keep it warm. Anything would taste good by this time. After eating, and in extremely dark conditions, Joe and Marvin helped us set up the camper in a spot Marvin had ready for us. By eleven o'clock, we are headed for bed, and I was passing out aspirins to my family so we could try and get some sleep.

Within a few hours, the hunters took off. When they left, I stepped out of the camper into the peaceful cool morning twilight, and I discovered tall majestic mountains surrounded the area with the road running in front of the camper. Looking to my right was the small hunter's cabin nestled between tall pine trees. I took in a deep breath to smell the cool freshness of nature. Looking up over a tall mountain peak that rose majestically into the dark sky was a single star shining brightly. I called it my "morning star." I then believed if we all calmed down, we would have a good time.

In the quiet hours while Pilar slept, I spent time writing a letter to Juliet of our hunting trip to this point and found myself laughing at yesterday's events. Pilar had now been up for a while, had enjoyed her time playing house, and was getting ready to go to the cabin and see if the people were up and if Emma would like to play.

Now that the morning sun was up, I discovered some of the conveniences of our campsite. Attached to the front of the cabin was a small porch people could sit on, and secured nearby was a picnic table, campfire site, and some kindling had been chopped. Inside was a rustic one-room open area that had sleeping and cooking facilities.

While Emma and Pilar began exploring the campsite, we three ladies enjoyed a pleasant morning with a cup of coffee over casual conversations. Ava was a very gracious host, easy to like, had a sense of humor, and loved to cook. As the morning warmed up, we enjoyed our breakfast outside at the table in front of the cabin. I was now really glad we made the effort to be here.

Late morning, the hunters returned without them having any luck. After eating breakfast, the three men decided to get some sleep, so we ladies took Pilar, Emma, and Luke, who was too excited to sleep, on a hiking trail up the mountain to a place with a waterfall. The trail was well-marked but became increasingly steep, and in less than thirty minutes, I heard the sound of a rushing waterfall. Emerging out of the forest and on a steep incline, we viewed a waterfall that cascaded at different levels down the mountain. The three kids were so excited to play along the different edges of the cascades. We ladies found a shaded spot to listen to the tumbling waterfall, the sounds of happy children, and the silent sounds only a forest can make. I didn't think the day could be any better.

Returning to our campsite, we found the hunters up, hungry for food, and making plans to return to the mountain for another attempt to use their muzzle-loading rifles. When the men left, Luke came to me with a question.

"Mom, I brought my pocketknife along with me, and I know of a game that us kids could play if you and Patricia would allow it."

"Luke, are you talking about the game Mumblety-peg? I think my brother, Logan, and I played it as kids."

"Mom, I don't know what it is called, but I've played it a few times with my friends. It's fun, and I thought us three kids could play it."

"Luke, the way Logan and I played it was we stood opposite each other beginning with our feet together. Then Logan would begin by throwing the pocketknife a few inches away from my feet as deeply into the ground as he could get it. If the knife stuck, I would move my foot to where the knife was stuck. I would then grab the knife and do the same to him with him moving his foot in the knife's direction. The next throw would be to the opposite foot. Logan always had better luck with the knife sticking than I did, so my feet were sometimes far apart, and his was not. The first whose feet were stretched out as far as possible and eventually fell down lost that round, which was usually me. Is this the game you want to play?"

"That's it, Mom! What do you think?"

"Well, I'll give you and Pilar permission to play if she wants too. Let's go and ask Patricia about Emma and see if she wants to play."

Patricia was in favor of the game and thought it might improve their skills and courage. So the game was on. They played it for about an hour with Emma giving Luke good competition, but he still won overall and was happy the girls played.

Later in the afternoon, the hunters returned without luck and sat around the campsite, sharing stories of previous hunts. Luke spent some time chopping more wood for the campfire that was being planned after a steak dinner around the picnic table. Joe had brought some of his fresh processed meat, and with Ava adding her culinary skills to a couple of side dishes, everyone was looking forward to the evening meal here with more hunting stories and laughter around the campfire.

Sunday morning, Luke joined the men for one last attempt to use their rifles, but they were unsuccessful. They never saw a deer the whole weekend. A final noon meal was planned, and Patricia's oldest daughter came up to join us for our final hours on the mountain.

As we packed up and headed down the mountain, large black clouds appeared over the mountains, and before we were completely off the winding mountain road, it began raining. The last couple of miles down were slow going. It was raining hard all the way into Gunnison, and as we approached the edge of town, we looked to our right, and on small hill near the edge of town stood a buck deer in all his majesty.

Driving into our place, it was raining on all the bales we had left in the field. We would now be spending days rolling them over and standing them up to get them dried out before they could be brought into the hay shed. However, the weather and work ahead didn't dampen our spirits. We were glad we went on this hunting trip.

**48**

When Juliet left for college, I went through the heart-wrenching pain all mothers go through when they send their oldest child out into the world to become the person God intends them to be. This is the child I gave roots to and was now giving her wings. Memories flooded my mind of our special times alone together, times with my mom and dad, the many adventures with friends on weekends, camping trips, skiing on winter weekends, and a special trip to a foreign country. I watched her achieve both academically and athletically while growing more beautiful each year. Then there were the years with Josh, the mistakes I made, and her resilience to believe that when life gave you lemons, you make lemonade. It was then I realized I was truly happy for her and the freedom she now had.

After she left, the first phone call I received was telling me that the flight from Gunnison to Denver went well, and with the help of her Uncle Nathan in Denver, she had arrived safely at her dorm in Boulder. She was alone in her room and very happy to be at CU in Boulder. She wasn't sad to be alone; she was just so happy to be there and was so excited for the year ahead.

The second call I received was about a week later. She had been to a barbecue and played a volleyball game with girls from her dorm and had met some boys. She said she had decided to break up with her high school boyfriend. She wanted to be free to date since she was being asked out.

Luke, Pilar, and I made chocolate chip cookies, and we each wrote her a letter. It was the "Juliet Requires Energy" care package, the first of many we sent during the years she studied and earned a degree in nursing. I wrote her a letter every week, keeping her informed on the different activities the family was involved in, and she especially wanted to hear the latest about Luke and Pilar. Once or twice a month, Luke and Pilar would write to her also.

Luke liked to write:

> How are you doing? Well, I am doing good. The rooster is chasing me a lot. I'm almost ready to kill him with Dad's gun. Dad hurt his fingers with his hammer bad.
>
> Pilar went to suntan. The sun went down, so Pilar went to find the sun.
>
> I really like hammering nails into my tree house, riding the three-wheeler, and riding the horse is fun too.
>
> We vaccinated the cows. I did a good job working the chute. Dad says I only need to grow a couple more inches, then I can work the chute by myself. Mom fell in the chicken poop trying to get the cows in the pen.
>
> We went to the library, and now I have books to read which I don't want to. Mommy, Pilar, and I got chased by a cow. Mommy says it is going to the market. Daddy loves the cow. Mom is going nuts!
>
> Have a good time in Boulder.
>
> Love,
> Luke

Pilar liked to write:

> Hey, sis, how are you? I am doing good. I just got done with a book that has eighteen chapters, and now I am reading *The Chocolate Touch*.
>
> Thank you for the *Miss Saigon* tape. I really like it.

I am going to ride the horse today. My cats
are growing and getting cute.

Our family is going to Montrose, and we
are going to look at pianos. I am doing well in
school. We are going to get some pigs soon. I am
going to a kid's choir at the church.

Happy birthday.

Love,
Your sis, Pilar

Sometimes in the letters, I included money I would receive
from her father or a five, ten, or twenty-dollar bill from me to use
as she wished. It brought back memories of that five-dollar bill my
dad sent me each week. Sometimes she would read the letters to her
friends in the dorm or colleagues at work. We learned that when
Juliet announced that a "letter from the farm" had arrived, students
would gather around to hear the latest events from the "funny farm."

During the five years Juliet spent at CU, she had different living arrangements, always looking for ways to cut costs. She first
started out in the dorm with her roommate being a girl from northern Colorado. Even though they had completely different tastes in
clothing, they were the best of friends, and the friendship continues
today. She learned the farther a student lived away from the campus,
the cheaper the rent. So, one year, she moved into an apartment a
few blocks away from the campus with four other girls, and that was
the year she discovered when things broke or needed fixing, she was
able to fix them with very little cost. She attributed her knowledge of
how to repair things to the times she helped working on our rentals.

Another year, she roomed with six girls in a larger apartment
nearer the school. She discovered students came from family situations where they had live-in maids and butlers, and these students
never knew what a broom or mop was. They soon learned how to use
them and carried their own share of responsibilities. She also found
out this was too many people to live with, especially the strangers
that walked through, causing personal belongings to disappear. So

on her last year, she moved closer to the campus with one roommate named Maria, and this arrangement worked out well. In between all the moving to try and save money, she underwent a second surgery on her other knee and had a serious bike accident that left scars on her biceps.

June 1, 1995, before Juliet's graduation from CU, I became a full-time housewife and mother, and I found both roles challenging and rewarding. I had more time to spend with my family and was not so rushed anymore. As a family, we were able to do some more cleaning up of dead wood around the place and collected firewood in the high country. We also spent some time changing corner fences and putting in culverts to be able to cross the ditches during hay season. Luke and Pilar were glad to have Mom home full-time. They said the lunches especially improved; desserts were a surprise treat, and I found time individually with both kids.

With Luke, it was fixing or repairing something where he could use an extra hand to hold a board or help him measure correctly. As we worked together, we found a topic of interest to discuss and were always laughing as we did the work. With Pilar, the garden was our major project with either planting, weeding, or harvesting the vegetables. She loved snapping green beans, and they became her favorite vegetable. I had more time to listen to her play the piano as she continued to advance to more difficult pieces, and I learned about her friendships at school.

In August of 1995, Juliet would be graduating from college. I was extremely proud of her. Luke and Pilar were looking forward to attending the graduation, and Pilar especially wanted to see Juliet's and Maria's apartment. Pilar also wanted to do something special for her graduation, so in June, I wrote out the names and addresses of people I thought she would like to notify, and then Pilar typed them up. Pilar wanted Juliet to know that I checked them over and she was not to worry about mistakes being made.

After the graduation ceremony, a luncheon was planned back at Juliet's and Maria's apartment. Besides Luke, Pilar, and I attending, my two brothers and their wives came along, and Josh's sister, Victoria, and her two boys drove in from Evergreen, Colorado. I was so grateful for them all being there, and every one of them loved and admired her.

Josh allowed me to take the family car since after the graduation events, I planned to drive over to Evergreen to visit with Victoria and her two boys. I thought it would be a good chance for the cousins to spend some time together before heading back to Gunnison. I was hoping Juliet could go with us, but she was still working and had seven days to be out of their apartment in Boulder and be in California, ready to begin her new job. The cousins did have a good time, especially riding a four-wheeler around the mountain trails surrounding Victoria's home.

In the spring of 1995, before graduation, a position opened at a hospital in California where Juliet wanted to live. She applied, received an offer for an interview and, shortly after, was notified that they were offering the position to her. Maria, Juliet's roommate, decided she wanted to go with Juliet to California. Five days after graduation, Juliet and Maria drove into our place in Gunnison. Maria was driving a U-Haul truck packed with their belongings with Maria's car towed behind. Juliet was driving behind in her car. Juliet and Maria had come to pick me up, and the next day, the three of us spent two days traveling to California. They had found an apartment in Ventura, were very excited to be living close to the ocean, couldn't wait to walk on the beach, and wondered who their first boyfriends would be.

All she had accomplished was beyond the measure of everything I had ever dreamed for her. She was a very special person, and I knew God had someone special for her.

## 49

On an afternoon in July of 1996, I received a call from Juliet.

"Hi, Mom, it's me. I can't talk long because we're boarded, and the plane is about to take off. My colleague and I are leaving New Orleans, and we're headed to Los Angeles. I just want to tell you that if you get a call from a man named Philip, be nice to him. That's all I can say right now. Call you later. Bye!"

After she arrived home, she called me back to tell me about this man named Philip who had become a mystery to me, but my daughter was certainly excited about him. When she arrived home and was settled, she called me back.

"Did he call, Mom?" she asked.

"No, he didn't," I said. "Tell me about him."

"My colleague and I have been working in New Orleans. We were driving on the freeway when we came upon a car that had one of its taillights out. This really bugged my colleague, so we pulled up along the side of the car to inform the driver, and that was when we discovered the people inside the car were military servicemen. Surprisingly, we ran into them on Bourbon Street later, and I ended up having a nice conversation and evening with the one named Philip. He's a First Sergeant Marine stationed at the Marine Base in San Diego. Philip said he wanted to call my mother and let her know she has a lovely daughter."

"Well, that is one thing that he and I agree on. I've just learned he is a smart man if he knows that about my daughter. This is exciting news. Now that I know, I will be extra cautious and polite if he should call," I said. "Juliet, I've heard a lot about Bourbon Street in New Orleans. Is it as exciting and fun as people say it is?" I asked.

"It's in the historical French Quarter of New Orleans. Bourbon Street has a lot of bars and clubs. It's like a street that never sleeps at night. We went to a place called The Red Door that was known for its music and dancing. That's where we ran into the military guys. Mom, I hope we can reconnect. I really like this guy, Philip. We exchanged phone numbers and addresses, so I hope to hear from him."

And they did connect. Philip began by writing Juliet a letter, hoping she would respond. She did with a letter back to him. They enjoyed a fall romance, and in February 1997, Philip proposed, and they began living together. They wanted to be married the coming summer.

During the months they dated, Juliet would call me, and she would share more and more information about Philip and the life he had lived before meeting her.

"Mom, you need to know that Philip is nine years older than me, was married before, and has a ten-year-old daughter named Lia. She lives mostly with her mother since Philip's service career has had him deployed several times and traveling around a lot. During school breaks and summer vacations, Lia will be living with us."

"So what you are now telling me is you are going to be a new wife and stepmother at the same time? Are you looking forward to this dual role you are about to enter? I just don't want you to go through what we've been through."

"There is one thing I know, Mom. Philip and I love each other. I found a man that really loves me, and the few times I've been with Lia, we've done well together, and she seems to accept me. It's like being a big sister all over again. And you know how much I love being a big sister to Luke and Pilar. I am planning on loving her. There is also the fact that Philip and I will have a lot of time by ourselves while Lia is in school."

"Well, if he is good to you and this is what you want, I'm very happy for you. I just hope he knows how lucky he is to get you. I look forward to meeting the little girl that is going to become a big part of your life. How long has Philip been a Marine?"

"Almost eighteen years. He has seen a lot of the world like Africa, the Middle East, he was involved with the Gulf War in 1990, and was also stationed in Hawaii, which was his favorite place. He has wonderful memories of his family's time in Hawaii, especially their times at the beach, playing in the waves and tea parties on the front lawn with Lia.

"Wow! A Marine that does tea parties! I'm starting to like this guy of yours."

"Mom, I'm very excited for you to meet him. That's why I called. I got Andy's graduation from high school, an announcement and invitation to attend. Philip and I have decided to come to the graduation, and it will be an opportunity for everyone to meet him and Lia. I'm so proud of Andy graduating, and I want to be a part of his celebration."

"That's wonderful news! It will be wonderful to see you and get to know Philip and Lia also."

At the end of May, Philip, Juliet, and Lia drove to Gunnison to attend the graduation and celebration. Philip was a nice-looking man, tall, and built like a Marine. While sitting around and getting acquainted, he also proved to be intelligent, witty, and a big tease. I discovered that characteristic when I asked them about their future plans.

"Have you thought about the kind of wedding you both would like?" I asked.

"Mom, Philip and I have talked about having a garden wedding instead of at the church. I thought since I live in California, I would be responsible for my dress. I want to ask Virginia, my roommate from college, to be my maid of honor. That is all I have thought about at this time."

Then Philip surprised me with his idea on how they should be married.

"Gillian, I thought on our way back to California, Juliet and I could just drive through Las Vegas and go through one of those drive-through wedding services."

"I can tell you, Philip, that is not going to happen. My daughter is not being married at a drive-through service in Las Vegas. My daughter will have a proper wedding!" I said.

"Well, it would sure save a lot of time and money," was his response.

"Not happening, Philip," was my response.

Then he started to laugh. I have been known to be a gullible person, and I proved to be an easy target for Philip with my daughter's wedding being discussed.

Thursday night, we attended Andy's graduation, and then on Saturday, we gathered in Logan and Lucia's backyard for the graduation party. Logan and Lucia had spent many hours making their backyard into a private garden of beauty, landscaped with unique stones and rocks from their travels to the high country, and in the center of the yard was a beautiful rose garden. There was an intimate covered patio where many fun conversations had taken place. It was in this area that Logan, Lucia, Philip, Juliet, and I began to discuss wedding plans.

"Logan, your backyard is very nice," Philip said.

"Thank you," Logan replied. "I like to barbecue out here, and Lucia and I really enjoy coming out here to relax, unwind, and share a glass of wine together. It's a great place for parties too."

"Juliet, why don't we hold the wedding here in your uncle and aunt's backyard?" Philip asked.

Lucia, who loved to joke around also, was standing at the dessert table and overheard Philip's remark and said, "Sure, I could just make this graduation cake into a wedding cake really quick."

"Why not? Works for me." Philip said, "We could get married here tomorrow since everyone is already here."

"No, no, no," I said, "we will plan a proper wedding with a nice wedding cake and even a groom's cake on the side."

"I don't want a wedding cake or a groom's cake, Gillian. I want a pie," Philip said.

"*A pie!*" I screamed. "You're out of your mind!"

To which everyone did laugh. But to some extent, Juliet was thinking about considering the possibility of doing the wedding that weekend. That is when Uncle Logan took his niece, Juliet, aside and had a serious talk with her.

"Juliet, you're not going to do your wedding this way. You need to think about the two little sisters you have in Arizona that I know would love to be a part of your wedding and would want to see you get married. There is your mom, Pilar, and Luke also to think about. We all want to see you married in the right way."

When the joking stopped and the conversation got serious, it was decided the wedding would take place in Logan and Lucia's backyard on August 2, 1997.

"Mom, since we in live in California, I will take care of my dress and the dresses for my attendants."

"What two colors would you like for a color scheme?"

"Black and white. I always thought a black and white wedding would be pretty. Mom, beyond that, I have never been one of those girls that dreamed about her wedding day. So you and Lucia can have fun with all the other arrangements."

"I know your Uncle Nathan would love to marry you. Would it be okay with you if I asked him to perform the ceremony?"

"Yes, that would be great also!"

I had two months to plan a wedding. Lucia said she would love to help me with the planning and decorations. I was very grateful for her help, and I looked forward to us working on the wedding together. I have never been a visionary or creative person, and Lucia had those talents, so I was going to give her the lead on how she wanted to decorate her backyard for the event.

Back in February, when I learned Juliet was engaged to be married, I dreamed of giving her a nice wedding in Gunnison. When I told Josh about Juliet's engagement, his response was, "Don't look to me for any money for those plans. It's Ricardo and your responsibility to do the wedding for her."

Once again, the old Josh arose with not a word of happiness for me or Juliet. I wondered, *Why?* All Juliet did was achieve and do well during her college years, was advancing in her job, and now found a man who truly loved her. She brought no shame or disrespect to our family's name. She was a stepdaughter any stepfather would have been proud to have raised, but it wasn't to be in Josh's heart. I needed to find a job so I could give Juliet her special day.

I began searching for employment in the Gunnison area. There was a position posted in the accounting department at the school district, and I was really hoping to get that position. It would be a full-time five days a week with good benefits, and if I could get it, I thought some of my financial struggles would be over.

From a friend, I also heard about a bookkeeping position at the oral surgeon's office in town doing accounts receivable and payable. It was part-time with few benefits. Thinking about the two jobs, there were positives and negatives with both. The school district paid more, had better benefits, but my time was limited with my other responsibilities around our home, and I still wanted time with Luke and Pilar. The position at the oral surgeon's office was four days a week, nine to three, and it worked well with my family's situation.

The position at the school district came down to me and another girl who had more accounting experience. We each had to do an oral interview before a panel. I was nervous about the interview because I believed I didn't interview well, and I couldn't always express myself with enough confidence to reveal how capable an employee I could be if given the opportunity. Leaving the interview, I didn't think it went well, and in two days, I learned the position was given to the other girl. I called the oral surgeon's office, spoke to the office manager, and said I would accept the bookkeeping position. I was to start on Monday. God made a way for me once again.

50

Entering the office of an oral surgeon opened a new career for me in the field of dentistry, and it was one of the best jobs I ever held. To do the accounts receivable and payables, I had to learn the medical vocabulary associated with the mouth, especially the teeth and the number assigned to each tooth. However, my job also included other responsibilities to help the office run smoothly. I became familiar with my new working environment through on-the-job training procedures. I learned how to operate a panoramic x-ray machine and develop the x-rays in a dark room through a dental x-ray machine. I was instructed in the proper procedures for cleaning instruments, bagging them, and putting them through an autoclave for sterilization. Once sterilized, I set up new trays and prepared rooms for the next patient.

The most interesting part of my new job was being able to assist in the different surgeries by holding the patient's head still. I was amazed at the different surgeries performed inside the mouth. As the doctor operated, he was always open to any questions asked which furthered my knowledge of oral surgery.

The first two things I wanted to do for the wedding was to have an engagement announcement placed in the local paper and then get the invitations ordered. I had asked Juliet when she returned to California if she would send me a picture of her and Philip that I could use for the announcement. The one she sent to me was taken of them at the Marine Ball held last November and is one of my favorite pictures of them as a couple. When family and friends called congratulating me about the engagement, they also spoke about the nice picture the paper had printed. I also sent Juliet samples of invitations, and she chose one that was simple but elegant with a single red rose on a black vine.

When I received my first paycheck, Lucia and I had scheduled a day to visit the different craft stores in the area. She already had several ideas on how to keep costs down with the different garden-theme decor she was planning for the tables. As she selected different items, she shared her ideas with me, and I became more excited as a vision of what Juliet's outdoor wedding could look like on a small budget.

With my next paycheck, we visited a local flower shop. The florist gave me different ideas to consider and especially wanted to know Juliet's three favorite flowers. So I called Juliet the following weekend, told her what Lucia and I had already been planning, and asked her about the flowers she would like.

"Mom, I have always loved lilies, orchids, and roses."

"I thought for your bridal bouquet, I would have you carry an arrangement of those three flowers."

"Mom, that is a lovely idea, so go with it."

"Have you had any more ideas about your wedding?" I asked.

"Yes, Philip and I talked about it on the way home. We want to keep it a small wedding, more intimate. So I am only going to have one main bridesmaid, and that will be Virginia, my best friend from college. Her dress will be black. We would like Pilar and Lia to be a part of the ceremony also. We already talked to Lia about it, and she loves the idea. And thirdly, I have already decided on the style of the dress I want."

"Wow, I'm glad that you have put so much thought into your wedding, and I love all the ideas," I said.

"I have to say, Mom, it's been fun thinking about it and planning the design of the dresses. Since it is outside and I will be entering the yard along plants, rocks, and steps, I would like Pilar to follow behind me assisting with the dress train so it doesn't get torn. After the ceremony, the train will be attached to the waist of my dress so I can walk around easily."

"Lia will make a cute flower girl, and I know Pilar will be excited that she is part of the wedding party."

"Mom, both Lia and Pilar will be in white dresses. So I am going to need Pilar's measurements. If you could send them to me next week, that would be great.

"I'll get the measurements tonight. What about the ring bearer?" I asked.

"Do you think Luke might do it for me? I know he is a little old to be a ring bearer, but it would be nice if he could be part of my wedding," she asked.

"I'll talk to him. I'm sure he will do it for you," I said.

When I hung up the phone, I had to agree with Juliet it was fun planning her wedding and I was thankful for how decisions were being made and falling into place so easily. I now had to start thinking about the wedding cake, food, drinks, tables, and chairs. August can be a hot month in Colorado, so I decided I would try and locate some umbrella canopies to shade the tables. But the first thing I needed to do was to talk to Luke.

Much to Luke's dismay, he was not happy about the request.

"Mom, I'm thirteen years old. I do not what to be a ring bearer!" he exclaimed. "That's for little boys to do, not boys my age! I love Juliet and I'm happy for her, but surely there is something else I can do for her," he pleaded.

"Yes, there is something you can do. You can support her. The families invited to the wedding do not have a little boy. If it was a larger wedding, then we would have been able to ask more relatives, and a younger boy might have been possible. But that's not what Juliet and Philip want. You are the only one we can ask. We need a groom, best man, preacher, and ring bearer. Three of those four roles are filled, and I haven't heard of renting ring bearers for weddings. And even if I could rent one, it's not in my budget. So that leaves *you* to help us fill the fourth role. So what do you say? Think about it. You can be standing up there with two Marines that have served this country. That should be an honor," I explained.

"Oh, okay, I'll do it, but I want you to know I don't like doing it."

For the wedding cake, I knew exactly who I wanted to ask to make it. Josh had a cousin who grew up in 4H, learning to make and decorate cakes. She was now married with a family of her own and had a successful business doing wedding cakes. When I called her, she was very happy I asked her to do Juliet's cake. She had seen the engagement announcement in the paper and was happy for Juliet. Lucia, she, and I sat down at Lucia's house one afternoon, looked at a portfolio she had created, and came up with a design we all liked. It would be three white tiers with black decorations, each tier would be different sizes, and the top two tiers would be on pedestals. When we began to talk prices, she said she wouldn't take any money. It would be her gift to Juliet. I will always remember her love and generosity to Juliet. On the day of the wedding, she and her husband came to deliver the cake and set it in place. It was beautiful.

The other beautiful hand-made gift was the ring pillow Luke would carry. Lucia was an exceptional seamstress, and she wanted to make the pillow as a personal gift to Juliet. It was gorgeous. It was made from white satin, and she had hand-stitched a special ribbon embroidery around the edges.

Lucia was given permission to use the tables and chairs at her church which would be displayed around the rose garden. And for food, we decided on a popular local barbecue establishment to cater the rehearsal dinner. For the wedding reception, Lucia came up with a menu the local grocery store could cater. Everything seemed to be falling into place, and every time I received a paycheck, I made payments or bought supplies. Logan and Lucia had added additional flowers with colorful foliage to their potted plants along the walkways which increased the beauty of the landscaped areas. It was now the last of July, the wedding was next Saturday, and while we were working and making final preparation plans, I started getting worried that I might have a huge problem concerning the outdoor wedding. The weather.

The winds came up, the sky turned dark, and it began to rain. By Sunday morning, it was pouring down rain, and it was still pouring Monday. Logan, Lucia, and I started realizing we might have to move the wedding to another place. On Wednesday, it was still raining, and with a heavy heart, I placed a call to the church Juliet, and I attended when I first came back to Gunnison and was raising Juliet as a single mother. The secretary invited me to come in and visit with the pastor. After a friendly visit and information was exchanged, he said the church was available to use Saturday. However, everything would have to be cleaned up and ready for services on Sunday. Very understandable, but I wasn't looking forward to the additional work.

I also knew Philip and Juliet didn't want a church wedding, but it was the only place I knew on a short notice that had the facilities I needed, and the rental of the church might be within my budget. My prayer was for the rain to stop. And it did on Thursday morning. The sun came out, the sky was a beautiful blue, and there was a fresh earthy smell as the ground was saturated with water. Logan wanted to give the grass one full day to dry out some, so his plans now were to cut the grass Friday morning, and then he and his family, along with one of Lucia's sisters and niece who came from out-of-town to help, would set up the tables and umbrella canopies.

Friday, out-of-town guests began to arrive. Members of the wedding party and their families were invited to Logan and Lucia's house for the rehearsal followed by a buffet-style dinner around the rose garden. The backyard environment created an enjoyable time for everyone to get acquainted. Plus, we all were looking forward to the men and lady's events scheduled for later that evening. For the ladies, a lingerie shower for Juliet was planned in Lucia's living room. The men were planning a bachelor party at a popular turn of the century bar downtown. I now knew where Philip got his sense of humor.

At the lingerie party, his mother told stories about Philip that really livened up the party. The party ended early, so the ladies decided to walk downtown and find the men. We found them at the famous bar, sitting around a table, having a good time laughing with Philip smoking a cigar, a gift from the men. Juliet walked right up to him and sat on his lap, placing her arm around him. I had to think that when Juliet and Philip were together, they enjoyed each other and knew how to have a good time. I was happy for them, and we all were excited about tomorrow's events.

## 51

After two months of actively preparing for the wedding, the day had finally arrived. It was a bright sunny day with white fluffy clouds moving across a deep blue sky. However, it was also very humid, and the weatherman predicted it would increase though out the day. I was thankful for the beautiful weather and glad I had the umbrella canopies for people to sit under. Juliet was wondering how Philip and Steve, his best man, would handle being in their wool Marine dress blue uniforms in the high humidity. I was very excited to see them in those uniforms and hoped there might be an afternoon breeze to combat the hot weather.

The morning of the wedding, the men had planned on playing a round of golf while the women had appointments to have their hair and nails done. Later at the wedding reception, stories began circulating that when Logan and Nathan, the preacher, went to pick up Philip and Steve, the best man, they found them sitting on a downtown curb, not feeling very well after a night of partying, and there was a whole game of golf ahead of them to play. Another story they told was as they played golf, they were informing Ricardo, the father of the bride, where he was to walk and stand since he and his family hadn't arrived until late Friday night and had missed the rehearsal. They said they received some funny looks from other golfers they were letting play through them.

Before the women's appointments, Juliet had arranged a meeting at a local restaurant with a couple of good friends from high school who lived in town and wanted to see her. It was a good time of reminiscing and a nice way for Juliet to begin her special day.

About half an hour before wedding guests were to start arriving, I was dressed and walking around the backyard, checking final preparations. Lucia had the buffet table beautifully decorated, and she even added her own special surprise. At one end of the buffet table, a special small round groom's table was overlaid with a beautiful white tablecloth, and on it sat the pie Philip wanted for his wedding. It was a pumpkin pie with whipped cream around the edges and a large "P" in the middle. Overlooking the pie was a white gazebo, and on both sides were Barbie-style dolls, one a Marine, and the other a nurse. Lucia knew how to make someone feel welcome when joining our family.

As I walked down into the yard, I turned to see who was walking down the side of the house. It was Philip and Steve, but they were not in their dress blues; they were in their green camo uniforms. I couldn't believe they didn't know that they were supposed to wear their dress blues.

"No! No! No!" I started yelling. "You can't wear *those* to the wedding!" I said.

"What are you talking about, Gillian?" Philip asked. "These are our uniforms," he said.

"No, Philip, I wanted you in your dress blues! Not the camos that belong in a field or at work! This is a wedding! Please tell me you're going to change and will be wearing you dress blues!" I pleaded.

"Well, Steve and I thought we looked good, Gillian, and we would be a lot more comfortable in these in this heat than in the more formal dress. Won't you agree we can wear these?" he asked.

"Philip, Juliet told me you brought your dress blues. Please, please go and put them on for the wedding," I pleaded once again.

Philip and Steve started to laugh, and then I knew. I was gullible once again when it came to Philip and how he liked to tease me.

"Gillian, I just wanted to see your reaction if we walked in wearing our camos. You didn't disappoint me. Steve and I will go change, and I think you will like what you see when we walk in for the ceremony."

I was looking forward to Philip being my son-in-law.

As the wedding party gathered in the living room, I had a few minutes to look at my beautiful daughter. She was a beautiful bride and so excited to be marrying Philip. As I hugged her, I noticed she was wearing my mother's special pearl necklace that I had given her.

"Mom, do you think Grandpa and Grandma are watching from heaven today?" she asked.

"I know they are. You were very special to them."

Guests began arriving to music that Logan and his boys had programed to play through their stereo system. These were people who Juliet had touched their lives in special ways. For some, she was their babysitter for their children, others were close friends of our family and who she played games with around our kitchen table, and there were the extended family and friends that lived close by that just loved her. Josh came to the wedding and sat with the Reynolds family members.

As I was escorted in and sat down and looked up, true to Philip's words, I liked what I saw. Philip and Steve were in their dress blues, and I was so proud to know them and the service they had given to their county. Now one was becoming a part of my family. Lia, the flower girl, entered, dropping petals along the rocks. She looked like a princess to me, and she would be my first grandchild. Virginia, the matron of honor, looked beautiful in her blonde hair and black dress. Juliet's father escorted Juliet into the music of Pachelbel's Cannon in D. She was a gift from God to me, and I was proud to be her mother. Pilar, my bonus gift from God, looked so pretty and did well protecting the train from being ruined. Luke, my answered to prayer gift from God, performed the duty as ring bearer but would not wear a suit coat. My brother, Nathan, performed a very nice ceremony.

As the reception line was forming, Lucia, her sisters, and Lucia's boys, who also had special culinary skills, were setting up the buffet line. As I entered the buffet, to my surprise, they had taken their talents and created a lavish arrangement of exceptional dishes. Philip and Juliet made the cutting of the cake a fun experience. There was just one incident while cutting the cake and opening champagne a balloon pop, and both Philip and Steve said later, it sounded to them like a gun was fired, a reaction from their time of service in the war.

The humidity stayed high, and we were beginning to run out of drinks, so people began to leave. I was concerned about Philip and Steve in their dress blue uniforms and knew they must be sweating profusely. There were a few friends and extended family members that stayed for the opening of gifts and to blow bubbles as the couple drove away.

There are no words to express how much I appreciated and loved Logan and Lucia for opening their home and helping me give Juliet the wedding she deserved. I will always think fondly of my nephews and Lucia's sisters for coming and giving of their time and talents to help when help was needed. When Philip and Juliet saw all that was done for them, they wanted to say thank you to Logan and Lucia in a special way. A dream that Logan and Lucia had was to visit Washington DC someday, see our nation's capital, and tour the famous monuments. Not long after the wedding, they received in the mail an all-expense-paid four-day trip to Washington DC, hotel and air fare included. They have been forever grateful to Philip and Juliet to be able to see that dream come true.

My brother, Logan, has a passion for the history of this world. For our nation's history, it's the Civil War time, and his favorite historical character is Abraham Lincoln and how he fought to save the Union. He shed a tear as he stood at the foot of the Lincoln Memorial.

Life had been busy at the ranch since the wedding. We had put over three thousand bales of hay up and still had another fifteen hundred to go, Lord willing if it didn't rain anymore. Areas around us had been getting severe thunderstorms, and our area had been receiving the tail end of them, which made it frustrating to get the hay up. The garden was in such neglect with weeds that I took drastic measures to make it look like a garden again.

Pilar said, "Mom, is it my imagination or are you using the lawnmower on the garden?"

"Seeing is believing, Pilar." I took the lawnmower around the edges, and two hours later, along with Pilar's help, it looked like a garden.

In August, both Luke and Pilar had joined fall sports teams at school and had early morning practices. Luke had joined the football team. His coach had been building up his players physically with running, pushups, and going through tires. He also started tackling which he thought was getting fun. Pilar started volleyball, and her coach had the girls running three miles a day. Both the kids had to get up, make their beds, eat, and feed their animals and be ready to go by 7:00 a.m. This was good practice for when school began in September, and they would have to get up at 6:00 a.m. and catch the bus at 6:40 a.m.

For my job at the oral surgeon's office, I was taking CPR classes after work to be certified, which was needed to work in a medical office. I was also watching tapes on taking x-rays and learning how to read them. This was a new field for me and very interesting. I was enjoying both my job and fellow coworkers.

Juliet and Philip made their home in San Diego, California, where Philip was a First Sergeant on the Marine base. From the conversations I was having with Juliet, it sounded like they were really fixing up their home nicely. Juliet was anxious for me to come and visit them. I promised her I would be there as soon as I could, but she needed to have patience with me and my schedule. I was honored they wanted us to visit so soon.

November came, and Josh told me he was thinking about building a small shed to hold garden machines and tools. He thought he and Luke could build it over the Thanksgiving break.

"Would you really need Pilar and I to help with such a small project?" I asked.

"Not really. Sounds like you want to do something. What is on your mind?"

"The doctor is shutting the office down for five days for the Thanksgiving holiday season. Philip and Juliet have invited us to San Diego for Thanksgiving. If you and Luke want to work on the shed, it would be a chance for Pilar and me to see them and their home."

"Well, I'm certainly not going, and I need Luke's help to build the shed. What about a Thanksgiving for Luke and me?"

"I could prepare you a turkey and some side dishes to bake. There would probably be plenty to even have leftovers to enjoy. You wouldn't have to worry about what to fix for meals while we're gone."

"Well, as long as Luke and I don't have to think about cooking while working on the shed, the idea sounds good to me."

"Great! I'll call Juliet tomorrow and tell her to expect Pilar and I for Thanksgiving.

Pilar and I listened to a book on tape while making the thirteen-hour trip to San Diego. By the time we drove up to the gate, a dark evening had settled on the day. Philip had informed the men on duty that we would be coming, so after showing my identification, we were allowed on the base and given directions to the First Sergeant's home. It was my first time back on a military base since my time in Alaska at Fort Wainwright. Pilar and I were both excited to see Philip, Juliet, and Lia.

Driving up to their home, we found Philip standing on the porch. After hugs and kisses, we were given a tour of their home. It was a one level ranch-style house with an open floor plan. Master bedroom, bath, and laundry room on one end with the kitchen, dining room, and living room in the middle, and two bedrooms and a full bath on the other end of the home. It was nicely decorated, and I was so happy for Juliet and Philip, happy they had found each other and the life they were living. It was wonderful to see Juliet so happy.

Lia was friendly. She showed us her room, and we discovered her interests. Philip wanted me to relax and enjoy the evening, so he made me a rum and coke drink. On my first sip, I found out how generous Philip was with his rum. I became very relaxed, was in bed early, and slept well that night.

Thanksgiving Day, one of Philip's favorite holidays, I found out how much Philip loved turkey and pumpkin pie. They had bought a twenty-six-pound turkey that Juliet had ready to put in the oven early Thanksgiving morning. So when I woke up, the wonderful aroma of a baked turkey was already filling the home.

"Philip, do you think you are going to have enough turkey to serve?" I asked.

"Gillian, I love a baked turkey and I want to make sure there is enough turkey left over to enjoy some good turkey sandwiches for several days after the Thanksgiving holiday."

While Juliet and I prepared some side dishes for the holiday meal, Philip went to the enlisted men's quarters to invite men who had not been invited to homes in the community to join us. He returned with one young man from Kansas who was grateful for the invitation. It was an enjoyable afternoon sharing stories of our different lives. Philip had opened my eyes to how easy it was to remember our servicemen and women and the sacrifices they make for our country.

Friday, after Thanksgiving, we spent time at the pool on base, had lunch at the bowling alley while playing three games, and after turkey sandwiches for dinner, we joined other military families, which included meeting their close friends, for an evening of fun and games at the Officer's Club. Saturday, we spent time shopping at the large outlet mall a few miles from town. Early Sunday morning, Pilar and I headed back to Colorado, listening to another book on tape. As the miles rolled by, I thought of all Juliet had achieved and how happy I was for her and the new life she now had with Philip and Lia. I was already looking forward to our next trip back to San Diego.

Arriving home, we discovered Josh and Luke had completed the shed and were laughing at some of their rough cuts. They said the turkey dinner was delicious and was one of the best meals they had eaten. It really was a time to count our blessings.

Over the next five years, farms and ranches in Gunnison and the surrounding areas were being divided up, and grazing pastureland was hard to find. Eventually, Josh purchased a hundred areas with a large pond in another county where we could pasture the cows during the summer months. To secure the property lines to the land, we needed to stretch five strands of barbwire a quarter of a mile north and south and another quarter of a mile east and west. To accomplish this task, Josh and I would drive the hundred miles on Wednesdays, my day off from my day job, work digging post holes or stretching wire, and then drive the hundred miles back. On weekends, Luke and Pilar would join us when they didn't have sports activities.

Once that large project was completed, Josh found different areas of pasture around the areas we lived in and made deals of building or repairing property lines in lieu of monthly fees for pasturing the cows. One summer, we missed our hometown July Fourth celebration, so a cross fence could be built on an owner's property. Work became our way of life, except for the kids, and I attending church on Sunday morning and Josh and I going to see Luke and Pilar play in their hometown games. I was in the trenches, trying to make every aspect of our lives succeed and never realized that my family was unraveling.

Luke and Pilar were good students and brought home good grades, both in sports, but their personal relationship was not good. It would be several years after they both graduated and left home when I would learn just how bad it was.

There were a couple of more trips to San Diego to celebrate Thanksgiving, and Luke would join Pilar and I on those trips, but Josh never wanted to go. By this time, both kids had their driver licenses, and I was in the back seat passing snacks and sandwiches forward from a large cooler. Fifty miles down the road, Luke was already asking, "Mom, what's in the cooler?" Those trips are fond memories for me.

One summer, Pilar would spend several weeks with Philip and Juliet earning money while taking care of Lia during the working hours. It was a great summer for Pilar to be with her big sister, Juliet, while building a friendship with Lia. Juliet and Philip would give the girls chores to do each day, and they didn't care when the chores were done as long as they were completed by the end of each day. It would also be the summer Pilar would discover and enjoy the TV series *M*A*S*H*. In this environment, Pilar discovered a new freedom she had never experienced, and it was difficult when she had to come back home to the regiment of her life on the ranch. She no longer wanted to be there.

In August of 2000, Juliet called me and said she was pregnant with my first grandchild. Lia was excited to be a big sister. I was so excited I was going to be a grandma. Luke and Pilar were excited to be an aunt and uncle. For Josh, it meant nothing.

Juliet had been an amazing big sister, was a good stepmom to Lia, and now she was going to give birth to her first child. I knew she would make a great mom. She was a girl that knew how to have fun.

The year 2001 would bring many changes to Philip and Juliet life. A healthy beautiful boy, Ryan James Anderson, was born March 26. I flew out to California to meet my grandson who felt like a special gift from God. The other addition to their family was a German Shepherd dog they named Rusty. While stationed at San Diego, Philip completed twenty years in the Marine Corps, and he decided to retire. But when 9/11 hit, his retirement was put on hold until it was decided that the enlistment numbers were up, and Philip was given the go-ahead to end his service with the Corps. A ceremony was held on base, and then Philip moved his family to Pasadena, California, where Juliet found a nursing position at the city hospital.

During the last few years in the Marine Corps, Philip earned a master's degree in business finance. Once the family was settled in Pasadena, it wasn't long before Philip received a position at a major insurance company and was enjoying working in civilian life.

June 2001, the doctor I worked for planned on taking his family on a vacation through Russia. He would be closing the office for two weeks. During those two weeks, I was scheduled to have a hysterectomy.

Juliet called and said, "Mom, I want to come and take care of you for a week when you first come home from the hospital. I'll bring Ryan with me. You will have some time to sit and hold him, and it will be fun to see Luke and Pilar play with him."

"That would be wonderful if you can schedule the time off from work. I know Luke and Pilar would love to see you and meet their new nephew. I'll talk to Josh about it and call you tomorrow."

After talking with Josh, he agreed it was a good idea to have Juliet come and help while I was recovering.

It turned out to be a very fun visit. Pilar loved holding Ryan and didn't shy away from changing diapers. Luke didn't change a diaper, but he enjoyed trying to get Ryan to smile and giggle while lying on the floor together. The week went by too fast, and when Juliet left, she even had a couple of casseroles in the freezer for us to enjoy.

Juliet hadn't been gone a week when one afternoon, while trying to do some walking exercises, my left leg began to hurt a lot. Going back inside, sitting down, and lifting my pant leg, I discovered my leg had swollen two sizes. Josh called the doctor and was told to bring me right in. I had developed a DVT in my leg which ran from my ankle to my groin. The doctor said if I hadn't come in, I could probably have died in my sleep that night. Now I was back in the hospital for another four days. Juliet wanted to come back, but I reassured her that the family would be okay. But the truth was we were not okay. Luke and Pilar's relationship with their father and each other was deteriorating. I just didn't realize it.

## 54

September 2001, Luke began his senior year of high school, and Pilar her junior year. Luke planned on participating in the basketball program while Pilar wanted to be involved in volleyball, basketball, and track. These two different schedules allowed Luke to spend more time with his dad, working on projects and when he had free time, enjoy mechanic work, and rebuilding cars while Pilar would be spending a lot of her time away from the ranch with her friends.

I thought both kids were happy with their schedules. What I didn't realize was as social and active as Pilar was, Luke wasn't. He was withdrawing away from his friends and any school events he could have attended. He was lacking in self-confidence, and I knew he was unhappy; I just didn't know how miserable he really was. I was praying that God would help me see him graduate high school. The other thing I didn't know was as much as I was praising him and encouraging him, his father was tearing him down by telling him he didn't have what it takes to succeed. Their relationship was seriously breaking down.

Josh had always been a tough controlling father who expected perfection, and when expectations were not met his temper flared. Under Josh's guidance, Luke learned that "hard work works." He began to possess a work ethic and a range of skills that were unmatched by his peers. Josh was now faced with losing his son to his own dreams. Those dreams didn't include living on the ranch anymore or working with his father.

The day after his high school graduation, Luke left home to spend the summer with Philip and Juliet in California. That is when he started to dream of a life beyond the ranch.

The one thing that Josh and I both wanted for Pilar and Luke was a college education. Pilar always enjoyed her academic studies and did well earning high marks. For Luke, school wasn't easy for him, and he had to work hard academically to maintain grades that kept him on the honor roll. Pilar looked forward to her college years while Luke wasn't even interested in applying to any college. His passion was doing mechanic work on automotive engines. He also spent the summer after his junior year of high school learning to fuel and maintain private planes at a small private airport near Gunnison.

While working there, he spent time talking with the aircraft mechanics and learned that working on aircraft engines was a lot cleaner job than on automobile engines. So his desire after high school was to go to NASCAR Technical Institute to improve his skills. He needed seventeen thousand dollars which included his own set of tools. Josh wasn't keen on the idea, but he gave Luke a choice.

"Luke, I want you to do that one year of college, and after that year, if college isn't your thing, I will help you go to NASCAR school. If you go to Western, I'll pay your tuition and fees, but I'm not going to pay for you to live at the dorms when you can live right here at home and commute."

Luke said, "I'll think about it over the summer and let you know."

The day that Luke left for California, I went with him. I wanted to spend time with him. I didn't want him to make the drive by himself, and it was an opportunity to see Juliet's family. Any time I was with Luke, we were always telling stories and sharing a laugh or two. One of my favorite memories of that trip was trying to keep on the schedule Luke had set for the trip. It took three hours to go from Gunnison to Cortez, Colorado. He gave me five minutes to use the restroom and be back in the truck. From Cortez, Colorado, to Flagstaff, Arizona, was another three and a half hours.

"Luke, I want to stop in Flagstaff and have lunch," I said.

"Sure, Mom, we can take a few minutes. No problem," he said.

While he filled the gas tank and paid, I used the restroom. Coming out the restroom, I asked him what he would like for lunch.

His reply was, "You want something to eat? Here, have a bag of pork skins."

"Pork skins. Pork skins! You are offering your mother *pork skins* for lunch!" I said indignantly. "Luke, I have just spent six and a half hours in a truck with no air conditioning, and some of that way was going with the windows down, hearing the wind blow while talking and laughing with you. I'm telling you right now we are going to take the time to get out of that truck and have a nice lunch, and you can stick your schedule and *pork skins* where the sun doesn't shine!"

"So you don't want the pork skins?" he said as he started laughing. He also agreed he was tired, wouldn't mind a break, and asked if I would drive for a while after lunch so he could sleep, which I was happy to do.

After eating and sleeping, Luke was more relaxed, and we enjoyed sharing stories and laughing. We spent the night in Kingman, Arizona, and arrived safely at Philip and Juliet's home the next afternoon. I stayed a couple of days enjoying our time together and had a special time with Ryan, seeing what he enjoyed playing as a toddler.

During the three months Luke spent in California, he worked two jobs and was able to save enough money that allowed him the freedom to make some decisions about his future. He wasn't sure he wanted to return home to the ranch. So I called him and shared my concern with him.

"Luke, one of the first big mistakes I made in my life was that I left home without my father's blessing. In many ways, I have had a good life, but it has not been an easy one. I really don't want to see you make the same mistake. I really want you to think about coming home and trying to work things out with your father."

"I know, Mom, and I have been thinking about it. The main reason I'm thinking about coming back is that if I do fail in life, my father will always say it was because I didn't do that year of college, and I don't want to give him that satisfaction. So I've decided to come back and try college for one year. But there are two things I want you to know. One, I'm not coming back to the ranch. I have made enough money that I can afford to live in the dorms on campus. Two, I am going to set boundaries with my father."

"I think those are two very good decisions, and I know God will honor you for them," I said.

I began praying that God would give Luke a good year at Western, that he would enjoy his roommate, make new friends, enjoy his classes, and even possibly participate in some of the sports programs. But it wasn't to be. Luke went to his classes, did his homework, spent most of his spare time at the gym working out, and he and his roommate went to blows with each other. In a small dorm room, his roommate spent every night on his computer on inappropriate sites, making it impossible for Luke to get a good night's sleep.

In November, I approached Josh about letting Luke have one of his rentals in town.

"Josh, you have a choice. You can either let Luke have one of your rentals, let him get a couple of roommates, be responsible for the utilities and collecting the rent, or you could visit your son in jail for almost killing someone in a fight. The choice is yours."

Josh gave Luke a three-bedroom apartment in one of the duplexes he owned in the middle of town. Luke moved in during Christmas vacation and began working part-time at the auto parts store in town. It wasn't long before Luke told his dad college wasn't for him, and he still had the desire to go to NASCAR school. That's when Josh told him he wouldn't support the idea nor pay for it. Luke now knew what his next step in life would be.

Luke had been talking to Philip about the Marine Corps and the opportunities it offered a young man if he was willing to work hard. One thing Luke wasn't afraid of was hard work. By being a Marine, he could challenge himself with his dreams, get the training he needed, and be part of a respectful organization. He talked with the Marine recruiter in town several times about being a helicopter mechanic and eventually enlisted. He would leave in October for boot camp.

## 55

In December 2002, Juliet called and invited Pilar and me to come to the Rose Bowl Parade in Pasadena, California.

"Mom, my friend, Riley, from work, who I've told you a lot about, has invited her mom, Eleanor, who lives in Texas, to come and attend the Rose Bowl Parade in Pasadena with her. Her mom is excited about the invitation and the event and is coming," she explained.

"That's really nice for Riley and her mom," I said.

"Yes, I'm really excited for her. Her mom will be driving out from Texas, and after the parade, she plans on staying and visiting for a while."

"Is she driving out by herself or is someone coming with her?"

"Not that I know of, Mom. It's my understanding she is comfortable traveling by herself," she explained. "So what I'm calling to tell you is that this week, Riley had a friend who heard about her mother coming and offered Riley a suite of special accommodations at a place she works at in Pasadena. The place is big enough to accommodate four to five people. Riley and I have always wanted our mothers to meet, and I'm always sharing stories about my brother and sister. So we thought it would be great if you and Pilar would also think about coming and going to see the Rose Bowl Parade in person with us. What do you say?"

"Wow! That sure is exciting and a wonderful invitation. I would love to come, and you know Pilar is always ready to pack her bags and leave. What is Philip's idea about it?" I asked.

"He's all for it! He said he and James, Riley's husband, could watch the parade together on television while our sons played with each other. It would also give the fathers some male bonding time with their sons."

"Let me talk to Josh about it, and then I will call you back," I said.

"Don't wait too long, mom. Riley needs to know your decision as soon as possible."

"I will try and call you with an answer tomorrow."

"Great, love you, Mom."

Josh was okay with us going but wasn't going to give us any money for expenses. That would have to come out of my own pocket. I saved my last paycheck in December for our trip. January 1 fell on a Wednesday that year, and both Pilar's schooling and my work didn't resume until January 6, so there was plenty of time to get back home after the January first holiday.

Pilar and I knew we could keep expenses down by making the trip in one day each way instead of two. Accommodations in California were already provided, so I called Juliet the next day and told her we were coming. Both Pilar and I were very excited about being spectators along the Rose Bowl Parade instead of seeing it on television. It was also another chance to visit with Juliet and Philip and hold that precious grandson of mine.

The day we embarked on our journey, Pilar asked if she could do most of the driving. This was fine with me. She was fully licensed, a good driver, and she knew I would rather be reading a book to her instead of driving as we traveled down the road.

"So, Mom, what's the title of the book you brought this time?" she asked.

"You know, I have been telling you about this series of books by Charles Swindoll called *Great Lives from God's Word*. Each book is a profile about one of the major characters in the Bible."

"Mom, really? You brought one of those books?" she said in a disappointed tone.

"Pilar, I have already read two in this series: one on the life of King David of Israel, and the other one was Queen Esther of Persia. They were both good reads, informative, and were written in a way that makes the reader curious to learn more about that person's life while reflecting on our own lives. I just got the latest one on Joseph, and I thought since I have you as my captive audience, I could share this book with you," I explained.

"What about a book by Karen Kingsbury? She's a Christian writer, and I really enjoy her inspirational stories" she said pleadingly.

"I tell you what I will do. Let me read the first couple of chapters, and if you aren't hooked after that, I'll stop, and I won't force you to listen to the rest of the book. Deal?"

"Okay, Mom, deal. You're pretty much right about a book, and I have loved the ones you have shared with me, so I'll give it a try," she said.

After two chapters, I stopped reading.

"Mom, why did you stop reading?" Pilar asked.

"That is the end of the second chapter. I said I would only read two. So what do you think?" I asked.

"You're right. It's good, mom. You can keep reading," she said.

"I knew I could hook you if you gave me a chance."

The miles passed by, and so did most of Joseph's story. I read until the night started coming on, and then I saved the rest of the story for our return trip home.

Once we arrived, we spent a fun evening with Juliet and Philip catching up on their lives. Ryan, now nineteen months old, was a little toddler, growing in his abilities, and Grandma especially enjoyed pushing him in his chair swing hanging from a tree in the backyard. I enjoyed singing all the nursery rhyme songs to my kids, and now I had a grandson I could play with and sing to at the same time. Pilar and I shared the swing time, and then Pilar would take Ryan and play with him on the living room carpet while we talked.

The next day, we drove over to James and Riley's house where we all became acquainted over a buffet luncheon. They were a family that was easy to like, enjoyed entertaining people, and it was a fun atmosphere for me to become acquainted with Riley's mom, Eleanor. Both Eleanor and I were happy about our children's friendships. In midafternoon, we said goodbye to the men, and we ladies headed for Pasadena. We checked into a beautiful hotel and found our suite roomy with upgraded accommodations.

The next morning, after breakfast, we headed to downtown Pasadena where Riley and Juliet already had our tickets for places to sit in stands at the beginning of the parade route. It was a beautiful clear day with mild temperatures. And when that B-2 Bomber flew above our heads, announcing the beginning of the Rose Parade, I was thrilled to be there. I felt truly blessed to share this event with my two daughters and new friends. The floats were beautiful with amazing designs, and I was looking forward to being able to see them up close on the Tour of Floats after the parade.

I enjoyed the bands, watching their rank and files and appreciate all their efforts both individually and as a band to march in Pasadena. It brought back special memories of the time my brother and I had marched in special parades with the Gunnison High School band. It was fun to hear famous people's names announced and to know we were that close to them. I was in awe of all the different entries moving along in front of us. All my life, I can remember gathering around a television to watch the Rose Parade, and now I was seeing it in person.

I wished the parade wouldn't end, but when it did, we climbed down from our seats in the stands and walked around the corner. I looked down the long street where the parade was still moving and saw the biggest mass amount of humanity I had ever seen in my life. I thought it would take hours to get to our car and onto the freeway, but to my amazement, with people's patience, it wasn't a bad experience.

We were now headed to where all the floats would be lined up, and we would be able to walk by them and see up close all the different flowers and vegetables used on the different floats. I was in awe of the creative talents of people to design and create such beautiful works of art. The vibrant colors enchanted me.

Once again, it was time to leave, and our adventure at the Rose Parade was over. We were headed to Riley's home where we would reunite with Philip, James, and the boys. Pilar and I would spend one more day at Juliet's house before heading home to Colorado the following day. Today, when I watch the Rose Parade, I'm around a television with family. As the parade begins, my mind wanders back to that beautiful day in Pasadena when I was one of the spectators along the sidelines. It's a good memory in my mind.

## 56

The year 2003 was the beginning of the end of my second marriage. And the spark began on a Wednesday morning. My day off from work. It was a cold frozen January morning, and Josh and I had just come into the house from feeding the cows and horses. We were sitting in the warm living room with our mugs of black coffee as I began to talk.

"Josh, I would like to tell you more about our trip to California and the wonderful time we had," I said.

"It was probably a good trip for you and Pilar to make," he replied.

"Besides the trip, little Ryan is the cutest kid and so much fun to play with. I'm sure you're going to enjoy being a grandfather to him," I said.

"You can stop right there, Gillian. I want you to understand I do not plan on being a grandfather to Ryan. He is not my grand-child, and I don't claim him. I don't want you to talk to me about him or encourage the situation in any way. I don't want to hear about him in this house. Do you understand?" And as he said it, his tone was cruel and cold.

I was stunned! I couldn't believe what I was hearing, and all I could say was, "No, I don't understand! Why? What did that little boy ever do to you to cause you to be so cold-hearted toward him?" I asked.

"He's not my grandchild. It's that simple," he said.

"Well, he's mine, and I love him! And I want him to be a part of my life! This is my house also, and I'm entitled to talk about my children and grandchild in my own home!" I said in a disgusted tone.

"Talk all you want to about Luke and Pilar or my family. Anybody else, I don't want to hear about them."

"Josh, I've dreamed about having my grandchildren come to this ranch. Seeing the different animals and learning about them. There is so much you know about farm and ranch life that you could share with children. They would love it," I said.

"Gillian, don't expect anything like that from me. Maybe with my own grandchildren someday, but nobody else. You're just going to have to figure out how you are going to handle it all. I've got work to do, and I'm going to go check on the stock," he said as he turned and walked out the door.

Something broke in me that morning. Besides being stunned, my heart was breaking apart in pieces. Just a few days ago, I spent time with this little boy. I played with him, sang songs to him, and held him close to my heart. Now, I daydreamed about seeing him again, only to find out he was not wanted in my own home. I felt like I had just entered another nightmare. Was this really happening? All I remember saying was, "Why, God? Why?" And the only thing I could think of was I had married a man with a very cold, hateful, and cruel heart.

I began thinking about all the years I had been with Josh and all the different situations and trials I had come through to try and keep the family together and stay true to my marriage vows. Vows I put before my children because I believed in my heart I was to honor and obey my husband above all others. And until this moment, I believed I had fulfilled those vows. I began to wonder that morning about the vows he said to me. He promised to love me. Now I knew that all the trials Josh had put me and my children through; there was no love in his heart for anyone. I began to wonder, *How could he even like himself?*

Then my thoughts turned to my children. With Juliet, he resented her being in my life. I knew he was jealous of the attention I gave her. But I thought he would eventually come to realize what a good kid she was and that I had more than enough love to spread between her and him. The truth was all he wanted to do was destroy our relationship. With Luke, at eighteen, I knew he was a bitter and angry young man, and I couldn't understand why. I was praying for him and that God would help him. It would be years before I would find out the whole truth of his situation during that last year of high school and the cruel remarks Josh was saying to him. However, I was to learn that God did answer my prayer with Luke in a mighty way. But, today, Luke went from being a small boy who was excited to be his father's right-hand man on any job that needed to be done to now having to set boundaries with his dad and didn't want to be around him.

With Pilar, she looked for every opportunity to be away from home. She was now a senior in high school with straight As and a top athlete also. She was looking forward to applying to a large university where she could get a degree and also play basketball. She was sure she would get an academic scholarship; she just didn't know how large a one. However, Josh ruined that dream for her when he made the rule about college if he was going to pay for it: the first two years at Western State rule.

During the fall and spring semesters, Pilar would get brochures from colleges and universities inviting her to apply for admittance. When he saw her looking at them, he would tell her, "Pilar, the only school you need to apply to is Western State. You can do your first two years of college there, and then I will help you go where you would like to finish your college education," he said.

Pilar applied to Western and to a college in Colorado Springs, Colorado. She was accepted at both schools, but when her scholarship came through, it only paid for half of what she needed at the school in Colorado Springs. Western was offering her a full tuition scholarship, and she received a second scholarship from the local utility company of full tuition plus a thousand dollars a year for book allowance. Each scholarship was for four years. She knew I didn't have funds to help her, and her dad wouldn't. So she complied with her dad's wishes and accepted the offer from Western. With the advanced classes she took in high school, she was able to register as a sophomore her first year of college.

Day by day, Josh and I started spending less time together. When he did ask me a question or try to start a conversation, my remarks were short and to the point. I kept thinking that I did not want to be a woman who had two divorces, but how was I to love a man who showed no love to me or my children? He just took from us what we could do for him. I felt more like an indentured servant than a wife and partner.

My thoughts now turned to Satan and the sermons I had heard about how he was the great destroyer. I remember preachers saying, "Give Satan a foothold in your life, and he will destroy it." I felt like Satan was attacking me and my family in a mighty way, and I knew there was only one thing I could do: pray. Rebuke Satan and pray. How many times had I heard that there was power in prayer? I didn't want another divorce, and I was sure God didn't want me to divorce either.

So the next time I was alone in my home, I did the only thing I believed would save my family. I prayed. I knelt in the middle of my living room, bowed my head to God, and asked him to help me. I needed his help. I rebuked Satan and told him to get out of my home and our lives. I prayed for Josh and asked God to change his heart to one that loved and showed the fruits of the Spirit instead of the wounded, bitter, angry man he had become. If God was going to help me fight my battles, I needed him now more than ever.

I began by changing my attitude. I was going to speak nicer to Josh and work beside him whenever he needed me, whether it was here at the ranch or going a hundred miles and walking a hundred acres spraying weeds on his land. Even with my improved attitude, there was a gap in our relationship that wasn't healing. In fact, now, when Juliet called me and we would have a conversation on the landline, the only phones we had, Josh would sit at the table and listen to my conversation, and when I hung up, he would belittle me for how I talked to her.

"Do you even listen to yourself with how you talk to her?" he would say.

My response to him would be, "You don't have to sit there and listen if you don't like how the conversation is going."

He would say, "That girl sure has you buffaloed" and walk out.

I wasn't praying only once a day. I now was having small conversations and requests before God several times a day.

Easter was approaching, and we always invited Josh's family from Cortez over for Easter Sunday dinner. His cousin and her husband were visiting from Georgia, and I thought I would call and extend an invitation to them as well. So I decided to talk to Josh about it.

"Josh, Easter well be in a couple of weeks, and I understand your cousin will be here visiting her parents also, so I would like to call them and see if they would like to come over for Easter dinner. Maybe Luke could get the day off from work and join us too."

His response was, "You just can't keep your nose out of Reynolds business, can you?"

"What are you talking about? I've been a Reynolds for over twenty years! What does me asking your family and our son to an Easter dinner have to do with your attitude about me being a Reynolds? You're not making any sense at all! I'm trying to do something nice for you! We have a lot of laughs and fun when we are all together."

"Well, if you think you need to have them over, go ahead and call them," he said as he walked out the door.

Besides Josh not making any sense, everything that was happening between us made no sense to me. By this time, all displays of affection had ended between us, and I felt it was hard for him to even be around me. I felt caught in a downward spiral of evil that I couldn't stop.

I placed the called to Josh's family, and they were happy to come. Luke came also, and it was so good to have us all together. Josh's uncle could tell the funniest stories about people and situations that happened around Gunnison, and for one afternoon, I was laughing and at peace.

After Easter, my thoughts turned to Pilar and her graduation from high school. She was the salutatorian of her class, and she would be speaking at the graduation ceremony. We had mailed out her invitations, and Juliet and her family would be coming for the event. My brother, Logan, and his wife, Lucia, said they would like to come, and my brother in Denver also responded that he was coming.

I wanted to plan a dinner at the house for everyone after the ceremony. Once again, I needed to ask Josh's permission.

"Josh, Pilar's graduation is in a few weeks, and I would like to plan a dinner here at the house for everyone that is coming to the graduation."

"Who all are we talking about?" he asked.

"Well, the ones who have RSVP are Juliet and her family, my two brothers, Logan and Nathan, along with Lucia and Luke who will join us also. I think Grandpa and Elly will come and join us after the ceremony."

"Go ahead and have your dinner," was all he said.

Once again, it was an enjoyable afternoon. We were all proud of Pilar's accomplishments. I was happy to have everyone come to the house for a celebration luncheon. During that visit, I took Ryan, now two years old, on a walk around the small pond behind the house. He had such a fun time throwing rocks into it and watching the water splash upward. After leaving the pond, we meandered down the winding dirt road which was bordered on both sides with tall pine trees and oak brush mixed in between them. Ryan would pick up a rock and throw it at a tree and giggle with delight. Just watching him filled my heart with such joy. I was glad I didn't know then that today would be my last day to have fun with Ryan on the ranch.

During the months of April and May, Josh had been searching for pasture around our area for a few of his cows. He found some available from a sheep rancher ten miles from our ranch. He told Josh he could bring the cows over on Saturday, May 31. Josh wanted to be sure Pilar and I were there to help him run the cows into the corral, load them up, and take them to pasture.

When Saturday arrived, Josh said, "Gillian, I'm going to go change water for the horses, and when I get back, I want you and Pilar be ready to run the cows in."

"While you do that, I am going to balance the checkbook," I told him.

I knew the balance in the checkbook was low, and I was hoping that we would be okay for the weekend, and then the rental money would come in. Sometimes in the past, I would have to ask Josh to transfer money to cover the draws, and at those times, he was not happy about how I was budgeting the account. The one thing I needed for him to do was either tell me he wrote a check or write it down because if he didn't, that would throw off my estimates. As I was making the calculations, I saw a check for fifty dollars that went through the bank, but it hadn't been entered in the check register. Or he never mentioned it to me since we hadn't been talking to each other very much. I now knew we were overdrawn. I would have to tell him about the overdraw when he came back, and it wasn't going to be an easy conversation to have with him.

So as he entered the house and asked me if we were ready to go, I told him I needed to talk about the checking account.

"Just don't tell me we are overdrawn," he said.

"Josh, you wrote a check for fifty dollars that went through the bank, and you did not tell me about it or write it down," I said firmly.

"Oh, yeah, it's my fault, right? You're supposed to be a 'detail-oriented person,' and you can't keep a simple checkbook balanced!" he yelled.

He looked at me with total disgust. Years ago, a former boss said I was a detailed-oriented person. Ever since I told Josh about that compliment, he liked to ridicule me with it, especially when he learned I made a mistake or found and error. I walked out the door, headed to the field as he continued to yell and get on his horse.

As we were maneuvering the cows toward the corral, Pilar ran ahead into the corral, quickly grabbed a bucket of grain, poured some into one trough, and turned to put some more in a trough across the way just as the cows were heading into the corral. Pilar's movement in the corral spooked the cows, and they turned back into the yard. Josh just started screaming at Pilar. I thought the tension couldn't get much worse. On our second attempt, as they ran into the corral, Pilar locked the gate as her father continued to yell at her. I looked at Pilar. She was looking at me with an expression of "When, Mom? When, Mom, are you going to do something?"

I turned to Josh and yelled at him, "Josh, stop yelling at Pilar right now! You are not going to talk to her that way. She was only trying to help entice them into the corral!"

"Gillian, you shut your damn mouth right now!" he yelled.

I stood there for five seconds as he tied his horse to the corral, and as he was walking my me, he said, "You always have to be saying some damn thing out of your mouth."

I pointed my finger right at him, and with the strongest voice of determination, I said, "Josh, I am not shit under your feet, and you can move your own goddamn cows!" I walked into the house, grabbed the newspaper, my purse and car keys, got in my car, and drove away.

## 57

Leaving the property, I turned south down the dirt road that took me to the highway. Then I turned east, headed for Gunnison. I was mad—so mad! I wasn't crying yet. I was too mad to cry! All I could think of was, *Why, God, why? Why didn't you answer my prayers and help me save this marriage! The last thing I wanted was an end to this marriage and to be a woman divorced twice.*

"Are you listening to me God?" But as the miles went by, I knew that was exactly what was going to happen and what I was going to be. And then I thought, *God, I know you don't want that either. But how am I supposed to stay in a marriage with a man that has nothing but contempt for me, my daughter, and can show no love to his own children?* As I continued to drive, I wondered where it all went wrong again.

Reaching the city limits of Gunnison, I was trying to think about the best place I could go where it would be quiet and I could spend some time pulling myself together. I then realized it was a Saturday afternoon, and the hospital in town would not be busy with a lot of people having appointments. Check-ins on weekends were in the front of the hospital through the emergency room entrance. The back entrance was where the doctors' offices were located and for people to enter who had appointments with scheduled surgeries. Today, that area would be mostly deserted.

So I drove to the parking lot in the back where I did four days a week and found only a few parked cars. Getting out of the car, I grabbed my purse and the daily newspaper. I walked across the parking lot, walked up to the building, pulled open the door, and glanced into the reception area. It was deserted. The only light entering the area was coming through the large floor-to-ceiling windows on the west side. I was so relieved that no one was there and that I could have some time alone.

I walked over to the chairs in the waiting area, sat down, placed my head in the palms of my hands, and now the tears came. Tears of "why" kept multiplying; tears of wondering what it was about me that the men that I gave my heart to could not return that love. Another why! I really considered myself a good wife, the kind of wife God wanted me to be. I was supportive of what both my husband's dreams and goals were, and I felt I gave 150 percent toward both men's expectations, especially Josh's. But instead of loving me more or even appreciating what I had done to help them, they had no desire to love me, be nice to me, or even to my children who had also helped. All of us had especially helped Josh achieve his dreams, and he showed us nothing but contempt. I said to myself, "I prayed, God, for you to help me. Why do I feel like you didn't want to answer my prayer? Have I been that bad?"

As I kept crying, I began thinking in my mind that nothing made any sense to me. Absolutely nothing! I started wondering why Josh wanted to be so mean all the time. What is it that I did or didn't do or possibly Luke and Pilar did or didn't do that would cause him to be so bitter, angry, and hateful to us? Josh couldn't have had a better son or a harder worker beside him than Luke, and he couldn't even be nice to him. Their relationship was now strained. He had a beautiful daughter who had also helped when she was asked, was a high achiever, and he had no desire to help her reach her dreams. It was always what Josh wanted done next to achieve his next goal.

"Where is my God? Why aren't you helping me?" I certainly knew where the devil was. He was in the center of my home and had successfully accomplished his goal of destroying my family. Twice now, he had done this to me!

Calming down, I needed to decide where I was going to go. How was I going to live? I had a few hundred dollars in my checking account which wouldn't go far. I began thinking what an ironic situation this was. With the ranch and the rentals we owned, a person would have thought I had the money to buy any room in town. The only problem was the ranch, the rentals, and the money all belonged to Josh. What was mine was the amount in my checking account.

I picked up the paper and turned to the classified ads on the last pages. I skimmed though the sections on houses and apartments for rent, but they weren't realistic situations for me. I remember praying, "God, if you are here for me, show me what I am supposed to do. Where am I going to go, God?" I looked back into the paper, and I saw the section on "Rooms for Rent," and they were priced at what I could possibly afford, but I needed one that was furnished. The first number I called, a lady answered.

"Hello," I said, "I am calling about the ad for a room for rent. Is it still available?"

"Yes, it is, but it wouldn't be available until Monday. My husband and I need the weekend to clean it and get it ready to rent. How soon do you need a place?" she asked.

"Monday would be great! Can you tell me where it is located and a little about your home situation?"

"We're in the northern part of town, near the park. Our home is a two-story. My husband and I live upstairs, and the downstairs we have converted into a kitchen dining area, one bathroom, and two bedrooms. You would be sharing the bathroom and kitchen area with another lady that is occupying the other bedroom. She is an older lady, lives quietly, and works at the college."

"If it's possible, I would like to come by and see it now, and if it is what I am looking for, I could give you a deposit to hold the room for me until Monday."

"Yes, my husband and I are both here right now, so it would be a good time to meet and talk about living arrangements and expectations."

I wrote down the address and realized the house was only about five minutes away. I then decided to call my good friend, Patricia, and see if I could stay with her for the weekend.

"Hello, Patricia, this is Gillian," I said.

"Hi, there, what are you doing today?" she asked in a friendly way.

"Patricia, I need a favor." I started trembling and continued to say, "I have left Josh. I need a place to stay for the weekend. Can I come and stay with you until Monday?" I asked.

"Oh, Gillian. Of course, you can. This is a perfect weekend because Joe is on the road and is out of town for the weekend. He probably won't be back until the middle of next week," she said. "It's just Emma and I for the weekend. Why until just Monday, Gillian? You know you can stay longer if you need to."

"Patricia, I may have found a room to rent in a home in Gunnison, but it won't be available to occupy until Monday. I just called the owners of the house, and they can see me now. So, before I drive out to your place, I'm going over there now and if the arrangement will work for me. I want to put a deposit down so they will hold the room for me."

"Where is the house located, Gillian?"

"On Second Avenue in the northern part of town by the park. I think it is a good location. It is not very far from my brother's house. Say a prayer for me, Patricia. I'm going to need all the luck I can get right now."

"I'll be praying. Come as soon as you can."

Leaving the hospital area, I drove the short distance, and within five minutes, I began pulling up to the front of the house. I liked the appearance of the home and its location. My brother's home was just up the hill and down the street. It was also one block from a small park and a landscaped area which ran directly behind the hospital where my work was located. The doctor's office I worked at was a short distance down a nice walking trail, so I decided I could save money and walk to work. I also thought the time walking alone would be good for me both mentally and physically. Getting out of the car and walking up the sidewalk and stairs to the front door, I said a small prayer, "Lord, let this work for me for right now."

As the door opened, I was met with a friendly smile and hello from a small-framed woman with black hair.

"I'm Sharon. Are you Gillian?" she asked.

"I am. I appreciate you seeing me today and letting me have a look at the room."

"It's perfectly fine. Come into the living room area. I would like for you to meet my husband, Michael. He is a teacher at Gunnison High School."

"I see you are also expecting a little one. When are you due?"

"The early part of September. It will be our first child."

"Congratulations," I said as I entered a large open area containing the living room, kitchen, and dining areas. Michael, a small-framed man with brown hair and a mild manner, welcomed me to their home.

Sitting in the living room area, Sharon asked if I would tell her and Michael a little about myself.

How many times had I asked that same questions to the many people that I had rented apartments and homes to, and now, as they say, the shoe was on the other foot. I knew from experience the only thing I could do was to be straightforward and honest about my situation. I was not going to start off telling a lie.

"The best way I can introduce myself to you is to be honest with you."

Sharon and Michael looked at each other and smiled.

"A couple hours ago, I just left my husband of twenty-three years, and I need a place to stay while I will be seeking a divorce from him."

Laura and Michael said nothing. They just sat quietly and allowed me to continue talking.

"I have lived in the Gunnison area for about forty years. I have three children. My oldest daughter lives in California with her family. I have a son who lives in Gunnison and works at the auto parts store. He will be leaving for Marine boot camp in October. And my youngest daughter just graduated from Gunnison High School and lives at home right now. However, I think her plans will be changing also. I have a part-time job at the oral surgeon's office in the hospital and will be working there four days a week. Wednesday is my day off. I am looking for a quiet place to be by myself, giving me time to think and plan my next steps. May I ask how long of a lease you require?

"Gillian," Sharon said, "we rent our rooms on a month-to-month basis and we don't require a signed lease. Michael and I are Christians, and when we bought this home, we dedicated it to God. We also knew we wanted to help people, and we thought the best way we could do that would be to give them a place to stay if they had that need. Over the years, we have rented to a variety of different people, so if you like the room we have available, you can stay as long as you like."

"Wow! That's amazing! I didn't know people in Gunnison who had property rented like that. It sure makes it easier for me already."

Michael said, "Gillian, I want you to know the room is small, but it is conveniently located close to the kitchen and bathroom areas. So if you are looking for something larger, this may not meet your needs."

"Michael, I'm not looking for big. Small will work just fine with me. I grew up in a very small bedroom and have good memories of that room. If you think you would both would be okay renting to me, knowing what my situation is, I would like to see the room now."

"Sure, I'll be glad to show it to you," Michael said.

Michael showed me out the front door. We went down the stairs and around the corner of the house that led to the garage area. He explained to me I would enter though this door that would lead me into the kitchen area. Entering the area, and just to the right, was a landline phone which sat on a cabinet that held books that were free to read. I noticed the room was very clean, adequately furnished with a nice dining table which could seat four people easily. A small full-sized bathroom was off the kitchen area, and Michael led me just around the corner to a small room that had a twin bed and a little side table beside it. A comfortable chair that reclined was next to the table. A closet that was covered by curtains was near the end of the bed, and the only window letting in light was a small one at ground level. I thought the place was perfect and just what I needed. I told Michael I would take it and gave him the deposit, and I would be back Monday to occupy it.

Heading out of town, I realized I would be driving by Sue's house, my friend and colleague I worked with at the doctor's office.

Sue and her husband, Joe, were also leaders in a small church on the Mesa just outside Gunnison. Over the years, I had attended women's Bible studies in their home, which Sue led, and the kids and I had attended their church on special occasions, and Joe was also a teacher at Gunnison High School where Luke and Pilar attended, and he had taught both. I considered them good friends and spiritual confidants. I decided I would stop and see if they were home before going on to Patricia's.

Pulling off the highway and driving around a paved curved road that went by the small church, I saw Sue out in the yard. She waved to me as she walked into a shed to put an item away. I pulled up in front of their home on the property, got out of the car, and waited for her to come out of the shed.

"Hi, Sue," I said as she locked the shed and started walking up to me.

"Hello, what are you out and doing today?" she said.

"Sue, is Joe also home?" I asked.

"No, he's out helping a member of our church with a project he has on his land. Why do you ask?"

"Sue, I've left Josh. I wanted you to know about it before I saw you Monday at work. I thought if you were both home, I could talk to you about it. I'm on my way to Patricia's to spend the night."

"Oh, Gillian, I'm so sorry. Please come into the house, and we will visit. I know it has not been an easy situation for you."

Entering the house and sitting in the living room, I explained again to Sue that I thought it was better if I saw her today and explained my situation rather than at the office on Monday morning. She agreed. Sitting there, drinking a glass of water, I explained what happened at the ranch earlier in the day, my time at the hospital, and the room I had rented. She was compassionate, understanding, and urged me to come back and visit when Joe would be home. I told her I would like to talk with him also. Driving away, I was looking forward to my next visit in their home.

I was now headed to Patricia's house. I felt good with what I had accomplished in just a short time in one day. I was really look-ing forward to that small room and time for myself. I'm not sure if I thanked God for helping me find that small room, but I do remember asking God, "Why?" Again, "Why?"

When Patricia opened the door, I fell into her arms. She held me as I cried and said, "Gillian, he doesn't deserve you. You have to believe he doesn't deserve you."

"I know," I said. "It's just so hard to believe that it's all over, but I just can't take any more of his hate."

"I prayed, Patricia, for God to help me save this marriage. Why didn't he help me? Oh, Patricia, I am looking at being a woman divorced twice! That is just so hard for me to accept."

"I don't know, Gillian. I just know that he does not deserve you for how hard you have worked for him all these years and the abuse you have taken from him, especially toward Juliet. You have worked so hard all these years to please him, and he just does not care about anybody but himself."

"Oh, Patricia, it just seems so unreal that nothing I ever do is good enough. But I just cannot stop the evil that he keeps dishing out. The only way I know how to stop it is to walk away, and then I don't know if it will stop then."

"Well, I'm glad you finally had the sense to walk away. I want you to come and take a shower, and I will give you some pajamas to wear tonight. We can talk some more later. Emma will be home soon, and she will be glad to see you."

*****

Sunday, I called Pilar. I was glad she was the one that answered the phone (None of us had cell phones at this time, only landlines). I told her where I was, and she said she was coming right over. When she arrived, she had brought with her a bag of my clothes and some toiletries she thought I would need for a few days. I told her my plans of getting my own place in town and the small room that I would be renting in a private home in town. Pilar seemed relieved that something was finally going to be done about the domestic situation.

Monday, after breakfast, I gave Patricia and Emma a goodbye hug and thanked them for being there for me in my time of need. I would stay in touch with them. Patricia said she would be checking on me and would also be coming by to see my new place as soon as I got settled. I hugged Pilar goodbye, told her I loved her, and said I would like to see her after she got off work. She was happy I asked her.

Walking into work on Monday was not easy. A lot of the things and stories I told in the doctor's office made our family sound like one that supported each other, worked together to get any job done, and on Wednesdays, my day off, was Josh's and my day for business in town with a lunch at a local restaurant and time spent working on the ranch together. And all those stories were true. But I never talked about Josh's other personality which displayed a quick temper that easily became angered and enraged over the slightest error or a mistake an animal made or one of us made helping him. The constant put-downs, belittling, and snide remakes about us, his immediate family, or extended family members he generally wanted nothing to do with, or other people in the cattle business that just did not measure up to his standards—it was these stories I never told was why now I would be telling my colleagues that I was leaving him.

Before the first patient was seen, I quietly told the doctor and nurse about my weekend. Sue was there to support me. Naturally, they were shocked and would never have thought it would have been possible with the stories I had told. They were sorry for me and my family and offered me their support.

Monday, after work, I went to the local department store and bought a pillow and some bedding and a few more toiletries. I also went and bought a few grocery items to have something to eat at the new house. I then drove to the home in town where I would be living, paid a month's rent, and moved into that little room. How long would I be living there? I just did not know. All I knew was right now was it would be on a month-to-month basis.

I made my bed and was placing the few toiletries that I had in my possession when an elderly woman walked by my room and introduced herself.

"Hello," she said. "My name is Barbara. I rent the larger room just down the hall. I have lived here for two years, and I work up at the college in the cafeteria."

"Hi, I'm Gillian, and I feel lucky to have found this room to rent."

"Sharon and Michael told me about your situation, and if you ever want to talk, I'll be glad to listen. Sharon and Michael are good people, and I think you will like renting from them."

"Thanks for the information. They seem like nice people. I look forward to getting acquainted with you. I just need a few days to move in and get my room set up. Everything seems to be happening rather fast, and I am a little overwhelmed at the moment."

"I understand completely having gone through it myself. I'm usually around in the evenings either playing cards or putting puzzles together, so feel free to join me anytime."

"Thanks, I'll do that."

Pilar came by after work. She liked my little room and the way the downstairs had been converted to meet the needs of the renters. We had a nice short visit, and before she left, I asked her to tell her father I would like to talk to him Saturday morning and that I would also be getting more of my things. She agreed to be there.

*****

Saturday morning, I drove out to the ranch, parked the car in front of the corral, and as I was getting out of the car, Pilar was walking out of the house.

"Is your dad here?" I asked.

"Yes, he's putting on his boots and said he would be out." She decided she would go back into the house so we could talk in private.

It wasn't long before Josh came out of the house and was walking up to me like I had disturbed his morning.

"So what do you want?" he said in a disgusted tone.

"Josh, I've come to tell you I'm not coming back."

"Oh, Gillian, I don't want you back! No way I want you back!"

"Josh, I came back once hoping things would be different. But nothing ever really changed. You have more now than you have ever had, and you're just bitter and angry all the time. I've tried hard to please you and give you what you want, but nothing I do pleases you."

"Well, you're right about that. You don't please me, and I don't want you. So you can just leave!"

"I would like to get the rest of my clothes while I'm here."

"I'm leaving to change the water. When I leave the house, you can go in and get your clothes."

"All right," I said.

I watched him walk away and was glad I was not going to be around when he came back from changing his water.

Pilar helped me pack up the car and said she would be by later to see me. I was looking forward to her coming to see me.

Driving down the gravel road and away from the property, I also made another decision. I was going to get my divorce. Josh had one savings account at a bank in town that I could deposit and withdraw money to carry out transactions for him when I was in town. I needed a lawyer and money to obtain this divorce, and Josh was going to be paying for it. Monday, I withdrew half from that account and set up my own account in another bank in town.

## 58

Walking the trail to and from work four days a week gave me time to reflect and think. My main thought as I walked was wondering why the men I gave my heart and love to were not able to love me in return. I heard once that to have a successful marriage, each partner had to give more than 100 percent of their devotion, time, and effort to the marriage. In both my marriages, I felt I had given 150 percent, and it still was not good enough.

I was also finding solace in the small room that was now my new residence. Instead of hurrying home go get supper on the table by six o'clock and also work on a "to-do list" to keep things organized each day in a home, I was leisurely walking toward that small room and eagerly looked forward to some quiet time alone behind a closed door. The main thought that consumed those quiet moments was, "What is it that I do or do not do that makes me a failure at marriage?" I believed in my heart that I supported and helped my husbands in their life goals to the best of my abilities. I believed I was not demanding nor greedy for more than what we had, was also a good mother to their children, and believed God had helped me to find ways to meet my needs for my children when they wouldn't. I felt like I had been the woman God wanted me to be in both marriages, but the woman I had been to them was not what they wanted.

Besides the special times in my room alone, I was enjoying sitting in the common kitchen area and becoming acquainted with the other tenant, Barbara. In the mornings, we were both hurrying out the door to our jobs, but around the kitchen table at night, as each of us was preparing our evening meal, we enjoyed friendly conversations, and we both learned we shared a lot in common.

"Gillian, I too am divorced and have been for a long time. I was in an abusive relationship also, so I know what it feels like to have loved someone and not be loved in return."

"Barbara, after pondering mine and possibly your situation too, I've come to the conclusion that I think I just don't understand men at all. I have watched the television series, *Reba*, about a dysfunctional family. And I asked my oldest daughter, Juliet, why would a man who could have a wife like Reba—who is beautiful, smart, intelligent, and does well running the family home—choose to want to be with a ditzy, emotional, needy woman who always has a problem?"

"What did Juliet say?" Barbara asked.

"Mom, the ditzy, emotional woman needs him. Reba doesn't. Reba is a confident woman who can handle any problem that comes along and keeps it all together. The other woman has a lot of insecurities, needs help, and she seeks it from her husband who solves her problems and makes her feel secure. Mom, men like to feel needed."

"I've also enjoyed watching the Reba show, too, Gillian, and wondered the same thing. I had a lady at church who is also divorced, and she told me if she ever marries again, she will not be as independent as she was with her now former husband. So there is probably some truth to what Juliet says."

"Barbara, I never felt like I was an independent woman or wanted to be an independent woman in my marriages. I felt like I was needed, and I enjoyed helping my husbands do whatever they wanted to accomplish, to build the life we were trying to have together."

"What about time for yourself, Gillian? What did you want to do or accomplish?"

"Barbara, I think the day that my desires and dreams ended was the day I resigned my teaching position in San Antonio, Texas. I wanted to be with the man I loved. His dreams became my dreams. When Ricardo and I started our life in Fairbanks, Alaska, I had just resigned my teaching position. I really enjoyed teaching children and knew it was what I wanted to do in life. So when we got settled in Fairbanks, I went to the local school district and inquired about a teaching position for the coming school year. I learned there were twenty-five applications for every teaching position. The only position available was to fly into the bush and teach in a remote village. I could be gone five days a week and be home on weekends. I was newly married, plus flying into remote bush area was not appealing to me. I asked why there were so many applications per position. They informed me it was because of the Trans-Alaska Pipeline System that was being built across Alaska and the top wages that were being paid which attracted single and young married couples. Alaska also paid higher wages than the lower forty-eight states to attract teachers who were willing to teach in remote rural areas.

"After learning more about the community I was now living in, I started applying for a job at the local banks. Same story there: lots of applications for one position. I walked the streets of Fairbanks for two days looking for waitress work. There was just nothing available. In September, I learned I was pregnant with Juliet, so I quit looking, and we tried to make it on the salary Ricardo brought home. We struggled that year in Alaska. It was with the help of friends that we made it.

"When my first marriage failed, I went home to Gunnison, went to the local school district, again nothing available, and that is when I got into bookkeeping at the local motel and eventually found a good job doing accounting and payroll at the local steel fabrication company. I worked there until I became pregnant with Luke two years after I married Josh. A year later, Pilar arrived. I loved raising my children and helping Josh achieve his dreams. The problem was Josh made it so hard for Juliet and me to enjoy our lives and dreams while living with him.

"It seems like after I resigned that teaching position in San Antonio, I was learning to survive with the circumstances I was living under and never thought about seeking my career or desires. Now, once again, I sit before you, trying to figure out how I will survive and what am I going to do in life."

"Gillian, I attend the same church that our landlords, Michael and Sharon, do. I ride to church with them on Sundays, and I know they would be glad if you would like to come with us. There's also a nice women's Sunday school class."

"Barbara, I was raised in a Christian home and have been going to church all my life. I've liked studying God's Word, helping in his church, and being in women's Bible studies. I've considered myself a Christian because I believe I'm a sinner in need of a Savior. Jesus Christ is my Savior. I have tried to live my life as one of his disciples, believed I was married to Christian men, raised my children to know God, Jesus, and the Holy Spirit. But as I also sit before you today, I'm not sure where God is right now in my life. I have read about the more abundant life God has for a person if they accept his gift to man, a Savior, his Son, Jesus, then follows and obeys him. At times, I think I had that life, but somehow, I always end up in a bucket of shit. Thanks for asking, but no, I do not want to go to church and I don't want to pick my Bible up and read it. I'll say goodnight, Barbara."

"Gillian, I would like to pray for you and what you're going through."

"I've always believed in prayer, Barbara. And I know he has answered some prayers in my life. Some he has not. I prayed for my mother when she was so sick with cancer for healing and a longer life. God took her home. I understand and accept not answering that one. I really prayed and believed God would help me save my marriage with Josh. Not only did he not answer it, but I also believe he wasn't helping me to save it either. You can pray for me, Barbara, but like I said. I'm not sure what God's and my relationship is right now."

In June, I received the name of a divorce lawyer in Gunnison from a colleague at the doctor's office. I placed the call, introduced myself, explained some of my circumstances, especially the prenuptial agreement, and he said he would be glad to meet with me. I arranged an appointment with him on Wednesday, my day off.

Arriving for our meeting, I discovered him to be young with a few successful years behind him. He was kind, responsive to my inquiries, and asked questions to further analyze my situation. He was up-front with me that the prenuptial agreement could be a problem. To me, this revealed his honesty. He explained how much it would cost for me to obtain him as my lawyer. He wanted half of it paid up front and the balance at the end of the proceedings. I agreed to his terms, wrote him a check, and left his office. I was glad proceedings were underway, but I also felt incredibly sad about what I was doing. After twenty-two years of trying to help a man with his dreams and make him happy, it all came down to "He did not want me anymore." And it would be years before I would learn the truth of what had been happening in my home and never realized it. A week later, I walked into his office and signed the papers to begin the dissolution of my second marriage.

Walking along the trail to and from work each day helped to combat my sadness, and I looked forward to going to work. The doctor's office was an environment of professional attitudes where close-knit and interpersonal relationships grew. The people I worked with were all Christians, and each day, one of us would share an experience we had at church or what God was doing in our prayer life or the different events happening in our family, especially with our children. For many years, I always had something to contribute whether good or bad to the conversations. Now when the conversations turned to God, I would remain silent or just walk away.

My friend, Sue, was quick to pick up on my changed demeanor. So one day before we opened the office up to patients, she approached me with a question.

"Gillian, are you mad at God?"

"I'm not mad at God, Sue. I'm more disappointed in God. In a way, I feel betrayed by him. I sincerely prayed and asked him to help me save my marriage. And I really believed he would help me because I know he does not like divorce, and neither do I. I have been through it once, and it's painful. Now, here I am again, and I am going to be a woman twice divorced. It even makes me feel horrible to say it. But that is what I am going to be. I really believe in my heart I am better than that image and my kids deserve better also. We've had enough hate in our lives."

"Gillian, I spoke to you once before about coming to dinner at our home and talking with Joe and me. We only want to help you. Will you come?"

"Yes, I'd like that. It would be good to talk about what I am feeling. Both you and Joe know our family, and Joe's been a teacher to both Luke and Pilar."

A couple of evenings later, I was sitting at Sue and Joe's table, explaining the events that had taken place and why I was seeking a divorce.

"Joe, I know I am breaking my wedding vows, and I know God doesn't like divorce, but I feel relieved that I finally made the decision to walk away. My kids tell me, 'I wished you would have done it sooner and not waited so long.' I really did not know they were that miserable. I am also feeling ashamed of having to divorce to bring sanity and a place of safety to our lives."

Joe responded by saying, "Gillian, the first thing I want you to realize is that Josh broke his wedding vows to you. He promised to love you, and he did not keep that promise. Second, I had concerns about Luke with his behavior his senior year. He seemed withdrawn, depressed, and angry. With what you're telling me was happening in your home, I now know my concerns were right. Children do not deserve to live in an unhealthy environment in their home, and a wife does not deserve to be abused, mentally or physically. I am happy with the steps Luke has taken to live on his own and to set boundaries with his father. He seems to be happy about becoming a Marine."

"Joe, he is extremely excited about his future as a Marine and he is working hard physically to be prepared for bootcamp in the fall."

"Did you have any concerns about Pilar?"

"I wondered more about Luke and Pilar's home life and what was making Luke so unhappy. But Pilar seemed more socially connected to her school activities and friends. She also did very well in her classes. Joe, things seemed to go from bad to worse last summer when I had to have major surgery and could not help in any way with the summer work. A week after the surgery, I developed a blood clot in my left leg that put me back in the hospital. A lot more responsibility was put on both Luke and Pilar. I remember days laying in the bed downstairs, and Luke would walk in so unhappy, and he seemed so miserable.

"When I realized that, I laid in that bed and prayed for him, asking God to help him and bring him through whatever he was going through. Even after I recovered, he still seemed unhappy going into his senior year. He was on the honor roll all year but did not seem to have much of a social life. I tell people, 'I prayed for him through that year.'"

We had a good discussion, and as I was preparing to leave, Joe wanted to give me some tapes from his library to listen to. Upon handing them to me, I noticed they were by one of my favorite Christian pastors and authors, Charles Swindoll. I had read several of his books and occasionally heard him speak on the radio as I drove to and from work. There were twelve tapes, each one dealing with a different struggle people face in life.

"I'll take the tapes, Joe, but I'm not sure exactly where God and I are in our relationship with each other. Right now, I am feeling betrayed, not only by Josh but God also. I know that what I am going to do will be breaking my marriage vows. I honestly believed God should have helped me save this marriage, and he didn't, and I do not know why. Is there anything on those tapes that will explain that to me?"

"Try looking at it another way, Gillian. Maybe he did answer and said no because he thinks you deserve better."

"I'd like to believe you're right, Joe."

I took the tapes, said goodnight, and drove to that little room that was my place of shelter and refuge. Little did I know that upon listening to those tapes and journalizing what I would be learning from them that it would be one of the first steps on a journey I would begin to building my new relationship with God.

The weekend I was staying with my friend, Patricia, I called Juliet to inform her of the events that happened and told her I was leaving Josh and seeking a divorce. I was surprised by her response.

"Mom, I knew you would leave him. I just didn't know when you would leave," she said.

"How did you know?" I asked.

"The last few times I have talked with you, you sounded so unhappy. You never really said what was going on. I could just hear it in your voice. So tell me how you're feeling right now."

"Juliet, you know better than anyone knows how hard he has been to live with, and now when he looks at me, it's with disdain, or when we would talk, which is very little anymore, he's usually checking with me to see that I am ready to help him. The request is more like a command. Ever since Pilar and I came back in January from seeing the Rose Bowl Parade, and he told me how he felt about the family, our relationship has spiraled downward. After that conversation, I admit I wasn't loving and warm to him, and he became angry and mean with his comments to me. I realized I needed to be the one to change if I was going to save this marriage.

"So I started praying for God to show me a way. I started trying to do nice things for him, but he would just throw them back in my face. By the end of May, what happened with the cattle was the final straw. His family does not deserve the treatment he dishes out to us."

"I'm sorry you're hurting, Mom, but I'm not sorry you're leaving him."

"Juliet, I am so disappointed in God. I really believed he would show me what I needed to do to save the marriage. The way I am feeling right now, I don't know if I want to serve him anymore."

"Mom, I will not allow you to do that! No way! You are one of the strongest Christian women I know, and I also know how much you love your Lord. You're mad and hurting right now. That's understandable with all the pain you're feeling, but you need him now more than ever to see you through with this decision."

"Juliet, I'm numb. I can't pray. I don't feel like reading my Bible, and I don't want to go to church."

"Mom, you have to trust him and know he is there for you. With all the struggles and hard times you have endured in the past, you have always trusted the Lord to lead and guide you. You have a great faith, and you will never ever convince me that you don't love your Lord."

"Well, right now, I'm taking each day as it comes. Not sure about anything else."

"Mom, why don't you to come and see us? Bring Pilar. We can talk, and you both can spend some time with Ryan. He would love the attention."

"That's not possible right now. I have my job, and I am going to need the money. I want to be here for Pilar and spend time with Luke before he leaves in October. They both support my decision and have plans to stop by and see me occasionally."

"Well, will you think about coming to California when the divorce is final?"

"Yes, I promise I will consider it. I just don't know when that will be."

"God loves you, Mom, and so do I."

"I love you, too, Juliet. Bye."

"Bye, Mom."

During the month of June, the effort I was putting into my days to not have anything to do with God seemed to only make me think more of him. Questions about him kept popping into my mind. Like, just who was this God that I tried to honor and obey, but I continually ended up feeling like such a failure? What is it about him that I do not understand? Why does he answer some prayers and not others? Why do I feel like I am always struggling through life, making wrong decisions, especially in relationships with men when I only try to be the best I can be for them? Many nights, I would fall to sleep, wondering, *Why?* During those nights. as I lay crying, I started telling God exactly how I felt.

"God, when I wanted to leave home at eighteen and go away to college, I was seeking a different life. All I really wanted was to have some of the same experiences other girls have, especially living in a dorm with other girls, and having dates with boys. Was that so wrong? Or was it going against my father's wishes? Did I not 'honor' him enough in my life? Is that the road of doing things my way and suffering the consequences for it? Oh, God, in both my marriages, I truly do not know what it is I do so wrong. But both husbands, instead of falling more in love with me as the years go by, they grow to have only contempt for me. God, you have got to know how bad I am hurting and how I have tried to serve you and please everyone, but I feel like I have failed everyone, and now I am so mad and disappointed in you. One more big failure! God, I am tired of failing!"

Then, one night after work, as I was deciding how to spend my evening, I thought about the tapes Joe gave me. I remembered they were by Charles Swindoll whose writings and teachings I enjoyed. I knew the tapes would be biblically based, and that seemed important to me, especially if I was going to find any answers to my questions about God.

I picked up the organizer that contained the tapes and started reading about them. They were on problems Christians face in life, and each one had a different title like "Wisdom, Inferiority, Temptation, Depression, Worry, Anger, Loneliness, Doubtful Things, Deflection, Facing Impossibilities, Death, Resentment, Discouragement, and Right Relationships."

As I reread the titles, I thought to myself that I have experienced each one of these emotions at different times in my life, and I did not want to give the tapes back to Joe and Sue without having a least listened to one or two of them. So that night, I listened to the first tape.

When it ended, I thought to myself, *This is good information!"* So I made another decision. I was not only going to listen to them, but I was going to write down what I would be learning. For the first time, I was going to start journalizing. I had the time and wanted to be able to review what I learned. That night, falling to sleep, I was not wondering why but was excited about what I might learn that I could apply to my life.

\*\*\*\*\*

The next day, after purchasing writing supplies and sharing an evening meal with Barbara, I began listening again and journaling the first tape which was on wisdom. Suddenly, I received a phone call from my friend, Patricia.

"Hi, Gillian! What are you doing?"

"I've just started listening to a series of tapes titled *You and Your Problems* based on biblical truths in the Bible. I went and had dinner with Joe and Sue, and before leaving, Joe gave them to me and asked me to listen to them, so I just started the first tape tonight. I've also decided to journalize what I learn."

"How are you liking the journalizing?" she asked.

"What I like about them being tapes is when I do not get all that is being said that I want to write down, I can stop the tape, rewind it, and go back and listen again. So far, I am stopping the tape rather frequently. I am finding it is a nice way to spend my evening. What's going on with you?" I asked.

"The pastor's wife at my church is going to teach a Bible Study this summer on the book of Exodus. I wanted to invite you to go with me."

"I'm not sure I'm ready to do something like that, Patricia. I'm not ready to be in a big group right now."

"Gillian, this isn't going to be a big group. It will probably be about six ladies meeting in a small room. Our pastor's wife is a good Bible teacher. I think you would enjoy being under her teaching. It is only going to be for an hour to an hour and a half on Wednesday mornings, which is perfect for you since it is your day off. Then we can have coffee together afterward."

"Oh, Patricia, I'm just not sure."

"Gillian, come with me one time, and if you feel uneasy or decide not to do it, I won't pressure you."

"Okay, Patricia, for you, I will try the first meeting."

"Good! I will see you Wednesday morning in the church's parking lot. We can walk in together."

"See you Wednesday morning." I hung up, turned on the tape and, that evening, finished the section on wisdom. I reread my notes twice. What I learned is that wisdom begins with God and not our experiences. It comes with the process of time. It is available and not hidden. When wrong comes, deal with it that day; do not let it go on. I feel asleep, thinking, *I have learned my first mistake.* I let the wrongs go on too long.

Accepting the invitation to Patricia's Bible study, which I enjoyed, gave me the confidence to stop hiding in my room and go back to the church and Sunday school class that I had been attending during my years on the ranch. I shared with my Sunday school class my family's situation and where I was now living. We prayed together, and I left church that morning, experiencing only love, concern, and support. Later in the fall, when Sue invited me to a Bible study in her home, I accepted the invite.

Most of my evenings were spent listening to the tapes and journalizing. I was discovering that many of the great characters in the

Bible had problems with feeling inferior, being depressed, became bitter, angry, or even disappointed with their circumstances and situations. I was led to understand that God had never left them or forsook them. He was working through them to accomplish his purpose for their lives. He could do the same for me. I was reminded that God is for us, not against us (Romans 8:31) and encouraged that when we are emotionally and spiritually drained, it is time to slow down and spend time with God. He will strengthen us and can give us victory over our circumstances.

*****

One Sunday, after lunch, while Barbara and I were putting a puzzle together around the kitchen table, Pilar came by and was anxious to talk to me.

"Mom, Dad asked me what I would like to do and where I would like to live."

"What did you tell him?" I asked.

"I told him that since I would be attending college in Gunnison in the fall, I wanted to move into town into one of the rentals and live with some of my friends. He agreed as long as I understood I would be responsible for collecting the rent and wants me to put the electricity in my name."

"I think it is an excellent decision. Which rental did you choose?"

"The one in the northern part of town. It has a good location to a grocery store, and it's a short drive to the college. I would be doing the same thing Luke is doing where he lives."

"Putting the utilities in your name will help you build a credit rating which will be to your advantage upon graduation. How soon can you make the move?"

"I'll move to town sometime in July."

"I'm happy for you, Pilar, and I'm glad you will be just down the road where it will be easy for us to see each other more often."

"I'll come by as often as I can, Mom."

"Good, do you have to leave right away? Or do you have some time to put a puzzle together with Barbara and me?"

"I'd love to stay and work on the puzzle with you and Barbara."
"Great! I'll make us all some tea."

*****

By the end of July, I had finished the tapes but continued to review the journal, was attending the Bible study once a week with Patricia, and going to church on Sundays. I had also spent more time at night just talking to God. I now knew what I needed to do if I was ever going to understand just who this God was that I served.

Walking along the trail after work, I was anxious to get to my room and have time alone with God. As I entered my room and closed the door, I looked at the Bible that was beside my bed. I walked over, picked it up, sat down in my chair, and laid that Bible in my lap. And I finally knew what I wanted to tell God.

"God, it seems like I have been learning about you since I was a young girl in grade school. Today, in my life, I feel like I do not really know who you are. So I want you to show me just exactly who you are and what it is you want for my life. This Bible tells me that if a person seeks God, he will not hide from them [Jeremiah 29:13]. With all my heart, God, I am now seeking you. But there is one thing you are going to have to give me for me to find you. God, I need comprehension. Learning in school was always a struggle for me because I struggled to comprehend what I read. I am not going to just read your Word, God. I am going to study it as I read it. I do not want the time I put into getting to know you better to be another struggle."

After asking God for comprehension, I took the Bible, placed it on my bed, knelt beside it, and began praying.

"Jesus, I am coming to the cross and giving you all the broken pieces of my life. Thank you for being my Lord and Savior. I ask you to forgive me of my sins and want my will instead of yours. I want to get to know you better and serve you. I ask you to lead, guide, and direct me through the circumstances in my life right now. As I read and study your Word, may it be a lamp unto my feet and a light unto my path [Psalm 119:105]."

That night, I began a new journey with God, Jesus, and his Holy Spirit. A new adventure was ahead of me, one that was far beyond all that I could ask or imagine.

## 62

One of the joys of being a mother to my son, Luke, was how he could surprise me with the different "old car projects" he found to work on in his spare time. It was pure enjoyment listening to him explain the "sweet deal" he got on the car that was for sale and how he bartered with the owner for him to reduce the price. Sometimes the owner was pleased to just give the car to Luke if he hauled it away himself. Luke never paid the full asking price on any of his project cars. He was meticulous during the rebuilding process, visited the local junkyard a lot, and usually made money on the resale, except for one time.

When Luke left home, he kept me in his life. His phone calls always brought a smile to my face, and we usually ended up laughing at the updates we told each other. One phone call I will always remember was a summer evening while I was reading in my room, and he wanted to see me.

"Hi, Mom, what are you doing?" he asked.

"I'm just sitting in my room, reading a book. What are you doing?" I asked.

"Well, I have something to show you. I want to share it with you, so if you have the time, I'll come by and pick you up."

"I certainly have the time. I'll be out front waiting for you."

"Great, see you in a few minutes."

I had no idea what he was going to show me, so I was curious about our evening together. Then I saw it coming around the corner. As he pulled up beside me, I also saw the big smile on his face. It was a gray jeep badly in need of repairs. As he pulled up and waited for me to get inside, I wondered if it was safe to get in.

Opening the passenger door, I asked him, "Is this yours?"

"Oh yeah! It's mine!" he said, and he was totally excited.

"Jump in, Mom. I'm going to take you for a ride on a road west of town."

As we pulled away from the curb, everything starting rumbling, and I was not sure it was going to make it out of town. I envisioned the engine falling out and parts strung along the road.

"So this jeep is your new project?" I inquired, and I had to speak louder than usual because everything was shaking, including Luke and me.

"Mom, this is not just a jeep. This is a CJ7 Jeep."

"Is that a good thing?" I asked.

"Mom, a CJ7 is an incredibly special jeep. When I get through cleaning this up and rebuilding it, you are going to see the sweet deal this really is. Besides, I have three months before I leave for boot camp, and I need something to work on," he explained.

"Well, I can understand you needing a project to make the time go faster. Do you think you can get this sweet deal in shape before you leave? Seems to me there is a lot of work to do on it."

"Oh, absolutely! Mom, what is really great is that I can get parts at a discount working at the auto store."

"That is to your advantage. Are you planning on working on it at the duplex?" I asked.

"Sure, I have off-street parking. It's a good place to work on it," he said.

"Well, I'm happy you found a vehicle to work on. Do you plan on this being a resale before you leave?" I asked.

"No, Mom, this one I am going to fix up and make it mine. I'll leave it with Dad at the ranch until I am able to come and get it."

That evening turned out to be a lot of fun driving round roads outside of Gunnison. When he dropped me back at my place, I wished him good luck and told him, "Luke, this jeep of yours will certainly have the neighborhood talking!" And for your information, we did not lose any parts along the road.

Besides working at the auto store and on the jeep, each day, Luke was also challenging himself psychically and had been for many months. The dream of becoming a United States Marine lived within him. Once he told me he wanted to be able to run five miles in thirty minutes at the higher altitude we lived in. To achieve that goal, he hired a running coach. He not only achieved that goal, but he also surpassed it. Daily, he was doing push-ups, sit-ups, and chin-ups constantly pushing himself through the pain. However, his greatest struggle psychically was swimming. He was not a good swimmer. So he spent several hours a week at the local community center with another coach working on those skills. Many times, he invited me to join him, encouraging me to work on my skills. I really did not have any swimming skills, but I could float and watch him. A fear he had to overcome was jumping off the high diving board. I was there the day he ran and jumped off. Then he continued to do it repeatedly.

I would stop by his place occasionally and catch him working on the jeep. During those last three months, the work Luke had put into the jeep showed that somebody really cared about that vehicle. Under the hood, it looked entirely new. Throughout the jeep, all the bolts and screws were tight, the interior had been upgraded, and with a new paint job, it was a swell deal. The day he drove it out to the ranch, he had his picture taken with it.

\*\*\*\*\*

October arrived, and it was time for me to say goodbye to Luke. The day before he left, he came to see me. I told him I loved him, would be praying God's protection over him, and I had a verse from the Bible I wanted him to take with him. That verse was Joshua 1:9: "Be strong and courageous. Do not be afraid, and do not be discouraged for the Lord your God will be with you wherever you go."

We hugged. He told me he loved me, that I had his support, and he hoped I would find God's purpose for my life. I knew in my heart that Luke had the drive, motivation, and courage to face the challenges ahead of him. He was now free to follow his dream and find his way in the world. My boy was now a man who would become a United States Marine.

# 63

As summer rolled into fall, and the different groups at the schools and churches were forming, I joined two different groups. I began attending Sue's Bible study on Wednesday nights at her home. The second one was a phone call from a dear friend of my mother's who, after my mother's death, had become my dear friend and confident.

"Hi, Gillian. This is Marilyn. Is it a good time to talk?"

"Yes! It's nice to hear from you."

"Gillian, I want you to think about coming to church with me on Monday nights and helping us at Awanas."

"I don't even know what Awanas is, Marilyn."

"It is a church club for kids learning how to grow in Christ. One activity the kids do each week is to memorize a Bible verse, and then, when they come to the group on Monday nights, they need to recite the verse to an adult. If they recite it correctly, they get paper money. The kids save the bills, and a couple of times a year, they get to spend their dollars at the gift store, which has nice prizes. We need more adults to hear the kids recite their verses."

"So all I have to do is listen to kids recite the verse and reward them?"

"Yes. Will you come with me tomorrow night?"

"Sure, I'll be glad to come and help. It would be interesting to learn about the program. Why don't you let me come and pick you up?"

"That would be nice. Be at my home around five-thirty. The program starts at six."

"See you tomorrow night, Marilyn, and thanks for thinking of me."

*****

Arriving at the church the next night, I saw a lot of people I remembered when I attended here. They were glad to see me and happy I could be a helper too. I was given the materials I needed and a small room which contained two chairs: one for me to sit in, and the other was for the child I would be listening to. Several kids were lining up outside the door. What amazed me was how excited the kids were to be at Awanas, and several were practicing their memory verses with each other. I listened to about twenty kids and then was able to watch several of the other activities. I understood why the kids liked coming and was already looking forward to being back next Monday night.

Wednesday night, I drove out to Sue's house and met about ten ladies that attended her and Joe's church. Sue passed out the study books we would be using, assigned our homework for the week, and then we listened to the first video by Beth Moore that accompanied the study. It was an easy evening of getting acquainted, and I also looked forward to the homework I would be doing during the week.

Driving home that night, I had to reflect on the number of ways God had opened different doors for me to get to know him better. I was reading and studying the Bible in my room each night, going to Bible studies, was listening to children recite God's Word, and before I left for work each morning, I was watching discussions by leading Christian evangelists on a small television that my landlords had given me to use in my room. I thought to myself, *God, you sure have flooded my life with different ways of getting to know you better. I asked you not to hide from me, and I realize you were listening to me. Thanks a lot!*

*****

During the summer months, proceedings with the divorce began, and my attorney was good at keeping me informed of the different procedures and papers that were filed with the district court. Josh had also been served and notified.

I kept my distance from the ranch and made no attempt to contact Josh. However, there was one time in July after he had been served papers that he asked Pilar to call me. When she made the call, we spent a few minutes catching up with how it was going with her moving into the house, getting roommates, and how her job was going at the electric company in town. She was excited about having her own place, living in town, and was enjoying her job.

"Mom, there is a reason I am calling you tonight."

"Oh, what's that?" I asked.

"Dad needs to come into town and fix my garbage disposal. It's not working. While he is here, he wanted me to ask you if you would meet with him. He wants to talk to you."

"Do you know what he wants to talk about?" I asked.

"No, I don't. He didn't say. I didn't ask."

"Pilar, I'm not going to meet with him alone."

"No, I'll be here while he is here, but I'll let you speak privately."

"When does he want to meet?" I asked.

"He's coming in Wednesday. He knows it's your day off, and he thought you would have the time to see him."

"Tell him I will meet with him, but not alone."

"Okay, Mom, I'll tell him."

*****

Wednesday morning at ten o'clock, I was at Pilar's house to meet with Josh. He was in the kitchen, working under the sink, and said he would be with me in a few minutes. I went outside into the front yard and waited for him by the tree. In a couple of minutes, he came out.

"Gillian, I wanted to ask you a question," he said.

"What would that be?" I asked.

"Do you really want this divorce? Is this what you really want?"

"Yes, it is, Josh, I really want this divorce. And you already told me you don't want me," I replied.

"Gillian, what are you hoping to get out of all of this?" he asked.

"Whatever is due me, Josh."

"You're not going to get anything from me, Gillian."

"Josh, we will let the courts decide."

He was mad now and upset. As he turned and walked away, he said in a very disgusted tone, "Gillian, you're not taking anything from me."

I did not say anything as I watched him drive away. I was glad I stood firm on my decision and knew whatever I did get would be enough.

## 64

In August, my attorney called and said we had a court date. It was set for the middle of September where temporary orders would be decided. On the day of the hearing, I met my attorney outside the courtroom. A few minutes after we entered the courtroom, Josh and his attorney came in. The attorneys greeted one another, and then we waited a few minutes for the judge and the court reporter to enter and take their places.

I was the only one who was sworn in and took the stand. I remember the questions being directly to the point, and I gave short answers. I remember my attorney giving a detailed account of the contributions I had made to the marriage to achieve our current standard of living. The judge asked me a few questions, and I was told I could step down.

Josh did not take the stand. He said nothing the whole time. His attorney did cross-examine me with a few questions. The judge spoke to both attorneys and then handed down his decision.

The judge's decision was that real property appraisals would be done on the ranch, including hay, cattle, and equipment because it had been my home. Plus, an appraisal on the one acre of land that was purchased for a rental. That property was in both Josh's and my name. I would receive half of the total appraisal amount. All the other holdings would remain under the prenuptial agreement. Josh would need to sell the ranch to give me my fair share.

The appraisals were completed by December, and that same month, Josh put the ranch up for sale and auctioned off all the equipment. The ranch sold in January the same month Luke was to graduate from Marine boot camp in San Diego. After not hearing from him for fourteen weeks, Luke was now placing calls home to invite us to his graduation ceremony. My son-in-law, Philip, a twenty-year retired Marine, told us that this was one ceremony we should not miss.

Pilar and I drove out to California, spending one night in Kingman, Arizona, before arriving in Pasadena. Philip and Juliet had now purchased their first home which we found nestled in town in a single-family residential area. It was a beautiful two-story custom-built home at the end of a cul-de-sac with a large landscaped backyard. My grandson, Ryan, was now a cute little toddler, two-and-a half years old, that both Pilar and I were delighted to see and hold again. I was completely happy to be sitting in their backyard, laughing, and enjoying my family. A new freedom was beginning to wash over me.

The next day, Philip drove us down in their car to Camp Pendleton, the Marine base in San Diego where the ceremony would take place. We were all so proud of Luke because of what he overcame and achieved to be able to graduate today. Many feelings were rushing over me. I was proud, but I was also nervous and excited at the same time. I just wanted to put my arms around him and hug him. As we were directed to the stands and started climbing into our places is when I saw Josh. The last time I saw him was in September when temporary orders were decided. He sat behind us a few rows up. All I thought was, *He did come.*

Josh did not support Luke's decision to become a Marine. He told him he did not have the "right stuff" to achieve that type of goal. Today, Luke would prove he did have the "right stuff" and dreams do come true.

When the announcer welcomed us and asked us to stand, the music began, then to our right, down on the ceremonial grounds, large doors opened to a large pavilion, and the graduates began marching forward. Tears started running down my cheeks. The graduates went through a series of maneuvers with accurate precision moving as one. It was an amazing sight to see. After the award ceremonies, the graduates were released to their families.

As we gathered around him, congratulating him, Josh walked up and did the same. Families were invited to a buffet luncheon on base. An invitation was given to Josh to join us, and he accepted. It was a pleasant sunny afternoon, sitting by the dock, hearing stories of life in boot camp. As the years would pass, I would learn some of the real hard and challenging times he did endure to stay the course and not give up.

When it was time for us to leave, Luke left with his dad to return to Colorado for two weeks, to get his personal belongings before he would return back to Camp Pendleton for three weeks of combat training. Arriving back home, the life that Luke had known was gone. The farm and all his personal possessions that a young boy and teenager would accumulate were gone. There were no clothes, and the CJ7 was also gone. It went in the farm auction with all the rest of the equipment. The only items he had were the ones issued to him by the military. When he asked his dad why, his only answer was, "I thought the military would give you what you needed."

Luke was devasted, angry, and he left his hometown again, believing that God had given him a vision of what his purpose in life could be. He would now move with perseverance toward that goal.

*****

March 3, 2004, my second marriage was dissolved, and a Decree of Dissolution was entered at the district courthouse. I was now free to accept Philip and Juliet's invitation to come and live with them and start a new life in California. I would wait until Pilar finished her first year of college, and then she and I would drive to Pasadena, pulling a small U-Haul rental behind my car that contained a few of my personal possessions.

April 1, 2004, I gave a month's notice at work that I would be leaving for California on April 30. I was privileged to work with an incredible professional staff that was friendly, held strong work ethics, and we were well-organized. At the helm was a caring doctor for both his staff and patients. He was always approachable, and there was never a dumb question. There was a registered nurse who was caring, detailed, and organized. The front office manager was very efficient at answering the phone, booking appointments, and collected payments. During the years I worked there, good friendships were developed, and even today, the front office manager and I remain good friends.

The morning of April 30, before I said goodbye to my landlords and thanked them for being there for me in my time of need, I sat alone in that small room that had become my refuge and shelter for almost a year. I asked God for travel mercies for Pilar and myself as we traveled to California. But I also came to realize just what that small room had become to mean to me. It was the place I rededicated my life to my Savior and found peace with my God.

In the Breaking Free Bible study, I learned how Jesus met the needs of people in different ways. Sometimes, it was with the multitudes with feeding five thousand; most of the time, he was instructing twelve disciples on how they would change the world with the Gospel, sometimes three with Peter, James, and John at his transfiguration, and he also went further still to meet one-on-one with Peter where he asked a fisherman to feed his sheep. That small room was my place of "further still" where my faith in my God was restored. I would be taking him with me today.

Before I picked up Pilar, I went and said goodbye to my brother, Logan, and his wife, Lucia. Many times during the last year, I had walked from my room to just up the hill and down the street to their home. Around their kitchen table, we shared memories, talked, and laughed. I had their love, and they wished me the best at finding a new life in California.

Pilar was waiting for me when I swung by to pick her up. She was excited about the trip ahead and wanted to do the driving.

"Hi, Mom, what book did you bring to read on this trip?" she asked.

"A book by one of our favorite writers, Julie Garwood's *For the Roses*. It's about a young girl that has a rough start in life but grows up on a ranch in Montana with her four brothers and eventually discovers who she really is."

"Sounds great, Mom. Start reading!"

# PART 9

## California

## 65

The afternoon of May 1, 2004, Pilar and I arrived in Pasadena, California. We began lounging in Philip and Juliet's backyard with cold drinks soaking in the Mediterranean climate. It felt so good to be here.

My grandson, Ryan, was now three years old, a cute little boy who was anxious to show us what he liked to play with around the house. It was his *Star Wars* lightsaber, his dog, Rusty, and balls. His Aunt Pilar was very anxious to start playing with him. I loved listening to him talk and watching him run around the yard. The last time I saw him, we took a walk together down a dirt road on the farm, and we threw rocks in the pond. Such an easy child to love and be with; now I could hold him and watch him grow.

A few days later, it was time for us to take Pilar to her scheduled flight from LAX back to Gunnison. I knew when I said goodbye, I would not be seeing her for a whole year. During her first year at Western, she discovered the college offered an international program where she could study abroad for one year. She applied to the program and was accepted at the Darwin University, located in Darwin in the northern territory of Australia. She would be returning to Gunnison for a month where she would prepare to leave in the first part of June for the continent of Australia. I was extremely happy for her to have this opportunity, and I knew it would enrich her life.

The first time Pilar traveled was when she was nine years old. We took her and Luke to Disneyland and Sea World in southern California. It was on this trip she discovered the ocean, fell in love with it, and realized that there were other places in the world to be discovered also. During her high school years, she traveled for two weeks with teachers and classmates throughout France and Italy. Now she would be traveling into the southern hemisphere, living on a continent where she would fall in love with its culture and people. I started thinking about Pilar as my beautiful butterfly that would fly around fluttering from place-to-place, examining God's creation. There was a deep love between us, and I would be looking forward to the phone calls and letters coming from the land down under.

My plan was to stay a few months with my daughter, Juliet, and her family until I could find a place of my own. I had come to enjoy my time alone in that one-room bedroom I rented in town. It was a time of reflection about who I was, what I wanted in life, and I had spent many hours rediscovering my God. However, my son-in-law, Philip, was not keen on that idea. So one night, around the dinner table, he shared what life was like for him as a boy.

"Gillian, I grew up in a small town where my dad's and mom's brothers and sisters lived also. My home was always full of my cousins, aunts, uncles just walking in to just say hi as they were walking by or stayed to share a meal, a conversation, and discuss their latest problems. I admit many times I felt it was too much family, but there are fond memories of them also. I want my children to know their relatives and especially their grandmother. Juliet and I have discussed it, and we would like for you to think about living with us. You can have a private bedroom to yourself downstairs with your own bath. Our bedrooms and bathrooms are all upstairs."

"Philip, I will tell you what I'm going to do. I'll stay for a few months, and if it does not work out, I will look for a place of my own."

"That's great!" he said. "It's all settled."

I knew that both Philip and Juliet had full-time jobs with large corporations, and my grandson, Ryan, was enrolled at the day-care facility where Juliet worked. They all left a little after 7:00 a.m. each workday and did not return until six in the evening. I had the house to myself, and their family pet, Rusty, was my companion each day. I was already enjoying time to myself and time with their family. I also wanted to be a help to them, so it was not long before I approached Philip with a question.

"Philip, I would like to cook supper for the family tonight. What is one of your favorite casseroles for dinner?" I asked.

"Gillian, anything you would like to cook will be fine with me," he said, rather shocked and very pleased. This was a totally new concept coming from a man that was a former Marine and for many years ate at the mess hall or microwaved a meal.

"What time would you like for it to be ready?" I asked.

"Six o'clock okay with you, Gillian?" he replied, still with rather a shocked look on his face.

That night, when Philip, Juliet, and Ryan came home, I had the table set with water and wine glasses, a bottle of wine opened, and a casserole and salad ready to sit down and eat. This was the beginning of a very nice relationship between the four of us. Eventually, Juliet started to make a menu for the weekly night dinners, which helped me a lot, so I would not be asking what their likes and dislikes were all the time.

Philip loved coming home to the evening meal already prepared and waiting to be served as they walked in the door. It gave more time for Juliet and him to sit and talk about their day in a relaxed setting while I took Ryan outside to watch him fight the bad guys with his brown cloak and lightsaber. This is when I discovered Ryan enjoyed fantasy play.

One night, while we were sitting and laughing at the table, Philip told Juliet he had decided something.

"What decision is that?" Juliet asked.

"I have decided if we ever get divorced, we will not be fighting over the money, but we will be fighting over who gets your mother."

*****

The first summer in California, I learned how amazing it was to go to the beach and walk along the shore as the ocean waves rolled in over a person's feet and up their thighs. It was during one of these walks that I decided I needed to add more structure to my day. So I began to pray to God that he would make a way for me in California. One night, as Juliet and I were cleaning up the supper dishes, I asked her a question.

"Juliet, what do you think I should do here in California?"

"Mom, anything you want. Many times, you have told me that you would like to go back into teaching. You told me how hard you had to work to get your degree and you were only able to use it one year before you married and moved to Alaska. Start seeing what it would take to get certified in California," she said.

"I know I would have to go back to school and take some classes to update my certificate and get credentialed here in this state. I certainly have the time during the day to study. I'll start praying about it," I said.

One store I enjoyed spending time at was *Barnes & Noble*. Reading was my hobby, and I enjoyed finding a good book written by one of my favorite authors. One day, while strolling through their aisles, my eyes saw a book titled *God Will Make a Way (What to Do When You Don't Know What to Do)*. I could not believe what I was suddenly holding in my hands. It was written by Dr. Henry Cloud and Dr. John Townsend, two popular psychologists. They were also Christians, and their writings were biblically based.

The year I lived alone in Gunnison, a friend had given me the book *Boundaries* written by these same two men, and I had enjoyed it a lot. The book gave me good insights on setting boundaries in our relationships. I could not wait to get home and start reading this new book by them. I already felt that God was working in my life.

*****

As May rolled into June, I had leisurely settled into the Anderson household and had also spent a lot of introspective quality time with myself. Now I decided I wanted to find a church. If I was going to live in Pasadena, I wanted to work and worship in the same town I lived in and become part of the community. A good friend gave me that advice, and I decided I was going to follow it. So, one evening, I asked Juliet about the churches in Pasadena and what she knew about them.

"Mom, I know you have been raised Baptist and have always attended a Baptist church. You even raised all three of your kids in that faith. I don't know of one in Pasadena, but we have occasionally been attending the Evangelical church in town. Philip enjoys the pastor's sermons, and the people are friendly."

"My mom was a member of an Evangelical church in Boulder, Colorado, and she always spoke about how much she loved being a member of it. I think that was the church her mom grew up in."

"Mom, take some time to visit the different churches and see where the Holy Spirit leads you."

So I did. I spent a few Sundays visiting different churches in nearby towns, but at the end of those visits, I decided I was not following what I had decided to do when I came to Pasadena. I wanted to worship in the town I lived in. Next Sunday, I was going to visit the Evangelical Church. I came away from that service knowing it was where God wanted me to learn more about him.

After attending a couple of times, and after the morning church service, I inquired about Sunday school classes. I was told that they were discontinued for the summer months so families could spend more quality time together. That was such a foreign concept to me, coming from the Baptist faith, where we were in church Sunday morning, evening, and sometimes on Wednesday nights, plus living on a farm working all the time. These people were taking time off and going to the beach! God showed me that taking time for your family is a good thing.

Two events happened in August on that summer that are wonderful memories and God doing his part. The first event was an announcement that Sunday school classes would be starting up in September, plus the church pastor was planning on leading a new membership class with people interested in joining the church. After the service, I met with the woman leading the Children's Ministries, told her of my experience with Awanas, and that I would like to serve in the Sunday school classes. She told me I could not teach because I wasn't a member, but I could be a helper.

I came home and thanked God for this wonderful opportunity in my life. This is when I met one of the best kindergarten teachers in Pasadena, and she and I together, for eleven years, taught the kindergarten class. I was helping children learn about God's Word, and I was meeting the families of the church. I also enrolled in the new membership class, and after six weeks of meetings, I stood along with the other people who took the class, and we were voted in as members of the church.

The second event was an announcement that there was going to be a "Women of Faith Conference" in Anaheim at the Pond Convention Center. I could not believe it! I had read so many books by these women; they brought so much joy to my life, and now there was the possibility that I actually had a chance to go see them. Sixty women from our church signed up to attend. I felt God had given me an incredibly special gift, and when I stood at The Pond with all those thousands of ladies, and started singing praise songs, tears ran down my face.

In September, my son, Luke, a Marine at that time, was stationed in San Diego, awaiting orders for his next assignment. After boot camp and combat training, Luke was assigned to be a helicopter mechanic. He left for Pensacola, Florida, where from February to October, he attended technical school, learning helicopter systems. He graduated in the top 1 percent of the class with top honors. I will always remember that call, Luke telling me he was headed for Iraq. He asked me what I thought.

I told him, "Luke, God's Word tells me your days were numbered in my womb. I could have lost you on the streets of Gunnison, Pasadena, or Pensacola, Florida. Just know you have a mother who is going to be praying for you every day."

When I told Philip and Juliet the news, Philip, a twenty-year retired Marine, told me, "Gillian, Luke doesn't need a mother here crying her eyes out. He has a lot to think about over there, and he needs to know you are supporting him."

So I was in Sunday school, and I had met a man named Richard Brown who was also helping in the kindergarten class, and I asked him if he knew anyone who might pray with me because I had a son going to Iraq. He said he had a grandson also going and would be glad to pray with me, and he might know of some other members in the church that had children serving. So, one evening, about eight people met in the associate pastor's office, and we started a small prayer group. We began meeting once a month. I became very active in it, serving as the secretary-treasurer and helping to gather items to send to soldiers overseas.

Over a four-year period, Luke went to Iraq three times. God not only brought Luke home three times but also everyone we prayed for came home and had served their country with honor. It has been a wonderful experience praying for our nation, the young men and women who serve, and the parents who support them.

In November, there was an announcement that the church's "Women's Retreat" was going to be at Forest Home, a Christian Church Camp in the San Bernardino mountains, and sign-ups were beginning. I felt God was giving me another gift. I was going to be able to go with some Christian ladies, and together, we would worship God in the mountains. Juliet and I signed up, but she became ill with a cold and could not go. So I didn't know who I would be sharing a cabin with. It was during our first evening meal in the camp's lodge that one of the organizers approached me about my cabin mate situation.

"Gillian, do you know Diane Ferguson?" she asked.

"No, I don't believe I do," I replied.

"Well, she had been a member of our church for a long time, and her roommate for the retreat also became ill and could not attend, so I thought you two could be roommates if that's okay with you," she said.

"That's fine with me if she is okay with it."

"I've already talked to her, and she would like to meet you, so let's go get acquainted."

We were strangers but also sisters in Christ. That night, in our cabin, we spent time talking and sharing our lives. Diane was friendly, kind, caring, and easy to talk to. Over the weekend, we attended the different meetings together. The guest speaker spoke about the "broken pieces of our lives," and when she held up a cross with broken ceramic pieces on it, I knew it was the very symbol of my life and why I was at this retreat. During the different meetings, I learned of God's faithfulness, even when we are not faithful, and the ways Jesus can mend those broken pieces. The last morning before leaving our cabin, Diane asked me if I would be her prayer partner for the coming year. I said yes, that it would be nice to have someone to pray with. She was another gift from God.

Over the years, since that retreat, she and I have met once a week, studying the Bible and praying for our families and our church. She remains a true sister in Christ and a very dear friend.

\*\*\*\*\*

In the spring of 2006, the pastor announced he would be leading a summer tour about "The Footprints of Paul" through Greece and Turkey. I would now be traveling internationally with sixty other people to step back in time to discover ancient cities that I had only read about in the Bible. I will never forget the first night in Athens. Some of us sat at the top of our hotel, and with the wind blowing across us from the Aegean Sea, we saw the Parthenon lit up in lights against a solid black sky. It was a sight to behold.

The next day, we walked around the solid rock wall of the Acropolis and then walked over to the marble hill of Areopagus (Mars Hill), first standing at its base where Paul preached a famous sermon, and then climbed on top of it and saw where Socrates and Plato discussed their philosophies.

We traveled by bus to the ancient city of Corinth, walked through the ruins of the Agora (marketplace), and stood where Paul stood before the tribunal. We set sail on the Aegean Sea to the islands of Mykonos, Patmos, and Rhodes. At Mykonos, we had time to shop, discover the quaint windmills on the island, and have supper at a seaside café, watching the sun go down. On Patmos, the island where the disciple John was exiled for preaching the Word of God, we walked its hills with white marble buildings and descended into the Cave of the Apocalypse, discovering where John wrote the book of Revelation. At Rhodes, we walked its ancient streets, visualizing the grandeur of medieval times.

Arriving in Turkey, we walked the ancient city streets of Ephesus, sat in its amphitheater, and viewed the historic temples. Traveling north of Ephesus, we toured several of the historic church sites of the first century and enjoyed a refreshing stop in Pamukkale. It was here we wadded through the famous healing blue waters that flow over stalactites into pools down a vast mountainside. Our last stop was Istanbul, a city rich in histories of ancient empires. We shopped in the great marketplace, toured the famous mosques like the Little Hagia Sophia of the Byzantine empire, and the inside of the beautiful Blue Mosque of the Ottoman empire.

Flying out of Istanbul, heading home, I knew the next time I read about all the cities, towns, and sites I had seen, they would not be a word on a page but a vision in my mind. I prayed to God to give me comprehension to understand his Word. One way he answered that prayer was by giving me an opportunity and a cherished memory to travel back in time to places where the Gospel would begin to change the world.

After a couple of years, and I do not know how long exactly, I had been a member. One Sunday after morning service, one of the leaders of the church came up to me and asked if I would consider being a deaconess for the church. I said, "Oh, I could never be a deaconess. My sins are many, and I don't have the qualifications to be a deaconess. You do know that I am a divorced woman not once but twice, don't you?"

She graciously said, "Oh, Gillian, that doesn't matter to us. We've seen the way you serve in this church, and we think you would make a good deaconess."

And so I told her I would pray about it. I knew I was a sinner saved by his grace, and I was beginning to feel worthy of being his disciple. Now God wanted me to know it. So I said yes to the kind request to serve as a deaconess, and one of the first things I learned was deaconesses help serve communion. I just did not think I could do that. I could pray for people and help them, but I did not feel worthy to stand at his table.

I will always remember the night I stood in the fellowship hall and held the bread and said, "This is Christ's body broken for you." I will always be so grateful to the people of God's church showing me what "grace" really is.

So not only did God make a way for me in this church and introduce me to some wonderful friends, but he also made a way for me in the community as well.

*My journey into special education*

In August of 2004, I decided I would go down to the Pasadena Unified School District's Administrative Office, introduce myself, and see if they could use any volunteer help registering students for school. Over the summer, people would occasionally ask me what my long-range plans were for living in Pasadena, and I would tell them I hoped to update my teaching certificate and possibly be able to teach in the district. Their answer was always the same. "Gillian, there are no teaching jobs available in Pasadena."

Some would say, "There is nothing available."

My response to them was, "I have been told that, and I am trusting God to make a way for me." So, that morning, after praying with God for him to lead me through the day, I approached the receptionist in the district office with a question.

"Hello, my name is Gillian Reynolds, and I was wondering if you needed any volunteer help in registering students for school? In May, I moved from Colorado to Pasadena. I have past teaching experience and would love to help with any needs you may have," I said.

She responded by saying, "We don't need volunteer help, but we still do not have all our positions filled at this time."

"Really? I was told there wasn't anything available," I said.

"All the teacher positions have been filled, but we need a few more aides in the classroom. Would you be interested in one of those positions?"

"Yes, I would," I said.

"You need to take a test and get a passing grade to be considered for the position," she explained.

"What kind of test is it?" I asked.

"It is the California Basic Educational Skills Test [CBEST] that tests your proficiency in reading, math, and writing. We are going to be giving it Thursday of this week, and you will be taking it here at the district office with others seeking aide positions. Are you still interested?" she asked.

"I am. Do I need to study for this test?"

"Didn't you say you were a teacher?" she inquired.

"I did. I was a teacher in Texas several years ago. Reading a book is my hobby, and I have a lot of bookkeeping experience," I said.

"You should be fine. Shall I sign you up?"

"Yes, please do."

After signing the needed papers, I left the office, feeling that God had just opened a window for me. I just needed to pass that test.

\*\*\*\*\*

I returned on Thursday and sat in a room with four other people. We were spaced out along a rectangular table. Given a test booklet, pencils, and four hours to complete all three sections, I completed the test with time to spare and turned it in. I felt confident that I would pass. I was told we should know our results by Monday, and I would be notified by phone. That was my first long, anxious weekend in California.

Monday afternoon, I received a call from the head of special education at the district office. He introduced himself, said I had passed the CBEST test, and would like to offer me a paid position in his department.

"Gillian, what to you know about autism?"

"Nothing. I don't know what it is."

"It is a condition related to brain development, and it impacts how a person relates to and socializes with other people. People that are born with this condition are usually rated on a scale of one to twenty with one being a very mild condition to twenty being a very severe condition. I have a student who needs to have an aide with her during her school day. She has high intelligence with a more severe condition of autism, which causes her to have social interaction problems with her peers and the classroom setting. We need an aide to be with her throughout the school day. I would like for you to consider being her aide. You will be working under a teacher that has taught in the special education field for many years, has a good understanding of students with autism, and she will be instructing you on how to help the student process her day. If she goes to another class, you will be with her in that classroom. If she goes to PE class, you will attend that PE class with her. Gillian, what are your thoughts about this position I am offering you?"

"It sounds interesting and challenging. Are you sure I'm qualified to be her aide?"

"You will be taking the position on a trial basis. Right now, you are the best candidate I have to help this student. We are not sure if she can continue to function in a classroom setting, and you will have to decide if the role fits you as well."

"Well, I certainly will try the position and see if the girl and I can learn together."

"Thanks, Gillian. Can you come down to the district office tomorrow and get the necessary paperwork filled out to be employed with our district?"

"Yes, I can. Thank you for this opportunity."

"Come by the special education offices tomorrow and say hello."

"Thanks, I'll do that."

*****

After filling out the paperwork at the district office, I was given the name of the teacher I would be under. I called her. She was glad I had contacted her, and she gave me a date and time before school started when we could meet in her classroom. So, a few days before classes were to begin, I walked over to the school's office, introduced myself, located the classroom I would be working in, and also introduced myself to the teacher that would be my guide with my special needs student. She would also open my eyes to a whole new approach on how instruction in a classroom could be delivered to students with special needs.

"Gillian, it's nice to meet you. Welcome to my classroom."

"Thank you. I look forward to helping you and at the same time also learn about special education. I taught school in the early 1970s, and this kind of instruction wasn't offered."

"It began in 1975 when the Individual Disabilities Education Act (IDEA) was passed. It gives students with disabilities the same education that students with no disabilities receive. The instruction is slowed down and meets the needs of the student. That way, the concepts are easier to learn, and the students make progress. That is how you will be helping me in this classroom."

"I know I could have used that type of instruction when I was going through school. I look forward to learning about it."

"Gillian, I would like to spend a few minutes talking with you about the student you are assigned to, how you will be assisting me with her, and some of the other duties I will have you doing to help the classroom run smoothly. There will also be another aide assigned to my classroom who will be helping assist the students. I will be the lead teacher on your student's case, and we will be working with some other classroom teachers as well."

"I would really like that."

My journey started with a notebook of duplicate paper and a pen on which I took notes about my student's behavior, class participation, homework assignments, and their due dates. When the school day ended, I walked the student to her parent and gave them a copy of those notes and the other copy to the lead teacher to review. There were many challenging days, but as my student began making progress, I was eventually asked to attend meetings to report my observations to other professionals who worked with her.

I began to learn how to communicate professionally between family, students, and teachers. When my student was working on assignments, I was helping to assist other students in the classroom. I was fascinated to see how the flow of instruction and visuals were helping the students' comprehension which also increased their participation. Eventually, I became an instructional assistant in the class, helping to provide direct instruction in reading classes.

During my second year with my student, we sometimes had a special time we would spend in the library. She started showing me books she liked, especially ones about animals, even ancient ones, and would explain to me many of their characteristics. I was discovering how intelligent and artistic she was and longed to see her involved in a general education classroom.

One day, as I was having lunch with the lead teacher, I asked her about the possibility of having my student attend a general education science class.

"Gillian, I agree with you that she is making good progress. We would have to get permission from several different sources, and she would have to be prepared for the transition. We would also have to find a science teacher who would be willing to take her in their classroom. I'll start approaching the idea at my next meetings."

"Thanks. I would just like to see her have the chance to try."

*****

Several weeks later, on a fall day, during my lunchtime, I was alone in the cafeteria, and another teacher walked in and started having his lunch also. I introduced myself and started a conversation.

"May I ask what department you work in?"

"Science. I teach biology," he responded.

"I have been hoping I could meet someone in the science department," I said.

"Why is that?" he asked.

"I am a one-on-one aide to a special needs student here at the school. She has high intelligence, and I have learned from our time in the library she enjoys animals and knows a lot about their characteristics. Given a chance, I think she would do well in a general education class."

"I'll need to talk to the lead teacher first. If she is interested, have her contact me."

I was overjoyed with meeting this contact. As I left the lunchroom, I was saying, "Thank you, God! Thank you, God! Thank you, God!"

Over time, with parents and professionals preparing her, she was included into one general education science class with me sitting beside her with prompts and incentives. She thrived on the instruction and eventually was included in all general education classes with me following her from class to class. I was back in the classroom, learning along with her.

\*\*\*\*\*

After spending the fall of 2004 in special education classrooms and being an aide to a child with autism, I knew I wanted to become a special education teacher. So, in January 2005, with the help of a contact at the county offices, I submitted the necessary paperwork to the State of California's Commission on Teacher Credentialing. They responded in March, issuing me a Preliminary Multiple Subject Teaching Credential with the necessary standards I would have to meet to become a fully credentialed teacher in the state. I now had the authorization to teach if an opportunity came my way as long as I was pursuing courses to become fully credentialed.

I began researching the different smaller colleges in our area, found one that had the program I needed, and it was only twenty minutes from where we lived. I applied for the coming fall semester and was accepted. At the age of fifty-seven, I was going back to school.

My days were now filled with helping special needs students during their school hours and, in the evening, attending classes on strategies used in a special education classroom. It was the technology classes that I had to work the hardest in. When I went to school, my classrooms consisted of blackboards, chalk, and typewriters that did not instantly correct typing errors. Now I had to learn about Wi-Fi, whiteboards, PowerPoints, iPads, and computers, and especially the terminology that accompanied each one of those devices like "cookies" and "pop-ups." "Cookies" were something I enjoyed eating, and "pop-ups" came in a children's book. Technology and I were not on friendly terms.

The other thing I had to learn was being creative with lesson plans. Besides PowerPoints that were to grab my students' attention, I needed additional visuals. I am not a creative person. My tulips and flowers I drew did not win any prizes at the fair. My artwork was usually an example of what things did not look like! Now I felt like God was saying to me, "I've given you a new opportunity in your life. Accept the challenge." So I did. I used all the gifts and talents God gave me to create lesson plans that would captivate a student's attention.

In May of 2008, I said goodbye to my student. She graduated, and the family was moving to a different state. I applied to the district's summer school program and was hired as an instructional assistant at the high School. For two months, I had no prospects of employment with the district for the upcoming fall semester. Once again, I was praying for God to make a way for me.

July 29, 2008, the district office called and offered me a full-time temporary position as an eighth-grade special education teacher at one of the middle schools in town. One of their certificated teachers was granted a leave for a year, and they needed to fill that vacancy. My preliminary teaching credential and being enrolled in a college teacher preparation program to become a fully credentialed teacher qualified me for this temporary position.

July thirtieth I signed the paperwork, and August 1, I walked into the middle school and introduced myself to a friendly office staff. The office manager walked me to the class that would become mine for the next nine years.

In May of 2010, I completed the Special Education Credential program, and in May of 2013, at the age of sixty-five, I received a master's degree in special education with an emphasis on reading comprehension. As I held that degree in my hand, I was remembering the day I prayed to God, asking him to give me comprehension. He answered that prayer far beyond anything I could imagine. As I taught reading classes and studied about reading comprehension, I was able to come up with a model so I could teach my students the basic elements of a story (setting, plot, characterization, theme). I knew if they could understand these concepts, their confidence would grow, skills would improve, and participation in all their other classes would improve also as they advanced through the grades.

In my class, we would read, discuss stories, write book reports, and present PowerPoints. I was blessed to have highly skilled aides that inspired art projects on the stories which filled the walls in my room. The aides worked well with Down syndrome students and knew how to encourage students to believe in themselves. My proof to the approach I took with my teaching instruction was when years later, I would meet some of my former students at the grocery store, and they would tell me how well they were doing at the high school. Many of them had tested out of special education and were now in all general education classes. Some were attending the local community college.

During my years at the middle school, besides teaching English, I also taught a reading class and an Ancient World History class to sixth graders. My mind was exploding with knowledge, and I was able to share it with children with special needs that I believe taught me more than I ever did them.

I was able to work as a teacher, using a degree I worked hard for while learning about the world of special education. The staff at the middle school holds a special place in my heart. Their professionalism was a wonderful thing to experience.

# PART 10

## *Retired*

**67**

In the spring of 2018, the school district was offering early retirement incentives. I would be turning seventy during the summer, and I wanted to spend more time with my children and grandchildren.

To begin my retirement, I was invited to spend part of the summer with Luke and his family in Colorado. Before I arrived, Luke asked me what I would like to do when I retired. I told him I would like to learn to swim. I explained to him that as a young girl, I took Red Cross swimming lessons, but I never got over my fear of the water or learned the skill. I figured I now had the time and would try to learn. So when I arrived at his home, he surprised me with six lessons in an adult class at the local city pool. I thought it was so thoughtful of him and was happy to be joining some other adults with the same abilities and fears that I had.

At the first lesson, we were asked to jump into the five feet water. I was afraid to jump, so I just sat down on the side of the pool and slid into the water. We were given blue kickboards to hold onto and were instructed to hold them out straight in front of us and start practicing the flutter kick as we pushed our way from one end of the pool to the other end and then back. I had the hardest time trying to get myself to move through the water. I had my board out in front of me and was kicking hard; I just was not moving. While most of the class was halfway down the lanes, I was only about four feet from where we started. My coach said I looked like I was riding a bicycle in the water. That was the vision I took away from my first lesson.

I did not make much progress on my second lesson either. So when I went to the third lesson, I went early because I was determined not to slide into the pool. I was going to jump into it. I made the jump and realized that my body adjusted to the water temperature a lot faster, and it was a much better approach to getting into a pool. I was so happy with myself, and I could not wait for my coach to come and see me already in the pool, ready for instructions.

As she walked up to our class, I said, "I jumped into the pool today!"

"Gillian, that's great. I am happy you did that, but today, I want you to climb out of the pool. I want you to lay on the side of the pool on your back and work on some exercises I am going to give you that I believe will help you move though the water better," she explained.

Besides my ego being deflated, I wondered if I heard her right. *I am going to be making progress out of the water instead of in it!*

While the rest of the class was making gains with their strokes and head movements, I was working on arching my back and learning to hold it in that position. When I went home, Luke asked me how I was progressing with my lessons.

I told him, "I don't think I am making much progress. Today, I jumped into the pool, which for me is progress, but then my coach asked me to get out of the water."

He just laughed.

I explained about the back exercises, and he encouraged me to stay with it and try and think about the position of my back as I tried swimming.

During the last three lessons, I did start to make some progress, and the class was cheering me on. "We can see you moving through the water, Gillian!"

I always wanted to swim like the people doing laps in lanes. They all seemed to move through the water with ease, being very relaxed. Today, the swimming lessons are a good memory, but I am content to sit by the pool or ocean and watch my children and grandchildren, without fear, move through the water like fish or surf the waves.

**68**

During my years of living in California, I had a little idea of what it must have been like for the Jews to lose their homeland and, years later, go back to rebuild what they had lost.

When the divorce with Josh happened, the life we had known was gone. I was living in California. Luke had served with the Marines for five years, three of those years spent in Iraq. Eventually, he married Anna, the love of his life. They lived in Portland, Oregon, and northern Colorado where their daughter was born. Two or three times a year, I was a guest in their home. After graduating college, Pilar worked as an accountant in California. During that time, she reconnected with Ethan, a male friend from Darwin, who was working in the United States, and he became the love of her life. They lived and worked in California for a while before deciding to return to Australia. When they decided to marry, they returned to Colorado for the ceremony but continued to live in Australia where their first son was born. During their time in Australia, I visited them three times.

While I lived with Juliet and Philip, they had another son, William, in 2005, but in 2010, Philip, the love of Juliet's life and Ryan and William's father, died of cancer. They live in the same home, and Juliet has dedicated her life to raising her sons and loving her family.

In 2016, I believe God started to move in our family and bring many of us back to central Colorado. In that year, Pilar and her family returned to the States. They stayed with us in California for a few months while they purchased property in Gunnison to build a home on. They moved into a rental in Gunnison while it was being built.

In November 2017, Luke and Anna surprised both their families when they bought a small farm a few miles outside Gunnison in the town they had grown up in and where they went to school. Luke and Pilar's families now lived forty-five minutes apart.

In May 2020, during the COVID pandemic which caused schools to shut down and families to move into isolation, Juliet and I decided if we had to be in isolation, we were going to go where the pandemic was not so severe and be with our families in Colorado for the summer months. We decided we would surprise both Luke and Pilar's families with our decision on Mother's Day. We only let two people know we were coming: Luke's mother-in-law, Carmella, who helped us find a house to rent, and Pilar's husband, Ethan, who would be prepared on Mother's Day for us to have lunch with them.

We signed the contract for the rental house on Wednesday before Mother's Day. Juliet wanted to make the fourteen-hour trip in one day and did not want me to drive, so she flew her son, Ryan, in from Boise, Idaho, on Thursday to drive my car.

For two days, we were busy preparing for our home to be cared for and loaded up two cars with computers, suitcases, two dogs, and their crates and food for the road. Saturday morning, we left early. Ryan and I were in one car listening to all his favorite Country and Rock music, sometimes with the windows rolled down and the wind blowing through our hair. Juliet and William were in the other car with our two dogs and listening to a book on tape. We stopped one time at a nice clean rest area in Arizona.

Driving into Colorado and going through Gunnison, Ryan called his mom and told her to drive on ahead to the rental because he and I would be stopping at our favorite barbecue place and would be bringing supper to them. The rental home fit our needs perfectly. We were ten minutes from my son's home and forty-five minutes from Pilar's. As we ate our barbecue sandwiches around the kitchen table, we were tired but extremely excited about tomorrow's unfolding events.

Sunday, Mother's Day, Luke called me and wished me a happy Mother's Day. He always called me once a week. We enjoyed updating each other on the events in our lives, and he wished me a good day. Little did he know that at two o'clock, we would be sitting on his porch, waiting to surprise his family when they returned from a picnic in the mountains. He also did not know his in-laws were going to make sure they did not get back until after two o'clock.

At nine o'clock, Mother's Day morning, I knocked on the door of Pilar and Ethan's home with Juliet and the boys behind me. Ethan was to make sure that Pilar answered the door.

When Pilar heard the knocking, she spoke to Ethan.

"Ethan, I'm getting the kids dressed. I think someone is knocking on the door. Can you answer it, please?"

"Pilar, I can't put this down right now. You'll have to get it," he said.

"Really, Ethan? Okay, I'll get it," she said, walking away, wondering who would possibly be delivering flowers at this time of day.

When she opened the door, I said, "Happy Mother's Day, darling!"

Her eyes began to fill up with tears, she put her hands over her mouth, and said, "You're here!" She took a pause and a big breath. "You're here! How are you here?" she kept repeating, and tears filled her eyes. She then looked behind me and saw Juliet. "You're here too!" Then she saw Ryan and William walk in, and she cried, "You're all here! How is this possible?"

"We decided just Wednesday that we were going to come and spend some time with yours and Luke's families. We decided we would surprise you for Mother's Day. We have rented a house in Gunnison for three months, near the high school," I explained.

"So you all are going to be here for a while? We are going to get to spend time with all of you?"

"Yes, dear, we are. The house we rented has enough Wi-Fi for Juliet and the boys to have Internet access for her job and their schooling."

"Who all knew you were coming?" she asked.

"Just Ethan and Carmella. She helped us find the rental house. We drove all day yesterday to surprise you today! We needed to tell Ethan, so you would be the one to open the door, and he said he would plan a barbecue for lunch," I explained further.

"I wondered why Ethan bought so many salads for today. I thought they must have been on sale," Pilar said. "This is such a wonderful surprise. Best Mother's Day ever!"

And it was a wonderful time together. As we sat around the picnic table, enjoying barbecue ribs and salads, my grandkids threw the balls to the dogs, played frisbee, and we were all excited there were more days like this ahead.

Shortly after one o'clock, we said our goodbyes and headed to Luke and Anna's home. At two o'clock, Juliet, Ryan, William, and I were sitting on their porch, and in a few minutes, we saw their vehicles coming up the road and entering their driveway. We were so excited!

When they parked the car, Anna jumped out of her car and exclaimed, "You're here! How are you here?"

Next, Luke came around the car and exclaimed, "You're here! How is that possible? I just talked to you on the phone this morning! How are you all here?"

"We drove all day yesterday. When you were talking with me this morning, I was sitting in the sunroom in the house we have rented in Gunnison for three months," I explained.

"You're staying three months? Who knew about this?" Luke said, being totally astounded while looking at his in-laws.

"Carmella and Jack did. Carmella helped us find a house. We were not sure we could find one to meet all our needs, but with Carmella on the case, she did not give up, and here we are. We are only ten minutes from your home."

As Luke's in-laws and brother-in-law, Richard, came up the porch stairs, Luke turned to them and said, "You knew about this and you helped plan all this!"

Carmella said, "Juliet and I had a wonderful time exploring the different possibilities, and I was able to find a house over here by the high school."

"It's Anna and I that always put one over on you two. You don't do it to us!" Luke exclaimed.

"That is what makes this extra special, Luke. Jack and I were finally able to pull one over on you and Anna for a change. It has been so much fun!" Carmella replied. Carmella further explained, "Anna and Luke were getting a little too anxious to leave the mountains and get home, so Jack had to play his part of 'the aging grandfather' needing to walk a little slower and take things a little easier. It totally worked."

We spent the rest of the afternoon, sometimes walking around their property, sometimes sitting on the front porch, reminiscing old memories and excited about making new ones.

With Luke and Annal's family, we looked forward to Friday nights. Juliet and Luke would shut down their computers around five o'clock, we would order pizza or barbecue chicken from a local restaurant, and the two families would sit around a table, swapping stories while drinking their favorite beverages. We were also planning a big camping trip into the mountains high above Gunnison during the July Fourth holiday weekend.

*****

Friday night of the July Fourth weekend, a large camper, pop-up tents, trucks, and ATV three and four wheelers surrounded our campsite. The grandkids enjoyed cooling themselves off in the shallow mountain river that flowed nearby. A full day of off-roading was planned for Saturday and half a day Sunday at nine thousand feet around numerous mountain trails that surrounded old mining sites, including a stop at an old ghost town. For two nights, we began our evenings playing cards inside the camper, then went outside, sat around a firepit, making smores while breathing in the cool mountain air as overhead, the black night sky was lit up with a magnificent display of twinkling stars. On one of the trails, Juliet took a picture of a beautiful mountain waterfall that now hangs in my office.

Saturdays, we were with Pilar's family, playing games and having lunch around the picnic table. But during the week, while other people attended jobs and schoolwork, I would drive over and spend time with her family, playing with my three grandchildren aged four, two, and seven months.

Pilar and I enjoyed conversing as we watched the little ones playing with their friends, riding bikes, and driving four-wheelers around the cul-de-sac or swinging in the backyard. We would take walks around the neighborhood and along the river, many times just stopping and sitting by the river while the kids played in the water close to the shore. We baked cookies, played board games, and walked the dogs. Some nights, I would stay and have supper with them. It was great to hold hands as a family and hear one of my grandkids say a short prayer before we ate.

My brother, Logan, and his wife, Lucia, still lived in Gunnison, and on Monday, following Mother's Day, I surprised him with a telephone call, telling him of our arrival. They were excited to know we were in the area and would be seeing us during the summer months. We saw them the following weekend, and eventually, Thursdays for lunch became my special time each week to spend with them and another friend on their beautiful patio in the backyard.

In 2019, I began praying to God to show me where he wanted me to "hang my clothes and lay my head." Since 2004, my permanent address had been with Juliet and her family, and at different times, I had spent extended periods of time with Luke and Pilar's families. Juliet was now preparing her boys to transition into college life, and she was considering downsizing into a smaller home and living abroad. It was time to find a place of my own.

Two houses down from the rental home we were living in for the summer was a home for sale, and the sellers were having open house showings on weekends. Juliet and I would occasionally walk by the house, making comments about it when we took the dogs for a walk. We had been living in the rental for about three weeks, and one Sunday morning, as Juliet was coming back from walking the dogs, she stopped at the house, picked up an advertisement, and brought it home for me to read.

"Mom, I stopped and picked up a flyer about that open house, and I think you should consider looking at it. I think you might like it, and it would be something you could afford," she said.

I looked over the ad and decided it was a home I should consider touring. We were having lunch with Luke's family and a close relative, so we made plans to view the house later in the afternoon. During lunch, Juliet and I started telling them about the property for sale. Everyone was excited for me. So everyone wanted to go and see it.

As we entered the home, a couple my age greeted us, and we informed them I was the interested party. They introduced themselves, explained it was an estate sale, and they were the sellers. We found the home to be one level and well cared for with a well-laid-out floor plan. There was a large living room with a fireplace, a nice-sized kitchen with a large island and dining area, three bedrooms, two and a half baths with a porch off the master bedroom, and the house was surrounded by landscape plants all under a sprinkler system that a person just had to turn a knob to water. It was simply perfect for me. After a family discussion, I made an offer and, in July, became the owner of my own home. God had answered my prayer. The sellers told me, "The minute we saw you, we knew you were the one that was to have the home."

I came to believe the couple must have been God's angels. They left all the appliances, and the kitchen was well-stocked with cooking and eating utilities. The living room had a couch, comfortable rocker, and end tables. Solid wooden frames and beds were in two bedrooms. I planned to make the third bedroom into my office. A mixed assortment of tools hung on the garage walls along with gardening tools and gloves for me to use.

Today, the walls of my home have pictures of my children and their families. Over the fireplace are pictures of my grandchildren. Hanging on my dining room wall are pictures of my travels around the world, and a beloved relative gave me a piano that fits perfect in my living room. A guitar is on a stand near the television. I look forward to the day my oldest grandsons play those instruments as my family and extended family members gather in that living room to sing all kinds of songs.

The third week in July, the family said their goodbyes to my oldest grandson, Ryan. He would be flying to Fort Benning, Georgia, to begin his boot camp training in the United States Army under the ROTC program at Boise State. It had been his dream as a child to serve in the military like his father did, and now he was on his way to fulling that dream. He was a high achiever, and we all knew he would do well serving his county.

August 5, the lease of the rental house was up, and we said our goodbyes to Juliet and William. They would be returning to California where Juliet would be preparing William for his second year of high school. I would be remaining in Colorado until December where I would be living in my own home and dividing my time between Luke, Pilar, and Logan's families.

During the upcoming fall months, I would be able to celebrate four of my grandchildren's birthdays with them. And my seven-year-old granddaughter would be spending one night a week at Grandma Gillian's house. She would be showing Grandma her favorite shows, we would play cards and board games, do some science experiments, and be cooking breakfast together. During Colorado's cold winter months, I would be living back in California with Juliet and William and spending time with good friends.

Like the Jews coming back and rebuilding the walls of Jerusalem, we have come back to a place we love and rebuilt new lives. I heard a sermon by Joyce Myer who told of how some of the great characters in the Bible ran away from difficult situations in their lives, and in each case, God told them to go back to where they ran from.

Hagar ran from her mistress, Sarah, Abraham's wife, and God told her to go back. Moses ran from Pharoah. He spent forty years in the wilderness when God told him to go back to Egypt. Elijah ran from Jezebel after killing her false prophets. He was hiding in a cave when God told him to go back. Jonah ran from Nineveh, and after spending three nights in the belly of a whale, God told him, "Now, go to Nineveh."

I honestly believe God is in control of our lives, and he has a plan and a purpose for each of us. Why he brought us back to central Colorado, I do not know. But I do believe there is a reason. Whatever that reason is, I know he will reveal it in his own time. God went beyond what I prayed for or could ever imagine for me and my children. I will continue to trust him.

## 69

*God and me*

It has taken me many years to come to peace with the failure of my two marriages. Having a deeper faith in my God, building a strong prayer life, reading and studying his Word, and experiencing his unfailing love has given me that peace.

My brother, Logan, who helped edit this story, sent me the following text one day:

> "I enjoyed reading your chapters. I think it tells the story of somebody escaping to a much better place. You never had any reason to feel ashamed of anything. In both instances with your husbands, it was their fault, not yours. They are the ones who violated their vows and left you with no real alternatives. The things you have accomplished since you went to California are amazing and proof that God has a different plan for you. I am so proud of you."

I loved being married, having a home, raising children, being part of a man's dream, and I tried to be a good wife. I just could not please them. But, in my heart, I know the failure of my marriages was not my fault. However, as a Christian, I will accept the sin and responsibility of harboring unforgiveness against them. Both asked me to come back, and I said, "No."

With Ricardo, I was too afraid, and with Josh, I came to a breaking point. I have confessed that sin to God. I know he has forgiven me, and by his blood, I have been set free from condemnation.

My two favorite verses in the Bible are:

> Teach me to do your will, for You are my God.
> Lead me forth with your gracious Holy Spirit on
> a firm foundation. (Psalms 143:10)

> Thy Word is a lamp unto my feet and a light
> unto my path. (Psalms 119:105)

If you asked me what I look forward to when I get to heaven, it would be to sit at Jesus's feet and listen to his voice and discover how he draws people in to wanting to hear more. I was a girl raised in a Christian home by loving parents, attended church and Sunday school classes, youth group activities, and went to a Christian college; and as an adult, studying the Word of God has become a passion in my life. I have a longing to share God's Word with people, but when I begin talking about it, to share what I have learned, I usually turn people off instead of drawing them in to wanting to learn more.

I talked to a minister about my desire to share the Gospel, and he told me, "Gillian, you do not need to have a lot of theological knowledge to share the Gospel. Just tell people your story. Tell them what God has done for you."

So that is what I have done with this book. I am so grateful to God for the life and family he gave me, and I want to bring glory and honor to his name.

Hebrews 12:15 says, "See to it that no one misses the grace of God and that no bitter root grows up to cause trouble and defile many."

There are people that I really care about, and I do not want them to miss the grace of God, so during my prayer time, I bring their names before the throne room of God in prayer.

Not long ago, I heard a preacher say, "Sometimes the prayer that we pray to God, asking for his help with people, he may use us to answer that prayer. Are you ready to be used by God?"

I decided I was not ready, but I was going to get ready. I love a good story, and I wanted to be able to explain the Gospel in story form, so I searched on the Internet and found a site, Our Kingdom Culture, that posted a blog of "5 Easy Steps to Share the Gospel with Others." It was exactly what I was looking for, so I printed a copy and started to memorize those five steps.

As I would take daily walks—sometimes alone, sometimes with our family dogs—I continued to memorize that Gospel story and practiced it often. The Gospel was coming alive in my mind, and today, I feel confident I could share that old, old story.

## 5 Easy Steps to Share the Gospel with Others

1. *God*: The story begins with a loving Father that created everything we see. Even you and me. He created us to have a relationship with Him, and to live forever with Him. He is a holy Father that sees all things, even what is in our hearts. (Genesis 1:27)

2. *Sin*: When sin came into the world it created a gap that separated us from God. No longer were we able to come in the presence of our Father. Because God can see everything. He can see the sin in our lives and the Bible tells us that the price for sin is death. (Romans 6:23) So, we were separated from our Father and destined to die.

3. *Jesus*: But God's love for us was so much that He could not let us die. He gave up His most beloved treasure, Jesus to die for us instead. Jesus, the Son of God, became a man so that He can suffer and die and pay the price that we were supposed to pay. After three days, He rose from the dead, defeated sin and death and is now sitting right next to The Father. Jesus is the bridge that we need to cross to go to our Father. (Romans 5:8)

4. *The Gift*: The blood of Jesus that was spilled on the cross is the one that washes away our sins. That is the gift to us. That gift makes us clean,

makes us righteous, forgiven and allows us to have a close relationship with our Father and access to everything that He has for us. This is the gift of salvation. It is up to us if we accept this gift or not. (Ephesians 2:8)

5.  *Believe:* Nobody is forced to accept this gift. If you want it, you need to ask for it; you need to speak it with you mouth and you got to believe it in your heart. Once you do that, you will be saved and a new you will be born inside of you. The Spirit of God will come live on the inside of you and will help you with everything you need. Never again will you be alone. Jesus will be with you wherever you go.

If you confess with your mouth that Jesus is Lord and believe in your heart that God raised him from the dead, you will be saved. For it is by believing in your heart that you are made right with God, and it is by confessing with your mouth that you are saved (Romans 10:9–10).

*Prayer of salvation*

Father, I recognize that I am a sinner, and I need a Savior. I believe Jesus is your Son. I believe he died for me and rose again. Jesus, I open my heart to you, and I accept you as my Lord and Savior. I want to follow you and love you. Please fill me with your Holy Spirit, and help me to be more like you. In Jesus's name I pray. Amen.

If you are a broken man or woman *who ha*s turned away from God, made wrong decisions, struggled, and gone through rough phases in your life, it is my prayer for you that you will come to the cross of Jesus, accept him as Lord and Savior of your life, pray "The Prayer of Salvation," and allow him to bring healing and joy back into your life. He is the way, the truth, and the life.

I accepted God's gift of salvation twice in my life. Once as a youth and once again as a broken women when I recommitted my life to Christ. I know my sins are forgiven because Jesus's blood covers them. I serve a risen Lord and Savior, and I daily try to help people. I study his Word and spend time with him in prayer. I look forward to fulfilling his plan for my life until he returns or calls me home.

# About the Author

Three years ago, Elizabeth retired from being a special education teacher, and now she spends her time writing while enjoying her children, grandchildren, and extended family members. She spends the summer and fall months at her home in the Rocky Mountains where two of her children live along with four of her grandchildren. The winter and Spring months she spends with her oldest daughter and one grandson in the warmer climate of southern California. She also enjoys following the adventures of grandchildren living across the United States.

For most of Elizabeth's adult life, she has enjoyed sharing stories of the very diverse life she has lived which tested her faith and led her to discover God's unfailing love, grace, and mercy.

Elizabeth loves reading a good book, being in small group Bible studies, playing cards, board games, and traveling around America and to foreign countries. *The Round Robin* is her first book.